ALL THE WORLDS
BETWEEN US

Visit us at www.boldstrokesbooks.com

ALL THE WORLDS BETWEEN US

by
Morgan Lee Miller

2019

ISBN 13: 978-1-63555-457-1

This Trade Paperback Original Is Published By
Bold Strokes Books, Inc.
P.O. Box 249
Valley Falls, NY 12185

First Edition: May 2019

CREDITS
EDITOR: BARBARA ANN WRIGHT
PRODUCTION DESIGN: STACIA SEAMAN
COVER DESIGN BY JEANINE HENNING

For Karlee—who I promised I would dedicate my first book to when we were twenty years old.

And Julie—who read this story three times in its draft stages because I forced her to.

Thank you both for not only being my first readers to all my stories' drafts but for also being constant rocks in my life.

CHAPTER ONE

Maneuvering my way through a crowd of hundreds of people heading in the opposite direction was as hard as the four miles I just swam.

The football game just ended, and as everyone celebrated another win on their walk to the parking lot, I ran against the current of spectators to where my twin brother said he would meet me after the game. Liam and I were forced to share the Camry, and my parents gave me the rights during the week because of my strict swimming schedule for the world championships in ten months. This was more of an inconvenience for Liam than it was impressive because that meant he couldn't get the car until the weekend, and if anything infringed on his Camry time, he turned into a petulant child.

And my being late meant that he would turn into a bratty seven-year-old whose toy was taken away from him.

So I sprinted faster to avoid his wrath.

When I finally emerged from the crowd, I spotted Liam with two of his friends, Gabriel Báez and Tom Felix. All three of them tall, built, and wearing their emerald green letterman jackets: a symbol of their popularity and top spot on the high school totem pole. Liam and Tom stood with tight crossed arms, and I knew then that it didn't matter how fast I ran through a crowd moving at a sloth's pace, it still wasn't fast enough for Liam. His pissed-off scowl was detailed on his face.

"There's my favorite mermaid," Gabriel said and flashed me the warm smile he always gave me.

"Gabriel, I just swam a bajillion miles," I said. "Carry me to the Camry, my prince."

"Yes, my queen."

His six-two self squatted down to my five-nine height. Taking a deep breath of the wonderful smell of his freshly used body wash, I jumped on his back, and he caught me by the hamstrings.

"Onward!" I said with a direct point to the parking lot.

Liam and Gabriel had been best friends since kindergarten. He lived a few blocks down the street from us. Even though Liam and Gabriel were way more popular than I was, he remained the levelheaded jock who was always loyal to his longtime friends, no matter how late I was at meeting them at the stadium gates. He was my platonic boyfriend, we'd both declared sophomore year. He was the only boy I knew I would ever love.

Platonically, that is. Let's not get too carried away now.

"Really, Quinn? Fifteen minutes late?" Liam said, breaking the moment I had with my pseudo-boyfriend. His voice was sharp and pissy.

"I'm sorry! Practice ran a little over—"

"Let me guess: Hot Lifeguard was working again?"

I hesitated. "No…"

"Okay, so we're all late to our party because you had to talk to Hot Lifeguard?"

"Hey, I was on my way out, and she came up to me, twirling her hair and everything. I was just an innocent bystander—"

"Nice," Gabriel said and put a fist up in the air for me to bump it. Of course, I accepted. I was proud of the progress I just made with Hot Lifeguard. She'd been working at the pool since the summer, and now it was the second week in October, and she finally had a conversation with me. While twirling her hair. A college girl was twirling her hair over me. That was an important detail. With this monumental step, I could probably find out her name by next week.

"I told Cassandra we were gonna be there with the booze at nine sharp." Liam continued his conniption. "Now we don't have time to drive you home."

"I'm not going to that party if that's what you're trying to imply."

No part of me wanted to go to Cassandra Jones's house. She was the meanest girl in our class, which apparently was the only qualification you needed to become captain of the soccer team. She was especially mean to me for reasons I couldn't even tell you, and for whatever reason, she was Liam's upcoming homecoming date. Men and their thing for snarky girls.

"Should have sprinted faster then, Miss Olympics," Tom said in his douchey tone.

"You should too, then; maybe you'd actually start for once," I said.

Gabriel let out his contagious cackle that made me smile, and Tom flipped me off. Tom was Liam's worst friend. He loved rubbing in the fact that I missed qualifying for the Olympics by three seconds any time the opportunity presented itself. Popular people loved making others feel less than they really were. That was why I couldn't go to that party. Tom wasn't even the worst person in Liam's friend group. The girls' soccer team was a whole team of Toms.

"Liam, I'm sorry," I continued. "But I can't go to her party. That's basically asking to be picked on the whole night. Can you drive me home, please, and I'll pay for gas next time? I promise."

I hopped off Gabriel's back and threw my swimming bag in the trunk when we reached the Camry.

"You get the car four days out of the week," he said. "I only get the weekend, so no, I'm not gonna cater to you and ruin my time with the car. If you don't wanna come, then go get Hot Lifeguard to drive you home. The world doesn't revolve around you just because you're training."

"It will literally take you ten minutes to drop me off."

"Nope. It's out of the way. Not driving you home."

"I'm not even dressed for a party. My hair is wet, and I smell like pool."

I was also in my swimming nationals T-shirt I got from the year before, black Nike track shorts, and flip-flops. My hair was in a damp messy bun, and my skin reeked of fresh chlorine. The kids Liam associated with were all deeply rooted in Aspen Grove's affluent suburban lifestyle of designer clothes, luxury cars, and snooty attitudes. The party would be comprised of the girls' soccer team plus the football guys.

Like hell I was going to that party.

"I've been up since four thirty. I'm so tired and—"

"Sounds like a personal problem to me."

He got in the car without giving me a chance to argue back.

Liam was either a really cool twin brother or a major douche. He was hanging out with the soccer team and his football friends way too much. It didn't help that he was super popular, and I was that freak at school with chlorine-dried hair and skin and who dedicated all my free time to training rather than socializing with my friends like a normal high school kid. I really hated seeing my brother turn into a prick just so he could impress his friends and girls. I was always the one who got the brunt of it.

"I'll punch anyone who gives you a hard time," Gabriel whispered to me. "And even smelling like pool, you'll still be the prettiest girl at the ball."

Gabriel gave me a wink, and we both slipped into the back of the car.

It was the first time I'd ever been to Cassandra Jones's house; I could have gone my whole life never stepping foot inside it and died a completely happy woman. But at least I finally understood why Liam and his friends were always over there. Cassandra's parents were both doctors who worked at the hospital. Oftentimes they worked nights, and as a result, their daughter threw house parties. Poor Mr. and Mrs. Jones. As they were saving lives, their house turned into a haven for the high schoolers.

The house was gorgeous. Big. Beautiful. Open floor plan. All hardwood floors. Decorated with furniture Mrs. Jones collected from all over the world. Their precious daughter converted the mahogany dining room table into a beer pong table because "it's the perfect length," Gabriel said. Liam told me that the couch in the family room was made of Spanish leather. As we walked through the living room, I found the whole soccer team on that couch, decked out in their green Aspen Grove varsity soccer T-shirts with green and yellow Mardi Gras beads around their necks and school colors in different designs on their faces. Their hair and makeup were decked out even more than the school day because a weekend outing was practically like going to a gala. Each girl had a drink in her hand, and every one of them eyed me carefully as I trailed a few paces behind my brother.

They knew I didn't belong in this house. And I agreed with them.

"What the hell is she wearing?" I'm almost positive I heard one girl whisper.

"Gabriel and Liam probably dragged her," a second voice said.

"Right out of the pool?"

"Talk about a fish out of water," Cassandra's very distinct voice said.

I wanted Gabriel to hurry up with his beer so I could cling to him and hope all the banter about me would end. No one would make any comments with him right next to me because all those girls had crushes on him and would swallow their opinions about me rather than lose a chance at dating him.

But I currently had to wait for my bodyguard to finish shot-gunning his beer with seven other senior guys in the kitchen. The beer dripped down their faces and onto their shirts as the three of them chugged whole cans. A group of guys chanted like frat brothers for the three to drink faster. Gabriel was the first to finish, and a few soccer girls cheered for him from the fancy leather couch. Complete suck-ups.

Watching all those guys attempt to be masculine by chugging crappy Bud Light was the most unappealing thing my eyes had seen in a while. And then Tom let out a loud belch, and that was a done deal. Sold to Aspen Grove High's tight end who didn't know the difference between *there*, *their*, and *they're*. Tom's whole being won the award for the most unappealing thing my eyes had ever seen. The amount of disgust I felt was strong enough to probably clear my skin for the rest of senior year.

I never felt gayer until that exact moment.

"Quinn, let's play beer pong," Gabriel said, attempting to give me his heartwarming, dark brown puppy eyes for extra convincing. "You and Liam versus me and Tom. Show this loser how athletic you are and pulverize him to a pulp."

"I don't think the athletic skills I have contribute that much to beer pong."

"Yeah, Quinn!" Liam said. "One game. I always wanted to dominate beer pong with my twin."

"Why should I be your partner when you threw a hissy fit a half hour ago? You don't even care that your homecoming date is out to get me."

He waved her off as if her bark was worse than her bite, but he didn't even hear the comments she'd already made. "She won't bother you."

"If I play, then we leave in an hour. Sharp. All debts paid."

He groaned. "Fine! If it gets you to shut up about it."

"Wow, you're seriously going to have a beer?" Gabriel said, suddenly even more excited. "Damn! This is, like, the first time I've ever seen you drink."

"Two summers ago, she puked in Lana Banner's pool," Liam said.

I slapped him hard on the arm, and he let out a yelp. "I didn't puke in her pool. I puked in her bushes, and that was the first and only time I've been drunk, and it was because I was mourning the fact that I missed the Olympics."

"I'm still excited for this," Gabriel said, "and honored I get to be a part of it."

As Liam and Tom set up the red Solo cups on the table, I already regretted the alcohol I had yet to consume. Two years ago, as a fifteen-year-old, I made it to the finals of the Olympic trials in the 200-meter and the 400-meter freestyle. I took sixth place and eighth place, respectively. Only the top two advanced to the Olympics. I was absolutely heartbroken I'd come so close and then missed the games by three seconds. It felt like a breakup. I sulked for two weeks in my room, refused to watch any of the London Olympics, and cried, bitched, then cried some more.

Then it hit me, I wasn't accomplishing anything during those two weeks I pitied myself. If anything, the more I stayed in bed, the more out of shape I became. So, by the end of the London Olympics, I came up with a plan. I had to go all in and exert all the time, energy, and dedication in order to accomplish my dream. That meant sacrificing parts of my social life: being the one friend in the group who missed a lot of the weekend hangouts, especially in the summer. I needed to really give it my all and let nothing get in the way because in order for me to make it to the Olympics, I'm pretty sure there was a quota for blood, sweat, and tears. It seemed to work because the following summer—right after sophomore year—I went to my first ever world championships in Barcelona, placing seventh overall in my 400-free. Just a month and a half ago, I was in Australia, finishing fourth in my 200-free at the Pan Pacific Games, and now, I was all in for winning my first medal at the world champs in Russia in ten months.

So, that meant anything that would get me arrested or mess me up physically, emotionally, or mentally was absolutely forbidden. No high impact activities. No getting into any serious relationships with a girl (but a fling or a quick hookup with Hot Lifeguard was completely okay). And that meant no drinking.

But I was stuck in the house of a girl who hated my guts, I got weird stares and whispers from the whole soccer team, and I was going to humiliate myself by playing beer pong for the first time ever with all the popular kids who could make it to the Beer Pong Olympics.

Yup. I needed a beer. Just one beer.

I quickly learned that if you sucked at beer pong, you didn't just have one beer, and you didn't just casually sip on it. Liam and I lost the game in ten minutes because we sucked that badly. Tom and Gabriel made at least one cup each round. Liam had about a 30 percent conversion rate, and I hit the rim every time and didn't make a single cup. Insert many failed Olympic jokes and many butt sex jokes by Tom and a few spectators. I was supposed to drink three of those cups, per the rules of beer pong, but I only drank one and gave Liam the other two. Someone had to drive, right? *Maybe I can use this moment of irresponsibility as a reason to get the car next week for homecoming.* Liam didn't seem to mind at all about drinking my beers, but Tom sure did. He called me vanilla, which garnered a few laughs from the people watching us, specifically Cassandra.

"If you're not even gonna drink, then go away so others can play," she said to me but directed it at her friends.

She was lucky I never aimed the ping-pong ball at her face.

After the game and all the mocking, I took that as my cue to just leave the scene altogether and find the bathroom and hide there until midnight. The first-floor bathroom door was closed, but light seeped through the crack into the long, quiet hallway. I expected someone to say they were in there when I knocked on the door. But just like I hoped for, I heard nothing but silence. So, I opened the door, eager just to sit, pee out all the beer, and play on my phone to pass some time alone. But when I flung the door open, I discovered Kennedy Reed resting her back against the wall, sitting with her knees tucked into her chest next to the toilet. Her dark green soccer shirt enhanced her bright green eyes, and green and yellow paint faintly colored her pale face and triangle-shaped jaw. Through her glazed eyes, she looked right at me, giving me a look as if I was the monster who'd haunted her nightmares.

And maybe I was because Kennedy Reed used to haunt mine.

I slammed the door shut.

She was a stranger who knew everything about me. Yet we hadn't looked each other in the eye in four years. Until that moment in Cassandra Jones's bathroom.

Once my heart went back to normal beating speed, I slowly opened the door. A burning pain in my stomach intensified when I noticed her giving me the same shocked look back. I couldn't tell you why I was so surprised to see her. In the back of my mind, I knew she would be at the party since she was the goalie for the soccer team. Maybe I was more shocked because she actually looked me straight in the eyes.

"Are, uh, are you all right?" I said while trying to swallow the lump that rapidly grew in my throat.

All the memories we shared—some we wished we'd forgotten—sucked up all the moisture in my mouth. But I really had to pee, and she was the only thing preventing me from doing that, so I had to fight through the lump to get her out of there.

Her eyes drifted off me to the tops of her knees. "Yeah, um, I'm fine. I think," Kennedy said softly.

"You sure?"

"Yeah."

A pause.

"Okay, because I need to pee really badly."

"Right."

The second she got out of the bathroom, I ran in, locked the door, and peed out the whole beer pong game. Right as I pulled out my phone to distract myself from the party, there was a knock on the door.

"I think I need to go back in there," Kennedy said on the other side.

I could hear another round of vomit brewing inside her.

An annoyed sigh seeped out of me as I pulled up my pants to acquiesce to her urgent needs. Right as I stepped out of the bathroom, she swept by me so quickly, I couldn't even catch sight of her face before the door shut.

Just go back to the party, I thought, my heart still rapidly pounding. *You don't owe her anything.*

Except I did the exact opposite of what my brain told me to do. I fetched her some cold water instead. She kind of needed the help. Any kind of help, really. Her friends didn't seem to notice she'd been missing for quite some time, ever since I got to the party at least. Which wasn't a surprise because most of her friends were assholes.

So, I got her that cup of water.

I knocked on the door, and seconds later, Kennedy opened it. She flinched at the sight of me again. I guess I was still the same monster she saw minutes before.

"Water?" I said, flaunting the red Solo cup in my hand.

I couldn't be a monster if I had cold water for a drunk girl, right?

Still without meeting my eyes, she snatched the cup and chugged it as if she hadn't had water in three days.

"You sure you're okay?"

"I'm fine," she said sharply.

Disengage. She's grown an attitude.

And on that note, I left.

"Quinn! Quinn, take this beer. We're playing Never Have I Ever," Liam said in his excited drunk voice when I pushed myself into the circle. He handed me a red cup filled with Bud Light.

The party now took the shape of a circle. Everyone had both hands raised. Some had more fingers up than the others. Liam only had six, Tom had four, and Gabriel had five. I was so curious to find out what they'd done to knock down those fingers. I knew Liam would tell me when he decided to be cool again.

"No, Liam, I wanna go—"

"Kennedy! There you are," Cassandra said when her best friend squeezed into the circle. Although Kennedy's face was still pale with very little remaining of the face paint, her face radiated beauty. Her defined jawline and her beautiful ash-brown hair. Even after throwing up, she was the most beautiful girl at the party—hell, she was the most beautiful girl at Aspen Grove High School.

You can't think she's pretty. She doesn't even like you enough to acknowledge you.

I could only dream of looking that beautiful after puking up alcohol. Could that be a new life goal?

She sipped on the water I gave her and avoided eye contact with me. Even though I could tell by the way she tried too hard to pretend as if I wasn't directly across the circle from her, I knew that her peripherals focused all on me. Because I did the same thing, and I could feel our awkwardness toward each other dancing around in the empty space between us.

"Ten fingers up," Cassandra demanded. "Now, say something you've never done. I wanna prove to Tom and Gabriel that I *can* win a game."

Cassandra only had three fingers left. Kennedy let out a sigh and put ten fingers up. Her friends cheered as if the game was about to get a million times more interesting, as if they already knew all the apparently crazy things Kennedy Reed was ready to reveal.

"Never have I ever cheated on a test," she said.

Yeah, so worth the dramatic buildup, I thought with an eye roll.

Cassandra slapped her best friend on the arm and put down a finger like every single person in the circle. She was now down to two fingers.

"That was a waste of a turn," Cassandra said. "You were supposed to help me out."

"Well, maybe you should stop cheating," Kennedy said.

"Quinn, your turn," Liam said with a nudge to the arm. "Noobs gotta catch up."

The whole party stared at me as if I had a third eye in the middle of my forehead. Everyone except for Kennedy, who looked down at her cup as if a bug had fallen into it, and she was watching it swim.

"Never have I ever," I said and studied the faces in the circle. I knew plenty of things to knock out almost half the party. Liam: never have I ever wet the bed after I was eight. Gabriel: never have I ever gotten a boner in gym class. Cassandra Jones: never have I ever hooked up in the school elevator. Melanie Krugel: never have I ever puked in a pool...during a raging pool party. Jennifer Stewart: never have I ever had a crush on a teacher who was over forty. Tom: never have I ever lied about having sex when I really was a virgin.

And then there was Kennedy Reed. But her secret was one I'd done. It's just that nobody at the party knew about it. If she could barely look me in the eye, then I knew for a fact her new friends didn't know about this secret at all.

Since she had just puked up her small intestine, I decided not to target her, and there was no way I would target Liam or Gabriel so that meant...

"Oh my God, just say something," Cassandra whined. "It's really not that hard."

Okay, well, that solves my problem.

"Never have I ever hooked up in the school elevator," I said.

The majority of the party laughed in shock. I hated admitting it, but having those people smirking because of my calling out a not-so-friendly girl did make me feel good. Mean girls deserved karma.

Then, just as quickly as I became popular for four seconds, I went back down on the totem pole of high school popularity.

"Never have I ever kissed anyone of the same sex!"

Just as a few people dropped their mouths in excitement of

possible drama, I rolled my eyes because of course someone like Cassandra Jones said this.

Being straight didn't define straight people. Why did being gay define me? Some people clung so tightly to the fact that I was gay more than the fact I was going to the world championships. And why did people have to describe me as their "gay friend" instead of just "friend"? No, cousin Sabrina, my being gay has nothing to do with the story you're telling your friends about the time we flushed Aunt Karen's cigarettes down the toilet when we were fourteen. So, stop starting the story with, "So, my gay cousin and I…"

And now, Cassandra Jones tried using that gay label as the jab to end all jabs because apparently, if you couldn't find a clever insult, just use the trump card of someone's non-heterosexuality.

Well, too bad it didn't work for her…because it was 20Gayteen, and she was a moron.

"Yeah, okay, nice one," I said. "And the sky is blue, and the grass is green. Glad we're going around naming the obvious. Nice try, though."

Liam and Gabriel cackled beside me, their glances and laughs directed at Cassandra. And just like that, her proud smirk washed away. I came out the year before. I had a girlfriend since then that I took to my junior year homecoming. Literally everyone at school knew I was a lesbian, so it was like shouting to the world that Gabriel was Puerto Rican and Liam had a twin sister, expecting a huge reaction as if those two truths uncovered the most dramatic plot twist.

Nice try, Cassandra. You even failed at what you do best: being Regina George.

But what pissed me off a lot more than Cassandra's failed attempt at an insult was when I found that Kennedy's eyes lost interest in the invisible bug in her cup and found their way to me, finally willing to acknowledge my presence in her circle of fellow, top tier, Aspen Grove totem pole people. All ten of her fingers were up with no plans on moving.

Now I was pissed.

And then the blood began to boil inside me.

"Oh, okay, fine then," Cassandra said to me, this time with a more threatening scowl on her face. "Never have I ever dreamed of going to the Olympics and then failed at it."

And there you have it. Cassandra Jones won. Even if Tom was the only one who was gutsy enough to laugh, she still managed to find a way to break me down into nothing.

Everyone else either pretended as if she didn't say that by looking away (like Kennedy) or stared at me, eager to hear my second comeback. I really hoped my brother was going to be my savior in this conversation, knowing how much getting so close to the Olympic team devastated me. Knowing how much I worked to get to the Olympic trials only to miss it by three seconds. But he didn't say anything. He just took a sip of his beer to fill the silence. I wondered if it was because he was going to homecoming with her next weekend and didn't want to ruin his chances of getting laid. I really didn't know.

I could have started crying at that point, but I wasn't going to let Cassandra get that satisfaction.

"She made it to the finals of the Olympic trials," Gabriel said with a sharp crease in his dark eyebrows. God, I loved that guy so much. "She's been to the world championships. All over the sports section of the newspapers, traveled the world to swim. Where has soccer gotten you? To Buffalo for a state semifinal? Congratulations."

Every girl that comprised the Aspen Grove High School girls' soccer team directed their snooty glares at Gabriel. For the first time in that house, my back straightened, and I felt the most confident I'd probably ever feel around that group.

"Well, thanks for insulting all of us, Gabe," Melanie Krugel said, still in peak glare.

I had a million other things I could have said to Cassandra to knock down her last finger, but it didn't really matter at that point. I was already berated in front of all the popular kids. Some laughed at me, others—like my twin brother—just stood there silently. But even given my humiliation and Cassandra's ever growing sneer, I refused to let myself get all the way down to her pathetic level.

"I'm leaving," I told Liam and Gabriel and then snatched the Camry keys out of Liam's back pocket. "I think you lost these rights for a while."

"Yeah, please do," Cassandra said. "Go back in the pool and train for something you'll never achieve."

"Okay, Cassie, we get it. Lay off," Liam said harshly. "I'll come with you, Quinn."

"Me too," Gabriel said, wrapping his arm around me as he guided me to the front door. He was always protecting me.

I got a glimpse into the world of the popular kids. Nothing about that party made me want to stay. It was a galaxy I hoped I never had to visit again.

CHAPTER TWO

I used to dread school dances. For starters, it just gave Liam and me another reason to break into a fight about who was worthy enough to have the Camry. Liam usually won because he always found a date. But since Liam was taking Cassandra to the dance, and the Wicked Witch of Aspen Grove got a BMW for her eighteenth birthday, I won the Camry by default. Because obviously, a brand-spanking-new silver BMW coupe was way better than a 2008 navy blue Toyota Camry. So, at least I got the car one out of the four homecomings.

Another reason why I used to dread school dances was because I felt pressured to go with a boy when all I wanted was to go with a girl. For three homecomings, I got anxiety about asking the girl who I really wanted to go with. It really wasn't until my senior year, this very homecoming, where I felt 100 percent confident with having a girl as my date.

Freshman year was the first year I actually had an interest in a school dance. Partially because all my friends found dates and seemed enthusiastic about going. Partially because I knew that was what I needed to do to enhance my high school experience. And partially because I liked Lana Banner. She was my first actual girl crush—the kind of crush that made you excited to learn about amoebas and mitosis in biology because she was your lab partner. I passed her plenty of notes in class containing flirty sentences, hearts, and winky faces, and she passed them back to me. During labs, she would get really close to me, and every time she did, the hairs rose on the back of my neck. When we dissected our first animal, I was so grossed out and traumatized because I was forced to slice open a dead baby pig because the Department of Education said it would be instrumental to my education. But since her parents were surgeons, Lana was used to blood, knives, and carving out organs at an early age; her soft, gentle hands assisted mine. She made me want to dissect dead baby pigs every day just so I could touch her.

Our fingers laced over the scalpel was the farthest we ever got. Why? Because we weren't out. The gay gods paired two closeted lesbians together, and I ended up going to the dance with Gabriel. My mom was so excited because she thought that I found my first boyfriend. She really wanted us to date, so clearly, I didn't think it through enough because it just convinced my mom that I was into Gabriel. Sure, he was the most attractive boy I'd ever seen, but he really wasn't my type.

Sophomore year, my heart was over Lana and all about Meghan Merritt, a freshman in my gym class. She was out, and I was still about five months from telling Liam. Meghan was this edgy freshman filled with confidence; she wore awesome neon blue Converse and had funky, layered brown hair. She had amazing gaydar because she noticed me a few days into gym class when everyone swarmed around me to find out what the Olympic trials were really like (even our gym teacher). Meghan came up and asked me—very matter-of-fact—why everyone kept talking about me.

"Oh, the Olympics were this year?" she said, completely serious, then proceeded to offer me the second cup of water in her hand. "Sorry, I don't really do the sports."

She went out of her way to hand me unsolicited cups of water with a wink every day. One out girl meant that yes, things could possibly happen. And they did a few weeks into school; after numerous water cup exchanges, we found each other going to the bathroom at the same time during gym class. She proposed that we make out in the shower with the curtain shut. The showers hadn't been used since, like, the 1970s, so we thought we would give them purpose again. She was my first real kiss—with tongue, passion, fingers underneath shirts, and pure teenage lust. She made first-period gym class thrilling the same way Lana Banner made freshman-year biology exciting.

Meghan wanted to go to homecoming with me, but I was still too afraid and deep in my anxiety about my sexuality sophomore year. Meghan was a year younger than me and already had so much more confidence in herself and her sexuality. I mean, the next year, she fully embraced her gender fluidity by chopping off her shoulder-length brown hair for a bleached blond pixie cut, and she was a million times happier when she shed the femininity that she didn't want. She was that confident in letting the world know she was gay and gender fluid, and I envied that part of her so much. I felt so bad I couldn't match her standards.

So, no homecoming dates for both of us that year. Just a large friend group.

Junior year homecoming was the first dance where I was out to my parents and friends, and I asked a girl on my swim team, Riley Scott, to be my date. I got a handful of our swim team friends to wear colored latex caps with a different letter from "Homecoming?" written in permanent marker on each cap. Instant yes and success. A few months after homecoming, I asked her to be my girlfriend. We dated for five months, then I broke up with her that May. She was so loving, affectionate, and nice. Maybe too much for me. I knew it wasn't a really good reason to end things with her, but sometimes, I felt as if she smothered me when I needed space. Lots of space. But we remained friends. At the beginning of our senior year, we made a pact that if we didn't like anyone at the time of homecoming, we would just go together.

So, there we were: homecoming dates for the second year in a row. It was the first time I didn't walk into the dance wearing a huge boulder of anxiety on me like a freakin' corsage. I'd been out for a full year, never happier with myself, and I was actually excited about going to the dance. It also helped that I was going with Riley and our awesome queer friend group, the only ones out at Aspen Grove High School. Lana Banner and Meghan Merritt had been going strong for seven months, and they were adorable together. And then there were Tanner Hayes and Erick Iglesias. All the girls thought Tanner was cute, and all the football players thought Tanner was this laid-back, amazing quarterback, then all those swooning girls became disappointed girls when they learned Tanner was 100 percent gay and dating Erick Iglesias, one of the most talented musicians at school. Erick was the best show choir singer, he played five different instruments, and I could always rely on him to update me on the current rage on Broadway. The two were total opposites but had been dating for a year.

The best thing about my friend group was that we were drama free, with the exception of complaining about the lack of Britney Spears songs at dances. Like, what was that even about? Even when Riley and I broke up at the end of junior year and had a few awkward weeks of dealing with it during the summer, there was hardly any drama at all. Unlike other groups, like Liam's. He made it sound as if they all starred in a daytime soap.

"Just one Britney song," Erick said. "That's all I'm asking."

"Patience, love," Tanner said.

"Screw it. Who wants to go bug the DJ to play her *Circus* songs?"

"I'll come with you!" Lana said.

"Babe, request 'Womanizer' for me, please!" Meghan begged.

Lana gave her girlfriend an air-kiss, and she and Erick skipped along, holding hands through the crowd.

I would have gone with them, but there was just something about the night that made me want to be with Riley. I guess school dances sparked magic in the air. And that magic meant Riley. I'd been waiting for the right time to tell her how pretty she looked. She always looked good in emerald green. Riley could have worn whatever she wanted, and she still would have looked good. She had a great smile, straight white teeth, and she would always brag how she never had braces, so her teeth were just naturally perfect. Big, chestnut eyes; straight, dirty blond hair a few shades lighter than mine that fell to the top of her breasts, and she knew how to wear a snapback and ripped-knee jeans that just screamed "cool, hot, gay chick." It was also a major plus that she was the only one in school who seemed to pick up longboarding in the summers rather than obsessing over skiing or snowboarding in the winters. The whole package was a done deal for me.

We danced closely. Her hands wrapped around my waist and shoulders multiple times that night, and I did the same. The more we danced, the more I wanted her. The more I thought about kissing her. The more I needed to kiss her.

My thighs were starting to hurt from all the swimming I'd done at practice the night before and from all the dancing I'd just done on the dance floor. So, I suggested we take a breather and get fresh air, hoping no Britney song played while we were gone.

We ran up the stairs to the parking lot, holding hands and pulling each other along. We burst through the doors, and the fall air immediately stuck to our clammy skin. I pulled Riley into me and finally kissed her like I had been wanting to ever since she stepped through my front door in that emerald green dress. My lips were filled with lust, nothing more. It was homecoming. The magic tricked me into thinking I wanted Riley back—but just for the night. Or maybe more. Maybe I did want her back. I didn't really know. I also didn't really care at that moment when our lips were locked because our lips were locked, and that was all that really mattered to me.

She pushed me into the brick wall of the building and continued to kiss me as the cool air dried our sweaty skin. Kissing her brought those five months we dated back. My hands grabbed hold of her clammy face as her body pinned me to the brick building. Her tongue slipped into my mouth, and she made me squeak out the softest moan, and when I grabbed more of her iron-curled hair in my fist, she did the same.

But after a few moments, I sensed that we weren't alone, not the only ones who needed fresh air. I pulled away and turned in the direction I felt the presence.

And there she was.

Again.

Hiding in the shadows.

Kennedy Reed.

From the annoyed look she gave us, I had a feeling she'd watched our whole kissing progression from start to finish. But once we both directed our attention to her, she turned back to the phone that lit up her face. She was in a black and gold-laced knee-length dress, her hair pinned into a low updo bun, and I could tell by how her shoulders curled forward that she had been outside long enough for the air to sprout goose bumps on her skin.

If she looked beautiful five minutes after she threw up, I'm not sure what words I could have used other than "wow" followed by a few moments of speechlessness. I always thought she was really pretty. But now? It was the kind of beauty that caught in your stomach. Seeing her in that dress and how gorgeous she looked really overshadowed the memories I had of her missing her two front teeth, her hair in pigtails, and oversized overalls. Kennedy Reed really grew up. She was so freaking beautiful.

"Quinn?" Riley said, snapping me right out of Kennedy's spell.

"Hmm?"

"Wanna go back in? Or maybe drive somewhere?"

"Let's drive somewhere," I said. I couldn't have Kennedy distracting me. Nope, wasn't in the mood to go there tonight. "The music sucks. They haven't even played any *Circus* songs. Where are the throwbacks?"

She raised her hand, biting her lip. God, I needed to go

somewhere so I could make up for the five months it had been since I kissed her.

"We could play some nineties slow jams while we, uh, well, you know…" she suggested.

"Yes, please! But my parents are home."

"Yeah, well, my parents don't know we dated, so we can claim my room as ours."

Riley was really smart. She only told her dad that she was gay and not her mom. She was an only child, and since her parents struggled to get pregnant with her, her mom's next goal in life was to have lots of grandchildren. She would have been heartbroken to find out Riley wasn't going to find herself a lawyer, doctor, or CEO husband who would give her all the grandkids who would share the same genes as her. Even though Mr. Scott knew his daughter liked girls, Riley was also smart enough to know if she told her dad (and especially her mom) that she dated me, we would never be able to be alone together. With the door closed.

We were just the most perfect gal pals, they thought. And that was the only time we wanted people to believe we were "just friends and nothing more."

"I still can't believe they have no idea," I said.

"I'm going to enjoy it as long as I can. Gotta take advantage of my parents not knowing about us, right? So, to my room?"

"Should we just leave?"

Riley looked up at the sky for an answer. "Yes. This can't wait. I'll text the group. I'm sure they'll understand."

This was true. They all had been pushing for us to get back together ever since we broke up. They would be celebrating if they knew we were bailing on them to hook up.

Right as I fished for my keys in her clutch purse, I turned back to check Kennedy. That was when I saw her looking straight at me. My stomach flipped. And her eyes quickly flicked back to her phone.

"Come on," I said, grabbing Riley's hand. No part of me wanted to be in Kennedy's presence. "Let's get out of here."

When we walked into the Scott house, the smell of freshly popped popcorn overwhelmed our noses. In the family room, Mr. and Mrs. Scott bundled underneath a blanket with a large bowl of popcorn, watching *Game of Thrones*. The Scotts were huge *Game of Thrones* fans for various reasons. Mr. Scott liked all the war and gore. Mrs. Scott liked watching for all the family dynamics. And Riley liked watching it because she was in love with Daenerys and spent way too much free time reading Daenerys lesbian fan fiction online.

Riley quickly let go of my hand that she'd held all the way from my car to halfway inside her kitchen. Her parents turned with intrigued smiles. Her mom paused the TV.

"Oh, you two are home early," she said. "We weren't expecting you for another two hours or so."

"Oh, yeah, Quinn's really sore from all that swimming," Riley said and gave me a sly nudge on the arm to play the part.

I relaxed my right leg. "Oh yeah, Leanne had me doing almost eight thousand yards yesterday. My hamstrings are killing me."

"So, we were just going to rest up and watch *Buffy*."

"Oh, okay then. Quinn, you need some ibuprofen or something?"

"No, I'm okay. Thank you, though."

"Would you girls like some popcorn for your show?" Mr. Scott asked.

"Nah. We're still full from dinner. Maybe later."

She continued through the kitchen to the stairs. When we were out of her parents' sight, she grabbed my hand, and we bolted up the steps. Once she locked the door, I pushed her onto her bed, crawled on top of her, and kissed her exactly the way I thought about for the whole night. I hadn't kissed anyone since her, so my lips were ravenous, to say the least.

We made out for what seemed to be forever, then decided why the hell not have sex. Afterward, we dove into our normal routine of late-night, deep conversations, and I vented about how much I couldn't wait to go to Berkeley, to ditch the East Coast and relax on the West Coast, hoping to get a full ride scholarship and maybe be fast enough to medal in Russia at the world championships. But then I began to doubt myself because the Olympic trials still haunted me on my vulnerable nights.

The worst part about swimming was that you could work so hard that you had no effort left, and you could still lose by something as small as one hundredth of a second.

"Oh my God, Quinn," Riley said with a slight laugh; her arms wrapped around my naked body pulled me closer to hers. "You're only seventeen, and you've already done so much."

"Yeah, like failed to medal in anything."

"Oh my gosh, your life is so hard. Woe is you."

I playfully slapped her in the stomach. She grunted. "Shut up," I said.

"You were so close to medaling this summer. Your time will come. I mean, you gave up Swensons fried chicken sandwiches, for crying out loud. You better medal next summer."

"And what if I don't?"

"Well, if you keep playing this 'oh my God, I'm never gonna do anything and boo-hoo the Olympic trials,' you're not gonna do anything. How about saying 'hey, fuckers like Cassandra Jones, I made it to the finals of the Olympic trials when I was fifteen, and then went to the world championships when I was sixteen while you tried passing your driver's ed classes, and then I was on the cover of *Swimming World* magazine when I was seventeen, and now I'm the number one recruit for Division One swimming. Take that.'" She raised both middle fingers.

I laughed and shoved her middle fingers back down. "Okay, I sounded like an asshole."

"But I get why you're scared."

"I know, but I just don't wanna waste all this time training for something I'll never experience. What if I fail? What if I always get so close to qualifying or medaling, and I just become a flop? God, what if I have to stay in New York for the rest of my life?"

"Well, one, you're not gonna be a flop. You gave up fried chicken sandwiches and swim every hour you're awake for a reason. Two, despite just insulting me because I like New York, I'll still allow you to sleep in my bed when I live in the city."

"Can you give me free Broadway tickets as a party favor?"

"Just as long as you admit you think it's hot that I'm going to turn into a weird art student."

I rolled my eyes and let out a long, overly dramatic sigh. "Fine! I'll admit it's going to be really sexy when you turn into a weird NYU art student. You'll have paint all over you, and your hair is always going to be messy."

If her longboarding hobby intrigued me, the fact that she wanted to be a stage designer intrigued me even more. Who wanted to major in design for stage and film at NYU? Riley. Because she was Riley. She was so unusual in the best possible ways.

Just as I slowly leaned in to kiss her again, I heard my phone ringing faintly, buried underneath our dresses scattered on the floor of Riley's bedroom. I wanted to ignore it. It was two o'clock in the morning, and Riley and I were having one of our good, deep conversations again. We could have talked about grass blades and would somehow end up discussing it for four hours. I really missed our six-hour conversations about everything and anything and nothing.

But something told me to answer my phone. I thought, what if there was an emergency, and I didn't pick it up just so I could make out with my ex-girlfriend; I would live my life forever in extreme guilt.

"One second," I told her and searched for my phone on the floor. Once I found it underneath my dress, I saw it was Liam.

Then I had this awful feeling something was wrong. I couldn't tell if it was our twin instinct or just my two-in-the-morning paranoia.

Either way, I picked up. I wasn't going to risk it.

"Hey, are you all right?" I said.

"Quinn? Hi, I'm fine. Are you busy?"

The tone of his voice didn't sound at all urgent. If anything, the words stuck together like glue. My heart slowed down when I realized it was just a drunk call.

"Um, a little."

"Could you pick me up, pretty pretty please?"

Clearly, I must have misheard him. The one weekend night I won the car, he wanted me to stop what I was doing to pick him up when he didn't have the time or energy to drop me off a week before so I could avoid Cassandra's party?

"Um, why?"

"Because I'm drunk and wanna go home."

"Can't you just crash at whatever house you're at?"

"I'm at Cassie's, and no, I don't wanna stay at her house. She's drunk and crying."

"Why is she crying?"

"Because Tom and Gabriel broke her mom's vase she got from Madrid, and she's freaking out about it."

"Well, stay and help her clean up. You'd be such a gentleman."

"Quinn, it will only take, like, twenty minutes, and then you can go back to Riley."

"Remember that time it would have only taken you ten minutes to drop me off after the football game, but you dragged me to Cassandra's only for her to call me out on missing the Olympics to everyone, and then you literally stood there and did nothing to stop it?"

"Yeah, but—"

"I'm busy. I'm enjoying my night out. Have someone else take you home or call an Uber."

"Or you pick me up now, and I promise you can have the car every weekend until the New Year."

Okay, that was a game changer and quite the offer. He must have really wanted to leave if he just offered me the car every weekend for the next two and a half months.

"God, how miserable are you right now?" I said.

"Miserable. I'm tired and wanna go home."

"I'll be there in ten." I hung up the phone and glanced at Riley, who looked equally annoyed. "I need to borrow some of your clothes."

"Seriously? You're picking him up?"

"He offered me the car for the rest of the year. I'm taking it. Clothes?" She pointed to her dresser. "I'm so sorry. Maybe we can do something next weekend to make up for it?"

She rolled her eyes. "Sure. Fine."

After I stole a clean T-shirt, sweatpants, and flip-flops from her, I gave her a kiss on the lips and quickly ran out of her house.

When I pulled into Cassandra's neighborhood of McMansions, I spotted the cars of all the partygoers parked strategically and sporadically throughout the neighborhood, trying to be discreet from nosey neighbors. Pulling up into her driveway, I couldn't even tell there was underage drinking, sex, and drugs going on inside her ritzy house. Just a few lights were on but no blaring music, no red Solo cups in the front yard, and no stumbling high schoolers. Nothing like how they portrayed high school parties in movies and TV shows. Cassandra was a pro at the high-school-party-when-the-parents-were-out-of-town-slash-working thing. I expected nothing less.

When Liam stumbled out of Cassandra's house, he wasn't alone. Kennedy walked behind him, a little less wobbly than he was. His black tie was in his hand, and his dress shirt was unbuttoned at the top button and slightly wrinkled. Kennedy was out of her black and gold dress and wore jeans and her green soccer hoodie, her updo unraveled down to her chest in messy, loose curls. Both of them definitely looked like people usually did at two thirty in the morning. Drunk, forced to sober up, and up to no good.

Don't ask me to drive Kennedy home. Don't ask me to drive her home.

"Could we drive Kennedy home too?" he said as he opened the passenger door. "She's on the way."

He really didn't give me an option to say no.

"Sure." *Crap.* "Gabe doesn't need a ride home?"

"Nah, he's too wrapped up with Melanie."

Gabriel and Melanie went together. As much as I thought Gabriel could find himself a better girl, at least he was finding success with his crush. It just sucked he couldn't save me from the awkwardness shoved into the Camry.

Liam motioned Kennedy into the back seat and even opened the door for her. When both of them hopped in, they brought the stench of all the alcohol they'd devoured. With them combined, it smelled like Bud Light, coconut rum, Jäger, and Smirnoff. The air thickened in the car as Kennedy settled into her seat right behind the passenger's side. I partially hated myself for watching her get in the back through the rearview mirror, but I couldn't control my curiosity. Even in a hoodie, she looked so beautiful. I was also a sucker for the femme tomboy look, so her hair, makeup, and hoodie grabbed my attention when I didn't think it ever would, and I hated the feeling that erupted in my stomach any time I saw a pretty girl. And apparently, Kennedy was no different. My stomach was traitorous. And then her eyes found mine in the mirror. When we made eye contact, the feelings in my stomach rushed full speed to my chest. My eyes darted back to Cassandra's house in front of me, and I started the car.

Enough of that.

"Ah, look at you," Liam said with a teasing smirk on his face. "An NYU T-shirt? Are you wearing Riley's clothes?"

As I backed out of the driveway, Kennedy and I made quick

eye contact yet again before I immediately faced the front and put the car in drive.

"You owe me so much right now," I said to Liam.

"Oh, you're in your ex-girlfriend's clothes on homecoming night. Something happened! Did you hook up? Did you? Did you?"

"I don't sleep and tell."

He let out a laugh and smacked me playfully on the arm. "How did I know that was gonna happen? So, does that mean you two are getting back together?"

"I can't have fun for one night just for the sake of having fun?"

"Of course you can. Just remember why you broke up with her. Don't want her to latch on to you again."

"I know. I think we're good, though. Hopefully."

"You should probably talk to her."

I grunted. How about we didn't acknowledge it just in case the thought hadn't run through her mind?

"So, did you hook up with Cassandra?" I asked.

He scoffed. "Hell no. She was drunk the whole time. I didn't even know she was hiding a flask in her boobs until halfway through the dance. Does she always do that, Ken?"

Ken. Her family called her that all the time when she was younger. Ken or Kenny. I used to call her Kenny way back when. She called me Quincy, an ode to my first name and middle initial C. Now, I don't even remember the last time I said her name out loud, and I didn't even know Liam was close enough with her to get away with calling her Ken.

His head turned around the passenger seat to check on her. I glimpsed back too. She was curled up on the door, huddled into herself. I figured she was cold, and as much resentment I held towards her, I still cranked up the heat just a little to make sure it got back there if that was the case. Her face was long, and her gaze watched the passing tree line outside the window. Clearly, both of us were uncomfortable by how close we were to each other. If I wasn't driving, I'd probably look the same as her.

"Hey, you all right?" Liam said. "You got really quiet all of a sudden."

Kennedy's eyes fell on mine first, and then immediately darted to Liam's. Mine snapped back to the dark road ahead, and I turned on my brights to make sure I didn't hit any animals. I should have been paying better attention to the road than a pretty girl in a hoodie in my back seat—I mean, I should have been paying better attention to the road than Kennedy Reed.

"Yeah, uh, I'm fine. Just, uh, just tired," she answered.

I recognized that voice, and if Liam knew her as well as I used to, he would have known something was eating away at her mind. She only tripped over her words when she was worried about something or feeling guilty. Guess that part of her still lived inside her seventeen-year-old body.

"It's a left up here," Liam said. "This one. The one with the red door."

She can't even direct me to her house. That's so pathetic.

Her house sat modestly in the darkness with one giant oak tree in the front. No lights were on except for the garage lights to help guide her home.

"Good night. Sleep tight," Liam said as I parked the car. Kennedy wasted no time opening the door to escape, as if that was all she could think about doing the whole ride. I wondered if it was because the thick air between us weighed down on her lungs like it did for me. Or maybe she needed to throw up again. Who knew?

"Good night," she said to Liam, grabbing hold of his shoulder, then releasing it. He smiled. I rolled my eyes. "And thanks for driving me home, Quinn."

Something about how she said my name in a reticent voice did something to my stomach. Again. Because my stomach didn't get the memo that we didn't do backflips for Kennedy Reed. No sir. Kennedy Reed was not in the same category as Hot

Lifeguard, Lana Banner, Meghan Merritt, Riley Scott, Kristen Stewart, Demi Lovato, Lexa from *The 100*, and Alex Vause from *Orange Is the New Black.*

Even though I secretly knew she was.

But when she said my name, my stomach sank—or maybe it burned a little. I wasn't sure if the feeling was from the guilt of whatever I did to her that made her hate me or if it was a sign that I loved hearing her say my name.

Life was freakin' confusing.

"Not a problem. Bye," I said, quicker than I intended.

I needed her to leave so the butterflies on steroids in my stomach went back into hibernation. *You come out for Hot Lifeguard, not for Kennedy Reed, you morons.*

She closed the door and headed into her dark house. I wasted no time backing out of her driveway.

"Wow, that was cold," Liam said.

"What?"

"The way you answered her. She thanked you, and you were all, 'bitch, bye!' "

"I'll hug her next time. Say everything between us is squashed now."

"You're still not over that?"

"Really, Liam? It's not something you just get over."

"I think it is."

"You don't even know half of it."

"Then tell me so I can understand."

I couldn't tell him the other half. It was too…complicated. I didn't even know what it meant. Apparently something, though, if she felt the need to ignore me all this time.

"Look," I continued, "just know that she hurt me. Pretty badly. It's not something I can just forget about. I didn't do anything wrong."

"And she did?"

"It's not my story to tell."

"And it's hers?"

Yes, it was.

Meghan Merritt was my first actual kiss. One that lasted more than just a three-second peck. But technically, she wasn't my first kiss. That title belonged to someone else.

That someone else went by the name of Kennedy Reed: one of the most popular girls in school, co-captain of the soccer team, and the girl who all the guys wanted to date and all the girls wanted to look like. She was the one who initiated that three-second peck on her porch when we were thirteen. It was her story to tell.

As much as we both wanted to just forget about it.

CHAPTER THREE

I thrived on structure. My whole life was run on a precise schedule: from the very second I woke up, to my high school classes, to my swimming workouts, to what I ate every day. Some people might have gone crazy if they had a very detailed schedule they had to follow to a T every single day of their life, but I loved it. I looked at it as an easy roadmap to a medal at world champs. If I took an unsuspected detour, well, I was in trouble.

On Monday, Wednesday, and Friday mornings, I woke up at four thirty to train with my club team. This team was comprised of elite swimmers who dreamed big, usually nationals and Olympic hopefuls. So, on those days, I drove across town to that pool, spent forty minutes weightlifting, and then spent an hour swimming. Or on Tuesday and Thursday, I woke up at the same time for an hour-and-a-half morning practice session with my high school team. So, every day, I had some kind of morning practice. Then I did the whole high school thing. I followed my eating habits during lunch, filling my stomach up with healthy fats and proteins, and depending on if it was a meet day, carbs. I plugged my macros into an app tracker, then spent two and a half hours practicing with my high school team if the day was Monday, Wednesday, or Friday. Tuesday and Thursday afternoons, I trained with my club team since the workouts were more intense.

And then I had weekends off. But not in the summer. I gave my soul to swimming in the summer.

Sound confusing? It was, but I had a daily planner I geeked out over and used colorful pens to color coordinate my whole week. I'd been doing it for five years, so it wasn't confusing to me anymore. It was just my life. And my life and schedule had been running smoothly, uninterrupted for the whole five years. It was smooth sailing. Just follow the path, and you're on the right track. Just like Google Maps.

The Monday after homecoming, everything was shaken up by just one minuscule detail. No, I didn't like surprises—unless Xanax was involved. Maybe. I'd never taken Xanax or any kind of drug so I didn't really know if that was true—but that was beside the point. The point was, if something out of the ordinary was going to happen, I needed a reasonable amount of time to mentally prep myself.

That minuscule catalyst that shook up the rest of my week happened in fourth-period calc—the worst subject in the history of school subjects—the class right before lunch that I had to suffer through with Cassandra Jones, Tom Felix, Jennifer Stewart, and Kennedy Reed as my classmates.

That group decided that Monday after homecoming, they were going to be extra obnoxious. It was normal for Mr. Carmichael to shoot them at least one glare during the period because they kept whispering and texting, but this Monday, Mr. Carmichael had enough of their crap. Cassandra and Jennifer kept giggling, and Tom thought he was slick by showing Kennedy something on his phone underneath his desk.

Mr. Carmichael stopped writing on the whiteboard and directed his attention to the group's recent snicker. All four of them were guilty, and when he shot them his death look, they tried to hush but failed to hide their smiles.

"Please, share with the class what's so funny about indefinite integrals," Mr. Carmichael said.

This made it harder for them to hold in their laughter. Quite frankly, I didn't blame them. Mr. Carmichael really took calculus seriously in his sweater and tie. Taking a Mr. Rogers wannabe seriously was as difficult as making the Olympic swim team.

"All right, I thought you four were mature seniors who could handle sitting by each other, but I guess not. Mr. Felix, please switch seats with Miss Donahue. Miss Stewart, how about you switch with Mr. Shea. And Miss Reed, please switch with Miss Nahar."

My stomach dropped so hard, I almost had to let out a cough. Keely Nahar sat directly in front of me. This wasn't part of the script. Keely Nahar passed my homework to the front every class period. Keely Nahar was the person who occasionally asked me if I solved (insert the number of the hardest problem on the calc homework) before the bell rang.

Not Kennedy Reed.

With annoyed sulks on their faces, Tom, Jennifer, and Kennedy packed up their belongings and switched seats. Keely Nahar did the same, and I wanted to grab her hand and force her back down in that seat. Kennedy slipped into Keely Nahar's seat without giving me any eye contact. Directly in front of me. Close enough for me know what she smelled like. Her breeze smelled like a mix of McIntosh apple body spray and floral shampoo. Probably Herbal Essences.

Four years later and she still only wore Bath & Body Works body spray.

I sank in my seat. I could feel my pulse thumping through my neck.

"These will be your permanent seats from now on," Mr. Carmichael said. "Now, Mr. Felix, how about you show the class how well you've been paying attention? Come solve this indefinite integral equation."

And there went my concentration for the rest of calc.

After lunch, I always stopped at my locker to drop off my morning books in exchange for my afternoon of complete boredom: physics, AP History, and econ. But that Monday wasn't an ordinary Monday—maybe because of Mercury in retrograde? A ruptured star? A full moon? Who knows what was going on in the universe, but whatever it was, it was severely messing up the structure of Aspen Grove High School on Earth. So, of course, that meant complete boredom would be shaken up with Kennedy Reed approaching me at my locker. It was as if my body knew she was coming because I looked up when sliding my three textbooks into my book bag to find her eyes zeroed in on me. I felt so stuck. There was no way to escape.

"Hey," she said when she reached my locker.

Embarrassingly enough, I actually turned around to see if Cassandra or Jennifer were behind me, but they weren't. She was looking and talking to me, something she hadn't done in four years.

Once upon a time, before puberty either blessed or cursed kids, before cliques and labels determined the success or failure of said puberty, back during a time when all you needed was colorful chalk to spark a friendship, Kennedy Reed had been my best friend. From first through seventh grade, she lived only five houses away from us. Gabriel lived two blocks in the opposite direction. Kennedy was to me as Gabriel was to Liam. My best friend. My chosen person of the neighborhood. The person who I spent every daylight hour during the summers with, and the person I spent school nights marathon texting about the daily struggles of elementary and middle school. Liam, Gabriel, Kennedy, and I called ourselves the four musketeers. I couldn't recall a school weekend or summer day without one of them over at our house. Kennedy and I were inseparable. Then, right before the start of eighth grade, the Reeds moved to New York City for Mr. Reed's new job. We both were devastated. It was the end of an era. We had no idea how to finish middle school, and we couldn't even fathom high school without each other. We planned how we would text every day and talked about how we would make sure we applied to the same colleges and would request each other to be roommates. We had the next six years of our lives planned out the second we knew that she had to move away.

But after the Reeds moved to the Upper East Side, I never got a single text from her.

Two years later, when they moved back, I saw my long-lost friend in the high school hallways unannounced. Despite the silence, broken promises, and the random appearance without any sort of warning, I still called her name with an ecstatic wave because my best friend was back, in my high school, with a book bag strapped to her back and a class schedule in her hands just like the rest of us. But she took one look at me and turned the other way too quickly for me to fully process what happened. As if her silence for the past two years wasn't enough, I had to watch her reject me in front of her two new popular best friends: Cassandra Jones and Jennifer Stewart. And I had no idea why.

My childhood best friend rejecting me devastated me more than not qualifying for the London Olympics. So, no, as much as Liam thought I should have been over it by now, I wasn't at all. It absolutely crushed me because I had no idea what I'd done for her to write me off like that. She remained friends with Liam and Gabriel. Look how convenient that was for her: two of the most popular guys in our class.

Now, in the very same hallway as the first day of sophomore year, in almost the exact same spot, stood Kennedy Reed. Eyebrows raised to perfect her friendly face, but the space separating us showed how scared, hesitant, and unsure she was of the situation she'd just created with a simple "Hey."

I was completely nonplussed that after all this time, she stood just feet in front of me. The only word I could formulate was "Hey?"

Question mark fluctuation and all…like an idiot.

"Hey," she said softly and airy, looking as if she couldn't believe she was talking to me either. "I just want to thank you for driving me home this weekend. I know you didn't want to, and it kinda ruined your plans—"

"It's fine. It's not a big deal. Really."

"Yeah, well, I'm sure it was a little irritating ditching your date to drive two drunk people home. Also, thank you for giving me a drink at Cassie's party. You really didn't have to fetch a drunk mess a cup of water."

"We've all been there before. It's really not a problem."

"It was still a really nice thing for you to do. Both times. I really do appreciate it."

Her sincerity unraveled the frown I wanted to give her. She was being so…nice and genuine. Like the Kennedy I knew as a kid who was nice to even the meanest kids in the neighborhood. It almost felt as if I was talking to my best friend after a little fight.

"Well, I'm glad I could help," I said, and I thought it was weird that she made me actually glad that I did give her water and drive her home.

She gave a small smile. "Well, that's all really. Gotta trek over to American Lit now."

Okay, she's being totally nice and normal. I can be nice and normal too.

"Do you have Mrs. Dexter? For AP?"

She'd taken a step forward, but when I asked the question, she faced me again as if shocked that I continued the conversation. I was pretty shocked that I said more to her too. But she didn't have to walk up to me and thank me for the two good deeds. Yet, despite clearly being uncomfortable approaching me, she did it anyway. So, I thought I would acquiesce.

"Yeah…" The corners of her mouth rose slightly as if she was glad I stopped her.

"There's a pop quiz today. First four chapters of *The Awakening*."

Her eyes widened. "Seriously? Crap, I didn't read it!"

"B, C, C, D, A. Those are the answers. She goes over them right afterward."

"And you remember them?"

"I have a good memory."

"B, C, C…" She attempted to remember.

"D, A."

She looked up at the ceiling, her head doing a nod every time she said a letter in her head. "Okay, I think I got it. Thank you."

The next day in calc after the bell rang, Kennedy quickly took her new seat in front of me. The smell of apples and flowers sent me into my first trance: watching her settle in her seat, pulling out her textbook, notebook, pencil, and calculator; and noticing how shiny and straight her light brown hair was. Mr. Carmichael called for us to pass forward our homework. Instead of Keely Nahar taking mine, Kennedy turned around with a small smile, snapping me out of my trance.

"Thanks for the tip yesterday," she said with her palm out. "Got them all right. I'm still impressed you remembered those answers."

I ripped my homework out of my notebook and placed it in her hands. "Now you gotta put your finger down to never cheating on a test next time you play Never Have I Ever."

And then she laughed, and for whatever reason, I couldn't shake that moment from my head for the rest of the day.

For the rest of the week, she flashed a friendly smile when she turned around to collect my homework. The first time, it caught me by surprise, but I wasn't complaining at all by the end of the week. A slight alteration to the structure never hurt anyone, right?

Friday, after just coming from Mrs. Dexter's American Lit class:

"Another pop quiz today," I said when I gave her my homework.

"It's a good thing I read the chapters."

"Need the answers? I've got them all in my head for anyone who needs them."

She thought for a moment as she passed forward our homework. "Nah, I think I got it. Don't make me have a guilty conscience."

When she faced the front, the smirk I tried hiding stretched across my face. She was always a good girl, always obeying the rules. It was no surprise that she admitted to everyone at Cassandra's party that she never cheated on a test, and it was no surprise again when she refused to take my answers for a guaranteed A+ on a pop quiz. Cheating just wasn't in her vocabulary.

Maybe a part of the Kennedy I knew did still exist.

❖

Riley, Madison Olivares, Gia Rotella, and I stood behind lane four right after the national anthem to get ready for our 200 medley relay. It was our first home meet of the season. I was ready to see how successful my summer and fall training had been, spending five hours a day in the summer swimming and another hour of building muscle during dryland training. I had ten months to get my times as perfect as possible for the world champs, and if my times were fast enough, I would qualify for the Olympic trials. I had to start the season off right.

The timers and officials huddled near the timer's table, and the four of us stretched out our arms and legs. I used Riley's shoulder to balance on as I stretched my left thigh, watching people still trickling into the natatorium. Just as I switched legs and placed my left arm on her shoulder, I spotted Kennedy Reed walking through the doors.

My arm slipped off Riley's shoulder, but I quickly gathered myself before I could tumble onto the slippery pool deck.

Kennedy stood in the entryway dressed as if she was ready to hang out with friends. If you went to a swim meet, you wore jeans and a T-shirt because the humidity was that of Florida in the summer, even if it was snowing outside. But her hair was straight and shiny just like at school. She was in jeans, knee-high brown boots, and a navy sweater, and I knew it would be about five minutes until she regretted wearing that...despite looking beautiful in it.

Okay, so about this Mercury in retrograde or a ruptured star in the galaxy—it had to have been the real reason why all these things started happening, right? Kennedy sitting in front of me. Kennedy giving me smiles every day when she collected my homework. Kennedy randomly showing up at my swim meet by herself. I repeat: by herself. That was a gutsy move in high school, just waltzing into someone's world who wasn't on the same totem pole level as you.

I couldn't even go to the bathroom by myself without asking one of my friends to go with me. There was no way I would show up to a soccer game without a friend to protect me from popular girl ridicule.

She looked like a fish flapping desperately out of water as she tried to find a place to sit. It was probably the first time in high school that she felt like a fish gasping for ar. Liam spotted her, stood, and waved to get her attention. I wanted her to squirm just a little bit more. He looked just as surprised as I was, but his friendly smile told me he wasn't complaining at all. He was probably relieved someone in his world stumbled into the oh-so-scary one I subjected him to.

The expressions on my parents' faces reassured me that I was being completely rational with my confusion as to why Kennedy Reed now decided to reenter my life. Voluntarily. They didn't recognize her at first as she walked up the steps and approached them, and I assumed the words I couldn't hear Liam say introduced the nostalgic name to them. Their faces lit up, and they hugged her as if no time had passed. She hugged them back.

"Madison, is Mercury in retrograde right now?" I asked, still watching Kennedy interact with my family in the stands. Madison was really into astrology. Last year, during a girls' swim team sleepover, she did every girl's birth charts and stayed awake until three thirty in the morning explaining what it meant to everyone.

"No, we're in the post-shadow phase. Mercury was in retrograde in the beginning of October. Why?"

I sighed. "No reason," I said.

Needless to say, I didn't get my head together properly for the race. Swimming was 90 percent mental, 10 percent physical. I think that was why I couldn't pull through in placing first or second in my events at the Olympic trials. I was simply too overwhelmed by all the veterans I'd spent years admiring, all the people packed in the stands as if it was a Division I college basketball game championship, and the huge-stake-huge-reward that would come out of the meet. My mental game wasn't as strong as my swimming times at the Olympic trials, and that was what fucked me over.

This meet Kennedy decided to go to on a Friday night? Yeah, all my times were nowhere near where I wanted them to be, and I tried telling myself that my summer and fall training were fine. I was just completely thrown off by overanalyzing whatever game Kennedy was playing. I was so infuriated about letting myself get tangled up with her mysterious intentions. Letting my mind control my races still triggered me. So triggering that I even skipped the cooldown. That was a big no-no in the swimming world, especially since I was a co-captain with Madison, and our coach, Leanne, held us to a higher standard for underclassmen. But it was worth the risk. I could handle a lecture from Leanne. My brain going on sensory overload? Not so much. I needed a blue raspberry slushie to calm my anxiety down.

After I changed, I met up with my family, and Kennedy was still talking to them. You would think they would have been caught up on each other's lives during the two hours of the swim meet. Because, like, what did they have to talk about? Oh hey, you moved to the city? How was that? How's high school? How come you and Quinn don't hang out, but you and Liam always do? You could wrap that up in ten minutes max.

But nope. She. Was. Still. There.

I wasn't sure whether to be happy or pissed. Maybe I was a little bit of both.

"Quinn, dear, good meet," Mom said, smiling.

"The meet was awful," I said. "My times were awful."

My dad laughed. "Hon, I don't think your times can be awful. You have seven school records and two state records."

"They weren't good enough to medal at the world champs. They're not good enough for the Olympics."

"Don't be so hard on yourself," my mom said and wrapped her arm around me. "Everyone has a bad meet. You still have plenty of time to get the times that you want."

"I'm gonna go drink my sorrows now. I'll see you later."

When I got outside, I buried my hands in my jacket to search for my keys. The air was cold, and my wet hair started to freeze. All I wanted was to grab a blue raspberry slushie from the Swensons drive-thru to drown my swimming sorrows, crawl into my bed, light some candles, and listen to some angry songs.

"Hey, Quinn!"

It wasn't a voice I recognized, which meant it could only be one person. I was an inch away from my car yet so far. I took a deep inhale of cold, early November air, hoping that would kill all the anger I had raging in my body. When I turned, I saw Kennedy heading toward me. She still had a hint of a smile from catching up with my family, yet the closer she came to me, the more anxiety mingled into that smile when she noticed my less-than-enthused facial expression. I took a deep breath, trying so hard not to sound as angry as I felt. We'd made small but tremendous progress over the week, and I couldn't let my competitive temper damper that.

"Hey," I said.

"I thought you did really well. You lapped almost everyone."

I forced out a smile. She was trying to be nice even though whether I lapped people or not wasn't going to get me a medal at the world champs. But she got points for trying. Five points for Hufflepuff.

"You've taken an interest in swimming?"

"Well, kinda. I'm here for the school paper."

"The school paper? The school paper cares about swimming now?"

"Well, Ms. Kramer wanted to spice up the paper this year with things we normally don't cover or talk about, so I suggested swimming."

"We're the only sport that performs half-naked, and still, no one cares. I don't think anyone is going to care about swimming."

"But we can try? One of our swimmers is the number one ranked seventeen-year-old swimmer, went to the Olympic trials and world championships, and is going again next summer. That's kind of a big deal."

I was taken aback that she even knew about both world champs. She really did her homework. Another five points for Hufflepuff.

"People only care about the Olympics," I said. "I didn't make it to London. I think most people know that. Cassandra sure does."

"Cassandra is petty. Don't let a petty person bring you down from, like, the biggest accomplishment of your life."

Why is she giving me good advice? Why is she being so nice to me? Again?

Just a little bit of anger simmered. Just like when we were kids, whenever my quick temper or competitive side took over the best of me, Kennedy—the voice of reason—was always able to calm me down. Once when we were ten, the neighborhood kids played Capture the Flag one summer night in our backyard. I touched Danny Windell fair and square on the back, and he refused to go to jail. His team ended up winning, and I made a big stink about how he cheated and how he was supposed to be in jail because I touched him. *It's just a game*, Danny said, and most of the people agreed with him. *It's okay, Quinn*, Kennedy told me in her calm voice. *We'll team up on him next time, tackle him to the ground, and give him a wedgie.*

Two weeks later, we did exactly that, and Danny cried his way home. I didn't feel bad like I probably should have. Karma is a bitch.

Sometimes it really bothered me how much I let stupid things annoy me. But Kennedy was the only one who truly understood my competitive nature. Even after all this time of not talking to each other, she still understood my competitive side and tried calming me down.

"Well, it's easy to let her get you down when she hits you with two low blows in a night," I replied.

"Yeah, that was a really shitty thing for her to do. I'm sorry that happened to you."

She still played the innocent card when it came to kissing a girl. I couldn't hold the words back any longer.

"Eh, what can you do? I was the only girl at the party who kissed another girl so…"

Why did you say that? Your conversation was going so well, and you let your anger ruin that. Cool, Quinn. Very cool.

Her jaw tightened, defining her cheekbones and jawline even more. Her friendly demeanor quickly changed, but I wasn't fazed by her glaring eyes or the clench in her jaw. "Don't," she said sternly.

The friendly Kennedy Reed I'd experienced the whole week finally turned herself in, causing me to let out a laugh. "Don't what? Call you out? Acknowledge that we used to be best friends until you moved back?"

"Yeah, exactly that."

"Why? Does it make you uncomfortable?" I said, rather amused.

Okay, I knew I was a little harsh on her. But I was also infuriated with my swim, and that anger just brought up the grudge I'd shoved down for the past week while I enjoyed Kennedy acknowledging me to the most minimal degree—that also felt so rewarding.

But none of that changed how'd she treated me since she moved back, with no explanation. I deserved an explanation, and why not use my bad mood to finally get it?

"I don't know what I did that was so wrong for you to act like I'm nothing to you," I continued. "We used to be best friends."

"I know—"

"And then you move, break your promise that you'll text me, and come back just to ignore me in the hallway on the first day of school sophomore year?"

"I know. I'm sorry—"

"Why are you finally talking to me? Because I gave you water? Drove you home? Gave you test answers? You know that doesn't make it okay for all your ignoring for the past four years?"

"I know—"

"You know? You know everything I'm saying? Then why the hell did you do it? I deserve an answer. You know how it feels to be rejected by your best friend? Best friends aren't supposed to do that. I actually believed I did something wrong for years. I thought there was something wrong with me because you didn't want me in your life. I'm finally at the point where I'm at peace with losing you as a best friend because I didn't match up to whatever standards you have now for friends. I've finally accepted myself and the situation, and now you realize I'm not a crappy person like you think I am?"

"I never thought you were a crappy person."

"Then why the hell did you do it?"

She looked down at her hands. I hoped that her approaching me meant that I would finally get the genuine apology and explanation as to what I did wrong that I needed and wanted so I could finally get my closure.

"I was confused," she said softly. "Scared. Embarrassed. I didn't know what to do."

"Embarrassed about what?"

"You know what."

My heart plummeted. The kiss. It was all about the kiss.

Right as my stomach twisted, people started to pour out of the natatorium doors. We weren't alone in the parking lot anymore, and I knew that in order to get all the answers to the questions I wanted, Kennedy and I had to run away from the crowd.

"I was gonna go to Swensons to grab a slushie if you wanted to come and finish the talk."

She glanced over her shoulder and noticed the swim team mingling with the rest of the crowd. Riley, Madison, and Gia busted through the doors, laughing and talking like their usual loud selves, making their presence known to anyone else having important conversations in the parking lot.

"No, I, uh, I should just get going."

"Really? You don't have a half hour to finish this? We're already this far—"

"No. I need to go."

"Quinn Charlotte Hughes!" Riley shouted as she walked closer to us.

That scared Kennedy even more—like a dog hearing fireworks on the Fourth of July. The ex-girlfriend full-naming me right when she wanted to talk about the kiss. Kennedy bolted.

"Was that Kennedy Reed talking to you?" Gia said, laughing as Kennedy's silhouette dissolved into the night.

"Yeah, I guess you can call it that."

"What did she even want?" Riley said.

"I don't know? Something for the paper?" She didn't even want that. She was completely enigmatic. Who knows what she wanted?

CHAPTER FOUR

I thought about it all weekend. What she said to me. How she couldn't even finish the conversation. How she booked it so quickly when she saw my friends come out of the building that I thought she should have taken up track for a spring sport.

And that night. It was all because of that one night.

It replayed on repeat in my mind all weekend. It was the night before she moved to New York City, a few weeks before the start of eighth grade. We took a walk around the neighborhood one last time, and she told me how much she was going to miss me, and I told her the same thing. She confessed how she was scared of making new friends, she was scared of taking the subway everywhere, and she was scared that all the kids at her new school would be pretentious pricks, even more so than Aspen Grove. She promised how she would text me and how we would keep in touch because we were best friends. Nothing could ever change that, she said.

And then we got back to her porch. We hugged each other good-bye so tightly as we cried, afraid we would never see each other again. That was when it happened. So unexpectedly. She kissed me. My body froze in shock. It came out of nowhere, and I had no idea how to react but to kiss her back before I had time to process it or know what I was doing. I'd never kissed anyone before, and I'd always thought my first kiss—even then—would be with a boy. Not my best friend of six years. All I remembered from the kiss was my heart thumping against my rib cage, how her lips tasted like root beer from the floats we ate for dessert, and how soft her lips were against mine. They felt so…nice and comforting, and only in hindsight do I remember her kiss feeling scared and insecure. The kiss only lasted about three seconds, and after she pulled away, she quickly said bye and ran into her house. I didn't see her again until the first day of sophomore year when I ran up to her, and she walked the other way down the hall.

Unlike the week before, when Monday rolled around, she came into the calc room and chatted with Jennifer and Cassandra. When the bell rang, she took her seat in front of me; the sight of her made me feel so warm with guilt and confusion. And that was that. No smile when she collected my homework. Not even eye contact.

Just like what the original script called for. That should have made me feel at peace. The effects of the ruptured star finally wore off. But I didn't.

Tuesday was different. She came in right as the bell rang, and Mr. Carmichael told us to pass forward our homework.

This time, her eyes met mine.

"I want to finish the conversation," she said softly, holding her hand out for my homework. "Are you free Thursday night?"

Well, that was unexpected. Say something. Say words…

"I have a meet on Thursday night."

"What about Friday night? Maybe we could go to Swensons and talk there?"

Yes. Have a serious talk while having that blue raspberry slushie. Nothing could go wrong with a blue raspberry slushie.

"I have practice until six, but maybe after?"

"Okay. I'll just work out after school and meet you in the rec center lobby? At six fifteen?"

"Sure. That works."

I couldn't even tell you what we were supposed to learn about vectors that day. My mind was so focused on all the things we'd both held in this whole time that were now about to come out. That was when I really started doubting the healing powers of the Swensons blue raspberry slushie. For the rest of the week, when her hair was merely inches away from me and I was reminded of our looming conversation, I hardly took any notes on vectors and matrices. I caught myself daydreaming about all the scenarios that could happen during our talk, all of them ending with the cold hard truth that she hated me for some embarrassing reason, and I was the biggest loser on the face of the planet. No slushie would cure that humiliation.

But it was all about the kiss. It clearly meant something to her if she erased me from her life. I would be a liar if I said I didn't think about the kiss. I thought about it all the time, but as the years progressed, the more I remembered how I could feel her lips loosely against mine as if she was terrified. Terrified of losing me? Terrified of admitting her feelings to me? Terrified of liking girls? The only consistent part of the memory over the years was the taste of root beer. The weeks after the kiss, I kept drinking root beer because I missed her so much, and the taste of it was so vivid, I needed to drink it to preserve the memory of her and that kiss. But when my phone didn't have a single text from her, and she shunned me in the hallway sophomore year, I no longer ordered root beer when I had the chance. I avoided it like the plague instead.

I was able to put it out of my mind for my meet on Thursday. Thank God, because I don't think I would have forgiven myself if I couldn't compartmentalize my issues for yet another meet. My times were average, just a little faster than the first home meet. Good enough for me to be content for the second meet of the season, but nowhere near where I wanted them to be if I wanted to medal at the world championships.

"What are you up to tonight?" Riley asked me in the locker room, pulling up her jeans after Friday's practice.

Barfing up all of my insides.

I kept my eyes on my bag the whole time while getting changed. I knew that on the other side of the wall in the rec locker room, Kennedy was changing out of her workout clothes too. Was she as anxious and as in a hurry—yet procrastinating all at the same time—like me? Did she feel like throwing up too?

"Um, nothing," I mumbled. "Nothing important."

"Did you wanna grab something at Swensons? I'm really craving their chicken tenders."

"I can't. My mom wanted all of us home for dinner."

"Oh, okay," she said with slight disappointment in her tone. "You happen to be free tomorrow?"

"Maybe. I think we were supposed to go see my grandma, though."

"Oh, well, then never mind. Maybe next weekend."

I flashed her a fake smile since all my lying at that moment made me feel guilty. "Yeah, let's shoot for that."

After I threw my wet hair in my usual messy topknot, I found Kennedy in the rec center lobby, playing with her phone to pass the time. Her hair was also wet, pulled back in a messy bun, and she'd dressed in dark blue skinny jeans, those same knee-high brown boots, and her green Aspen Grove soccer sweatshirt. The jeans and boots were pretty fancy for after a workout…and there I was in a sweatshirt and sweatpants, looking anything but hot. Cool.

She glanced up, and I knew I was going to be in deep trouble when my stomach twisted at the sight of her looking directly at me. By her unsure expression, I think it was safe to say that her stomach felt the same.

"Hey," she said. Her greeting was breathy and nervous, but she was still able to smile.

"You ready?"

She nodded and led us out into the lobby.

Yup, we're doing this. This is actually happening. Holy hell did my stomach hurt. I needed a ginger ale instead of a slushie.

Or a Xanax. Or a new freakin' stomach. Jesus Christ. Why did it always move when I was around this girl? This was like Olympic trials stomachache bad.

We didn't utter a single word until we walked outside.

"My mom is going to yell at me for taking a shower and not wearing a hat in the cold," she said on the way to her car. It was her attempt at small talk to ease the elephant following closely behind, but I'd take small talk over silence in a heartbeat. I could easily give in to small talk. I was good at that.

"Right? I'm surprised after all these years of swimming, I've never gotten pneumonia."

"Well, just to warn you, it's going around. Cole Shea gave it to Keely Nahar, I'm almost positive. That's what Cole told me, at least."

"Oh great. We should probably buy doctor's masks now. Can't afford to miss a whole week of school and swimming."

"We absolutely should. Cole said he wanted to surrender his life to the clouds just to end his hundred-and-five-degree temperature."

"We might have to make a pit stop at Walgreens, then."

She just smiled and gestured to her dark red Volkswagen Jetta that lit up when she unlocked the car. It killed me how she had a Jetta because it seemed as if every basic, popular white girl had a Jetta just like every elementary schoolgirl had a Samantha American Girl Doll.

Come to think of it, I think she had a Samantha American Girl Doll. I don't know. They all looked the same to me.

We didn't resume our conversation until we pulled out of the high school parking lot. She asked me a bunch of small-talk questions about swimming. How much I swam in a day? (Between six and eight miles.) How awful was morning practice? (I woke up at 4:30 every day and didn't get home until 6:30 at night. So pretty awful.) Did I talk to any famous swimmers at the Olympic trials? (I was way too terrified to bother them.) How was traveling to Barcelona? (Amazing. Why was everyone there so attractive?)

After I answered all her questions, we finally arrived at Swensons, a drive-in diner with amazing cheeseburgers and milkshakes. The beauty of Swensons was not only their food but the fact you stayed in your car, and the waiters came out. You didn't need to dress up or do your hair. Kennedy was saved by staying in her safe space—her Jetta—so no other Swensons customers could see her hanging out with me. It was the perfect place to have a talk. Or the talk.

After swimming four miles at practice, my stomach cried out for some food in the midst of twisting and turning and aching. But since we were in the heart of swim season and I'd made a promise to myself to be more disciplined, I opted for a grilled chicken sandwich, a small fry, and a cup of water. Not the fried chicken sandwich, large fry, and chocolate malt that I wanted and craved. Of course, out of all the food combinations she could have ordered, Kennedy ordered exactly what I wanted.

"It's funny you get all of that because if I wasn't trying to eat healthy, I would have gotten the same meal," I said and pointed to her sandwich. "Like, my stomach really wanted all of that."

She held her fried chicken sandwich in front of me, offering a bite. The smell of the chicken. The oil. The toasted bread. I almost snapped at it like a starving alligator, then remembered I hadn't spoken to Kennedy in four years, so my mouth latching onto her food probably wasn't appropriate.

"Wanna bite?" she teased.

I held up my pathetic cup of water. "I'll drink my water instead. My cup of tears."

"Remember when we went out to eat with our families, and we would always order the same meal, no matter what? Guess that hasn't changed."

"Nope, but apparently you can read my mind."

"Apparently." She bit into her sandwich. "Mmm! Why is this place so good?"

"Because they fry their fries in crack."

She coughed while she laughed and then laughed at her cough. She quickly reached for her shake to ease the mild choking.

"What? It's the truth," I said.

"I used to crave this place when I lived in the city. Nothing was like it."

"Uh, you guys have Shake Shack. I don't even wanna hear it."

"But Shake Shack is everywhere in the city and overhyped. Chains have nothing on standalone restaurants."

"Okay, hipster. Maybe it was the nostalgia."

"Or maybe I'm into crack."

I laughed and then tried too hard to swallow it when I realized how naturally it came out. Kennedy smiled and reached for a French fry in her bag. No, I couldn't allow her to make me laugh. She was not allowed to make me laugh, and I wasn't allowed to make her laugh, and we had already failed at both of those just a minute into sitting with our food and acting natural. We couldn't get back to the familiarity of our past. Not when there was so much I had to uncover. Not until we were able to clear some of the smog out of the car. I needed to have closure, and the only person who could give me that closure with Kennedy was Kennedy.

"So," I said after washing my food down with another gulp of water. "What made you change your mind? About talking?"

"A whole weekend of thinking."

"You thought about it for the whole weekend?"

"More like obsessed."

My face reddened, and I was so grateful that it was already dark so she didn't notice. I obsessed too, but only because I was the rejected one. Why did she obsess?

"Okay...so, I guess we should finish our conversation, then?" I said. "Put both of our minds at ease."

"I'm not sure if it's really going to put both of our minds at ease."

There was a long pause. The cadence in my chest picked up speed just wondering why this conversation wouldn't put both of our minds at ease. I stuck a fry in my mouth, hoping Kennedy would continue without me nudging her. But whatever she needed to say to me, she struggled severely to get it out.

"What did it mean?" I said. "I didn't think it meant anything, but it clearly meant something if you wanted nothing to do with me anymore."

She didn't say anything. She just stared at her half-eaten chicken sandwich before putting it down in her lap.

"I don't know," she finally muttered and shrugged. "I don't know."

"Yes, you do."

She probably thought that because she hadn't looked me in the eye since the conversation started, I wouldn't have noticed her eyes blurring.

"Look," I said to break up the long pause. "The faster you let it all out, the faster we can get the closure we both need. I deserve to know why you haven't thought about me once since the day you moved to the city."

"Haven't thought about you once?" she said, and her eyes finally met mine with creased eyebrows. "I've thought about you every second, of every day, for the last four years." She said it so softly, I thought I'd imagined it.

The same stunned feeling froze my body, as if we were thirteen again on her porch and she gave me my first kiss. Actually, the stunned feeling was stronger. It was as if I ran into a brick wall that popped out of nowhere. It took my little remaining speaking ability to utter, "What?"

"I watched the Olympic trials," she said. "Every single one of your races. The heats, the semifinals, the finals. I watched them all. I was so excited for you and so heartbroken at the same time because I always told you that I would be—"

"Front row center, cheering me on, wearing a shirt with my face on it that says 'my best friend.'"

"Yeah, exactly that. I'm so sorry that I wasn't there to do that."

"It wouldn't have made a difference anyway, if it makes you feel any better."

"No, it doesn't. And I can only imagine super-competitive you probably wasn't happy with your performance, but if it means anything now, I was so proud of you for making it to the finals. As a fifteen-year-old, going up against people, like, eight years older than you. I watched you during the world champs and the meet in Australia. It's absolutely amazing how far you've gotten. I'm so impressed."

She smiled as if it was the most amazing thing she'd ever seen. The way her glossy eyes twinkled from the parking lot lights, her tears, and her joyous memory of my races spun my world around even faster the more she revealed. I sucked in my lips because my mouth wanted to form a traitorous smile.

She liked me enough to watch all of my swim meets.

"Sometimes, I planned my workouts on the rec center track around your swim meets just so I could peek through the windows to watch you," she continued, "and one time, I watched you get a school record, and it was amazing. The look on your face was priceless. I could see it from the window. Your big smile looking at the scoreboard."

"How?" I said. It didn't make sense. Nothing she said made sense. Never once did I see her. The two windows from the track that overlooked the pool were right above the scoreboard at the opposite end of the pool. I'm almost positive I would have seen her. Her face was hard to miss. "How is all of this even possible when you never once looked at me?"

"I looked at you. All the time actually. You just never noticed."

I was so confused that my stomach didn't even have enough room for the rest of my food. I just shoved the sandwich and fries back in the bag, set it in between my feet, and gripped my sweaty palms on my knees.

"What's the point of all of this? Tonight? Coming to my meet last week? Talking to me in calc all of a sudden? I know it's not for the paper, and you know that too."

She looked out the window. "I'm so tired of hiding." Her voice shook. "I'm so tired of all of it."

When I heard her cry, my anger and confusion unraveled my frown.

"Tired of what?"

"I'm so tired of pretending that you and I weren't friends." She took a second to collect herself. "I'm sorry for everything. I'm sorry for ignoring you and never texting you. I'm so sorry that I hurt you. I was just so scared."

"About what?"

She shot me a look like I should have been able to read between the lines. But I couldn't. Whatever she was trying to tell me wasn't resonating at all in my brain. Was it supposed to? Was I just being dumb?

"Quinn," she said, and my stomach did that tumble thing again when she said my name so sharp and flatly. "Come on."

"What? I don't know what you're saying."

"Oh my God. The night of Cassie's party when you found me in the bathroom, you were so close to me. You were talking to me. You were looking at me. The night we, uh, the night when we—"

"The night you kissed me?"

She hesitated. "Yes, that night. It all came rushing back to me. In that bathroom. I felt as if I was standing on my porch so nervous and incapable of saying the right words to you all over again. Then if that wasn't enough, we were both dragged into that Never Have I Ever game, and Cassie said that thing to you—"

"Yeah, and you lied. You acted like you didn't hear it. You fed me to the wolves, and they completely devoured me."

"What was I supposed to do? Put my finger down and have all my friends question me?"

"Um, yeah, that's exactly what you should have done. Just own up to it. It's really not a big travesty."

"All the feelings I tried forgetting came rushing back to me at her party. I didn't put my finger down because I wanted all of it to go away. The kiss meant something to me. That's why I didn't text you. I wanted to kiss you again and again and again, and I hated that I wanted to. I didn't talk to you in the hallway because seeing you brought all the feelings back, and I just wanted to be normal. I wanted to like boys and only boys, but no matter what stupid little crush I had on a boy, you and that kiss were still there in the back of my mind. And then I found out last year that you were gay and that you were going to homecoming with Riley Scott, and I was so excited and hopeful and heartbroken all at the same time. I was thinking to myself, 'Oh my God, I might actually have a chance with her,' but I had no idea how to even approach you. How could I after not saying anything to you since that summer? And then I told myself, 'No, she doesn't like you. She hates you. She can't even look you in the eye at school—'"

"Because *you* couldn't look *me* in the eye! Because you ignored me the first day of sophomore year, and it destroyed me."

"Yeah, well, seeing you make out with Riley Scott at homecoming destroyed me too. Because that could have maybe been me. Maybe I could have been your date. I could have picked out a corsage for you. We could have had matching dresses, and I could have slow danced with you, and I could have been the one making out with you. All of this could have maybe happened if I wasn't such a coward. If I just found a way to talk to you after you came out. If I never ran away from you after we kissed."

That lump in my throat? Yeah, it was the size of a watermelon now. Just lodged back in there, showing no signs of disappearing. Casually hanging out back there on this lovely Friday night as Kennedy Reed admitted to me that she liked a girl, and that girl was me, the weird girl who swam seven thousand yards on Fridays instead of doing cool things like going to football games or unsupervised parties. She'd liked me this whole time and pictured herself going to homecoming with me when she avoided making eye contact with me in the halls. I had no idea.

She wiped her eyes. "I just remember feeling so happy and hopeful when I found out you were gay. After you came out, I tried figuring out how to talk to you. I wanted to know how you knew that you were gay. Was it before I kissed you? Was it after? Did you think of me at all? Was I even your type?"

My hand suddenly had a mind of its own. It found its way onto Kennedy's leg. I couldn't sit there and let her put herself down without trying to console her. She stopped sniffing, and her eyes zeroed in on my hand. I knew exactly what she was looking at because I could feel it too. The tension that had forced us to be apart for so long vibrated in between my hand and her thigh. The two of us just stared at the source sending electrical currents throughout our bodies.

It was a feeling I never experienced before. It was another feeling I wasn't sure I liked, and yet again, I had Kennedy to blame.

"I thought about the kiss all the time, Ken," I said, and I was shocked by how easily "Ken" slipped out of me. Was I even allowed to call her Ken anymore? "And each time I thought about it, the more scared your lips felt on me."

"You make me so nervous, Quinn. Like, telling you this right now, I just wanna cry because I'm terrified, and I kept all these feelings locked up for so long, and now my hands won't stop shaking—"

That was when I grabbed her hand. She'd been talking with her hands during the whole conversation, so I thought they needed a rest, and I laced my fingers into hers to help her calm down. The feeling that shot through me when her fingers wrapped around mine was nothing compared to the feelings stemmed from her saying my name. The force running through my veins was a feeling I'd never experienced before—not with Lana or Meghan or Riley.

God, I'm in trouble.

"I know. I can feel them," I said. "You don't need to be nervous."

"Well I *am* nervous, and when I'm nervous, I run away from whatever it is."

"You're not running now. It's okay."

"It's not okay, Quinn. One hundred percent not okay. You're absolutely right. You didn't deserve it at all."

Her hand tightened around mine. Then our eyes met, and all the different kinds of feelings I felt just clicked right into place, as if we were supposed to be here in this exact moment. Her eyes fidgeted all around my face as if she was lost in the connection too. Her fingers squeezed my hand tighter as she slowly leaned in, almost as if asking permission to kiss me. I inched forward to tell her fuck yes, just kiss me. After everything she'd just told me, I needed to kiss her just as much as her longing expression told me she needed to kiss me.

And if she was too scared to make the move again, then I would do it. Fine. You didn't need to ask me twice.

I went for it. Forget thinking about the pros and cons of kissing Kennedy Reed; I just kissed Kennedy Reed. The second my lips touched hers, this jolt struck me right in the center of my stomach. Holy hell, if my stomach wasn't in enough pain, kissing her filled my stomach up with a low burn that felt so amazing. Her lips felt like damp silk—silk that caused my hair to stand up, goose bumps to sprout all up and down my arms, and my heart to bang like a timpani. I was amazed that after all this time, her lips were still so soft and gentle. By how delicately they moved on mine, I could feel how truly scared and nervous she still was. I didn't want her to be scared this time because there was nothing to be scared of. She needed to know that I wanted her lips on mine. Everything she felt in that car and the force that emanated from us, I felt too.

I placed my hand on her cheek and held her head steady in front of me. The kiss intensified, and our lips grew in sync. We parted slightly, and our tongues met for the very first time, and holy hell, the first time I felt her tongue, this electricity hummed all throughout me. Instead of tasting like root beer, she tasted like her chocolate malt, and my tongue brushed against hers methodically to taste her and the chocolate in her mouth. That was when her lips became more confident and sturdier, and her mouth formed a smile against mine. With every touch of her tongue, I wanted more of her.

Kissing her was a magical elixir I never knew I needed.

After what seemed like forever, she slowly pulled away, and I opened my eyes. The electric current flickered in my stomach when I saw those eyes on me, outlined with a grin in the parking lot shadows. My goose bumps were still alive even when her lips weren't on me.

"Wow," she said, exhaling raggedly. I wondered if her heart pounded as hard as mine did.

"Yeah," I said. I had no other words. "Wow."

I pulled her face back in for another, and we sank back into the kiss right where we left off.

If our worlds had crashed into each other, we didn't notice the bump at all.

CHAPTER FIVE

A nd that was when my love for chocolate malts started.
I craved one all weekend and was so bummed that I had this whole healthy-eating-and-being-more-disciplined routine. What the hell was that even about? Why did I make that rule? What was even happening in Russia in July?

I kid, but being kissed like that did a really good job of getting my mind off all my stresses about swimming. Because God, that was a kiss. She kissed me well into the next week. Every time I replayed the kiss in my head, I craved a chocolate malt. Then I checked my phone to see if she texted me since we swapped numbers. And this whole process repeated seventy thousand times for the rest of the weekend.

Finally, on Sunday night, in the midst of finishing twenty-five brutal calc problems, she texted me. Saved by the chirping of my phone. Her name on my screen made me pathetically grin. I might have even unleashed a few gleeful kicks in my bed, but that was going to stay a secret.

Kennedy: *Oh hey. How's your weekend going?*

I smiled and told myself, *act casually. Don't seem too eager.*

Me: *Oh hey. Completely uneventful. Dreading waking*

> *up at 4:30 tomorrow. I'm currently crying at the thought.*
> Kennedy: *4:30? Are you a masochist?*
> Me: *I think so. How was your weekend?*
> Kennedy: *Pretty boring except for my Friday night. It was pretty eventful. I can't stop thinking about it.*

I sank into my bed with a smile reaching both of my ears. I was at an all-time high of pure lust.

> Me: *Sounds like we're having similar weekends.*
> Kennedy: *Oh really? So I've thought a lot about it and I just wanted to say again how sorry I am for all the fucked-up things I did to you.*
> Me: *I accept your apology.*
> Kennedy: *Really? So easily?*
> Me: *All I needed was an apology and an explanation and I got all of that on Friday... along with an added bonus.*
> Kennedy: *I won't mess it up this time.*
> Me: *You can start by letting me know what you got on #4 of our calc homework.*
> Kennedy: *I don't cheat, remember?*
> Me: *You're not cheating but I am. So you're safe.*
> Kennedy: *x=7.8. Delete the text so the NSA doesn't tell Mr. Carmichael and ruin any chances I have getting into Syracuse.*
> Me: *Text deleted.*
> Kennedy: *Thank you!*

When I walked into calc that Monday, Kennedy wasn't there when I slid into my seat. Cassandra, Tom, and Jennifer yapped away in their corner before class. It only took a minute for her to step into the room. And her presence brought a new kind of tension. It wasn't smog anymore. More like warm spring air, the kind that instantly turned my face warm and made my palms sweat. *God, am I going to start looking forward to calc? Maybe I am a masochist.*

From the corner of my eye, I watched her sit in Cassandra's corner with her friends, just like all the other days.

"Where the hell were you on Friday?" Tom asked her. "Gabriel's bonfire was awesome. His sister got a keg, and Melanie got so shitfaced and skinny-dipped in the hot tub."

Gabriel always invited me to his parties, but I usually turned them down. A lot of the times, I was either busy with swimming or wanted to avoid Cassandra like the disease she was. He always understood, and even though I never showed up to his things unless it was just him and Liam, he never stopped inviting me.

"Wow, sounds like I missed a great time," she said with strong sarcasm in her voice.

"But really, where were you?" Cassandra asked. "Better be worth missing the party."

"Doing stuff for the school paper."

All three of them laughed as if that was the lamest excuse they'd ever heard.

"On a Friday night?" Jennifer said.

"Okay, totally not worth missing the party," Cassandra said.

"I've seen her boobs, like, a bajillion times. You give the girl one wine cooler, and she's, like, the biggest PETA spokesperson out there. I think I met my quota."

"Yeah, well, I don't think I'll ever meet my quota," Tom said.

Mr. Carmichael walked into the room, and all the talk about kegs, skinny-dipping, and Melanie Krugel's boobs instantly died. The sight of him made Kennedy, Jennifer, and Tom disperse to their new seats.

The last bell rang.

"Class has started. Pass forward your homework," Mr. Carmichael said.

"Hey, Quinn," she said softly when she turned around for my homework.

She gave me a wink before she faced the front of the class.

Class started, and my brain already died. That smile, that wink, the way she said my name. Her face.

I was so going to fail calc.

"Four hundred and fifty-nine," Mr. Carmichael said as he wrote the page number and section on the board. "Section eleven-point-four: matrices and linear equations."

But about twenty minutes into learning about matrices and linear equations, my phone went off in my book bag. If calc didn't bore me to sleep, I would have ignored it. My empty stomach begging for lunch and my mind wrapping around matrices, linear equations, and Kennedy made me so tired that I needed something to keep my eyes open. So, I slid my hand into my book bag and saw Kennedy's name on my phone screen.

Her text read, *Calc is the longest 40 min of my life. How has it only been 20 min?*

I bit my lip, and I was so grateful to be shoved in the farthest back corner so Mr. Carmichael couldn't see me smiling at my crotch.

I replied, *It's the reason why I cry at night.*

She responded, *Btw, you look really nice today.*

I immediately glanced up at the front of the class, trying too hard to hide my smile again. Unless it was a blue moon, I hardly ever dressed up for school. Waking up at the butt crack of dawn really killed any inspiration I had for impressing people. Didn't help that I was friends with all the out lesbians at school, so my pickings were very slim to begin with. So, I usually just wore a T-shirt or a sweatshirt, or if I was feeling half in the mood to look mildly decent, I wore a V-neck or sweater of some sort. I always wore skinny jeans, rotated my shoes between my Vans and brown leather combat boots, and 80 percent of the time, I threw my hair in a messy bun because I never had enough time or energy to do my hair after morning practice.

But since I was still floating on a cloud from that amazing make-out session with Kennedy, I was inspired more than ever to dress to impress. That day, I wore my favorite black cardigan with a white V-neck underneath, and because of that ruptured star or full blue moon, I even went a little crazy and straightened my hair in hopes of grabbing Kennedy's attention. Apparently, it worked, and I felt so accomplished.

God, was I pathetic? Maybe a little. Wasn't this really why I broke up with Riley? Because I thought she was too nice and affectionate, and it slightly disgusted and annoyed me? Now look at me. One amazing kiss with someone whose name I used to curse, and now I was all hypnotized and straightening my hair. I hated half of myself for acting this way.

Me: *Thank you. It will all disappear at swim team practice.*
Kennedy: *Doubt it.*
Me: *My hands are going to dry up too. All this swimming is going to turn me into a raisin.*
Kennedy: *Your hands felt perfectly fine when they were in my hair on Friday.*

Tingles. So many tingles.

Me: *I've been thinking about this whole second chance thing, and if we're going to do it right, I think we should give Friday night a second chance too. It's only fair. To us and our lips.*
Kennedy: *I'm all for this plan. Maybe we can plan another drive somewhere?*
Me: *We could. OR we can disappear today if you want.*
Kennedy: *That sounds even better!*
Me: *Side entrance of the performing arts center. Right after the last bell.*
Kennedy: *Oh wow. You know right where to go.*

"Miss Reed," Mr. Carmichael said.

Kennedy's head shot up from her lap. I quickly sank in my chair so I could hide behind Kennedy. I had an inch on her, and if Mr. Carmichael could spot Kennedy's phone through his thick old-man glasses, he could probably spot mine all the way in the back behind Kennedy.

"I already separated you from your friends. Do I need to confiscate your phone too?"

"No, Mr. Carmichael," she said softly and slid into her seat, sneaking her phone back in her book bag.

"Please, come up to the board and solve this equation for the class, then."

My eyes widened. Mr. Carmichael really didn't mess around.

Tom let out a chuckle.

"You can do the next one, Mr. Felix."

He hushed, and I instantly wiped the smirk from my face too. I didn't want to be Mr. Carmichael's next victim.

She slowly glided out of her seat and took the walk of shame to the whiteboard. Mr. Carmichael handed her his green marker and motioned her to the equation. A matrix times a matrix. Kennedy studied it for a few seconds and then attempted it. It was cute how her right leg relaxed as she tapped the marker end on her cheek, doing the math in her head while subconsciously being charming.

How I wished that my lips were the marker.

What I should have done was solve the equation myself for extra practice, but I didn't. I just watched her. Her layered ash-brown hair shining in the fluorescent lighting, stopping right below her shoulder blades. Those dark blue skinny jeans looked great on her—rounding out her skinny yet muscular legs and butt.

After she finished, she turned to Mr. Carmichael and gave an unsure look, but it was an adorable unsure look that told the teacher that she hoped it was right, then it told the class she couldn't have cared less.

"I have to say, Miss Reed, I'm impressed. M doesn't equal

three. It equals five. You were close. Here's where you went wrong."

He took the marker from her and circled the last line of her work where she messed up. She almost got it right, but she still didn't care.

"I underestimated you. You can sit down now. Next time I see your phone, I'll confiscate it."

"Sorry, Mr. Carmichael. It won't happen again."

He faced the board, and Kennedy gave a grin to her snickering friends. Then that grin directed at me, and she flashed another wink my way as she took her seat.

If she tried showing off to impress me, it totally worked.

No one used the performing arts center in November. It was an abandoned abyss perfect for making out. The only times you needed to avoid the PAC were the week of the holiday concert, the third week in December, and March through May when the show choir practiced for the spring musical. Though I knew for a fact the show choir snuck off and made out in every nook and cranny of the PAC. I knew this because Erick told me. We came to the conclusion that it would probably light up like the New York City skyline underneath a black light just as much as the band practice rooms.

She was right on time. Two thirty. I had only been at our spot for a minute, nervously tapping my fingers against the fabric wall when she opened the door, and a ray of fluorescent light crept through.

"Don't you have practice?" she whispered and let the door close behind her.

"Yeah, but it takes me two seconds to get changed, and the freshmen still have to put in lane lines," I said. "I got all my bases covered."

"God, I never thought this day would end. I've been thinking about that kiss since Friday—"

Before she could finish, I grabbed her shirt until her lips perfectly landed on mine. Her lips were sweet like honey yet so electric. Kissing her for the second time was just as good as kissing her the first time, and I didn't want it to end.

Every day for the next two weeks, we met up behind the side entrance door of the PAC. We only had ten minutes before I had to leave to go to swim practice. The ten minutes flew by. I felt as if I was only able to kiss her once before I had to go to practice with swollen red lips.

When I came home from practice every night, I shoved my dinner down my throat, locked myself in my room, and texted her. Homework could wait for study hall. We texted each other nonstop right when I got home to when we went to bed, just like we did when we were younger. What did we talk about? It started with calc, Mr. Carmichael's monotone voice and hideous old-man clothes. Kennedy said he dressed like an uncharismatic Mr. Rogers. We talked about how the school day would look if we were in charge: How to Write a College Application Essay. How to Do Your Taxes. How to Use Excel. How Not to Be a Shitty Human Being. How to Parallel Park. All classes Kennedy and I thought really needed to be taught in school. We contemplated why our parents decided to raise us in Aspen Grove, New York, when they could have literally raised us anywhere in the world. Hawaii? Orange County, California? Somewhere in the Florida Keys? Europe? That led to us discussing where we would want to live. Of course, I said West Coast for my twenties and then maybe on a Caribbean island so I could snorkel in the morning and check in on my wild dolphin who would always come visit me. It was also why I wanted to be on the national team. I would travel all over the world to compete. Kennedy called me a mermaid. Kennedy said she would love to live in a French village like in *Beauty and the Beast* or in Amsterdam where she could ride her bike everywhere and write poetry in a café, and that was when I found out Kennedy Reed wrote poetry.

God, my poor heart. On a wild high ever since our first kiss with no time to take a rest.

Those nightly text conversations gave me a glimpse of the new person she'd become over the years. She wasn't the friend five houses down who just loved riding bikes and playing *Mario Party*. Inside her lived a world traveler, a book nerd, a poetry enthusiast, and a girl who appreciated cozy, quaint places like French villages and Dutch cafés. She appreciated the arts and culture, and I knew it had to have been the two years she spent in the city that helped expand her horizons outside of plain ol', boring, white, upper-middle-class Aspen Grove.

I loved intriguing people. And she was so intriguing to me. She had me at poetry.

At school, if we caught each other's stares from across the cafeteria, both of our cheeks would turn red. After a few weeks of our PAC rendezvouses, I would wink at her anytime I caught her glancing over at me from the cafeteria, and every time I winked, she glanced back down at her food, biting her lip to hide her smile.

She made my ordinary world unordinary with just one simple movement.

CHAPTER SIX

B ehind lane four, I jiggled my arms and legs two events before my 500-yard freestyle. No matter how many times I swam it, it gave me the creeps. The event was a beast. I'd been swimming it for four years, and each meet I had to swim it was just as scary as the first time. It was the longest event in high school meets that tested endurance and mental stability. Anytime I had to mentally prepare for the event, my legs and arms turned to Jell-O, which then toyed with my mind, which then toyed with my legs and arms. It was a never-ending cycle.

Kennedy texted me at the beginning of winter break about how she wanted to watch one of my swim meets again because "winter break means a break from you, and that's just a really sucky Christmas break," she said. So, when I told her about our home meet just a few days after Christmas, she purposely scheduled her run on the rec center track to watch a few of my events from the window, and then the plan was for me to go back to her place to hang out (aka: make out) and meet her family all over again. But not at the same time, obviously.

Not only was Kennedy going to watch me, but a sports reporter from the *Buffalo News* sat with my parents in the stands so she could write a front-page spread in the sports section that weekend. So, on top of my regular 500-free nerves, I had Kennedy, reuniting with the Reeds, and the sports reporter nerves bubbling in my stomach that made for one hell of a stomachache at the worst possible time.

Your mental game played a huge factor in your race, and I wasn't about to have an awful swim in front of Kennedy or the sports reporter. So I took deep, long breaths to untangle the knots in my stomach. I had to swim well to impress this really pretty girl who, for some magical reason, was into me.

Oh, and impress the reporter too. I guess that was also important.

"You got this, Quinn," Riley said with a pat on the back one event before my race. She always wished me good luck before she ventured down to the opposite end to be my counter.

"I hate this event," I said, half joking. "Why do I swim this again?"

"Because you're a beast in the pool."

"I'm going to campaign for you to do this next meet."

"No, thank you. I have the 100-fly I swim to torture myself for fun. Unless you wanna switch?"

"Absolutely not. I'll stop complaining."

"I'll catch you on the other end of the pool," she said with a shoulder tap for good luck, but the tap lingered just a little bit longer than I expected it to, as if it was flirting or something.

"I'll make sure to splash you extra hard when I do my flip turns."

She winked and followed Madison down to the other end to prep the counters.

Nope. I didn't have time to read into Riley's shoulder taps and winks. Compartmentalize that issue. Save it for later. Think about times and kicking ass and Kennedy watching me and not drowning halfway through this beast of an event.

As I approached the lane four block, I buried my goggles as tightly as I could into my eyes. The worst thing that could happen to you during the 500-free—on top of your nerves—was having your goggles fall down your face when you dove into the water. It happened to me at districts my freshman year. My body felt amazing, as if I turned into a dolphin overnight. I got myself into the right mental state, I was ready to dominate the whole event. I was ready to shatter that seven-year-old state record. As a freshman. I dove in, my goggles slipped right off like a wet bar of soap in my hands, and I had to swim the whole event with the chlorine burning my eyes. Missed the state record by a second.

I was actually terrified that would happen again. Knowing my luck, my goggles would slip off while my crush watched me from the track.

When my goggles were snug in my eyes, I jiggled my arms and legs one last time before I glanced up at the other end of the pool. I spotted Kennedy through the track windows behind where Riley sat cross-legged and counter in hand. Her arms were perched on the middle windowsill. Her hair was back in a ponytail, white headphones dangled down her cheeks, and she wore a cut-off pink T-shirt that flaunted her amazing arms. She looked right at me with a tooth-revealing grin, forcing the corners of my mouth to rise. And she noticed because she gave me a thumbs-up. I had to kick ass just to show off to her.

Oh, and that reporter. Damn it. I kept forgetting she was there.

And I did swim an amazing race. Knowing that Kennedy was watching me from the track, I picked it up just a little faster. When I finished, I immediately turned to the scoreboard and saw that I got a 4:39 and won by a whole lap. I did even better than I wanted to.

Maybe Kennedy was my good luck charm.

My interview with the *Buffalo News* reporter only lasted about ten minutes. She'd interviewed me plenty of times since the start of high school. Usually, she wrote something about me right around the time of high-profile swimming events, like the Olympic trials, the world champs in Barcelona, and the Pan Pacs the past summer. Nothing really in the middle of a boring high school season. She basically just asked me questions about training for the world champs, my goals for the swim season, and how I was balancing training for an international competition while finishing my senior year and competing at the high school level, and we briefly talked about my desires to go to Berkeley.

After the interview, I made it my mission to make up for those past ten minutes. I quickly took a shower, dried myself off, and threw my clothes on as if it was a race. I paid the price for it because I guess I really sucked at drying myself when I hurried to be with a pretty girl. My jeans and bra stuck to my wet skin, and boy, did I regret not perfecting the quick dry.

"Quinn, wanna go to Applebee's?" Madison asked after the meet. She pulled her sweatpants underneath her towel wrapped around her waist. "Half off appetizers!"

I checked my phone for a text from Kennedy, and when I saw her three demanding texts in a row, hiding my smile was merely impossible.

She texted, *You were really hot winning that event. By a whole lap. Goddamn, you're fast.*

Followed by *I'm so lucky the fastest high schooler in the country likes making out with me. I did something right in a previous life.*

And her last text, the best text: *Hurry up! My lips need your lips!*

My cheeks felt as red as a quick sprint down the pool would have made them. Knowing I was being watched, I tossed my phone back in my bag and resumed getting changed. Riley studied me closely. Madison and Gia gawked at me with nosy grins.

"Ooh, who are you texting?" Gia said. "Who put that little grin on your face?"

"No one," I said, searching for my T-shirt in my swim bag.

"Lies," Riley said, "that's your smirk for 'I'm talking to a cute girl.'"

"I have a smirk?"

"You do. I think I would know for many reasons."

"Who's the cute girl? Who's the cute girl?" Madison said.

Her chants got the whole girls' swim team interested. My

face blushed, and everyone laughed. Except for Riley. Her eyes demanded an answer.

"Who in here is sending flirty texts to Quinn? Anyone?" Gia surveyed the locker room and the other twenty-six girls on our team, purposely trying to embarrass me. "Oh wait, are you two just fucking with us, and you're really just texting each other?" she said to both Riley and me.

Riley faced me. "Are you dating someone?"

My shirt slipped from my hands and fell in the puddle in between my legs from my wet suit. Madison and Gia laughed with even more curiosity in their eyes. Riley's face remained neutral, just wanting a straight answer more than anything.

I picked up the soaked T-shirt. It was a goner. It became one with the puddle.

"Shit," I said.

"Oh my God, are you?" Gia said.

"And her face is red," Madison said.

"Yeah, because my T-shirt fell in a puddle."

I wrung out as much water as I could from the T-shirt, but no matter how much I twisted it, it was done. Guess I had to brave the December air with just a bra and sweatshirt.

"That would make sense," Gia said to Madison. "She's straightening her hair after morning practice now. Ditching the signature Quinn topknot."

"Oh my gosh, you're right!" Madison said. "And she's wearing, like, all her best clothes."

"So, who are you dating?" Riley asked.

"Oh my God, no one!" I said.

Technically, that was the truth.

"You're lying," Riley said. "I know when you're lying."

"Tell us! Tell us!" Madison chanted.

"I'm not dating anyone. I'll see you guys next week."

While the team went to Applebee's to get half-off appetizers, I drove myself over to Kennedy's, clenching the steering wheel the whole way. I was excited and terrified at the same time because I'd never been inside her new house. I hadn't interacted with her parents since a few days before she moved. They'd probably wondered what happened in the world that made Quinn Hughes appear in their house again—besides that ruptured star.

"This is home," Kennedy said with a glowing smile, gesturing me to come into the mudroom of her new house.

Although it was a totally different house, the smell of it instantly brought me back to my younger years. Her mom loved candles and air fresheners. Their house always smelled so good, depending on the season. Even though Christmas was three days before, pine needles and cinnamon still wafted throughout the house. Her family always went all out for the holidays. At their old house, their Christmas tree would light up their sunroom and glowed all the way from the street to say "Merry Christmas" to cars and people passing by. Now, it snuggled in the living room corner next to the stone fireplace. It always had red and gold ornaments with silver streamers and white lights, and it remained the same color scheme after all this time. The entrance into the living room was lined with silver garland and red ribbons. All the overhead lights were off with candles lighting up the whole downstairs as if electricity didn't exist.

Despite being in a different house, the same sights and smells transported me back to my childhood. The nostalgia brought a smile to my face.

"Hey, Mom," Kennedy said as she walked into the living room that glimmered in white Christmas lights.

Mrs. Reed turned around from the sectional sofa. She had a cup of warm tea in her hand and was bundled in a plaid blanket watching some *Dateline* episode, probably about a murder in some random state like Idaho. It only took her a moment to study me before she saw my thirteen-year-old self.

"Remember Quinn?"

"Oh my gosh, Quinn Hughes?" She got off the couch, set her mug on the coffee table, and joyfully walked over to give me a tight hug. "Oh gosh, it's been so long." She broke the hug and held me in front of her as if she could better study how much I've changed over the lost years. "You've grown so much. You're so tall now. Last time I saw you, you were at my shoulders. Easily."

Mrs. Reed couldn't have been more than five six. Even her daughter had about two inches on her. Oh, times had changed.

"I'm glad you think I'm tall," I said. "Some meets, I feel incredibly short."

Anytime I swam for Team USA, I felt like a child. I know I was still a child compared to the majority of the swimmers in their twenties, but I actually felt like a baby compared to them in size. Five nine might have been well above average in the normal world, but in the swimming world, it was pretty short. Most girls were about five ten at the shortest.

She waved my comment off. "No, you look great. It's so good to see you again! How are you, dear?"

"It's good to see you too. I'm good. Your house looks great, as always."

"Well, you know how much I love this time of year. Can't take the decorations down until the New Year is over and everyone is back in school, right?" She winked.

"Absolutely."

"Now, what have you been up to? Catch me up on all this lost time."

"Nothing really. Just the usual high school senior stuff."

She crossed her arms and raised her dark eyebrows. "Are the world championships and Olympic trials usual high school stuff?"

I blushed. "No, not really."

"Well, let me tell you that we're really proud of you—of all your swimming accomplishments. Isn't there another world championships again this year? Your brother mentioned it."

"Oh, yeah, um, they're in Russia next summer so I'm basically selling my soul to the swimming gods until July."

"She wakes up at four thirty in the morning, five times a week," Kennedy added.

"Oh yeah? Quinn, can I pay you to drag my daughter out of bed at a decent hour? She likes to sleep in until one in the afternoon."

I laughed. "One? Oh my God, that's a whole day wasted."

She smacked my arm. "Shut up. Stop siding with my mom."

"You kinda asked for it by bringing it up."

"Oh, Quinn, I'm so glad to hear that you're doing well," Mrs. Reed said. "Kennedy, I'm glad you brought Quinn around. I hope to see more of her." She shot her daughter a look, knowing it all fell on her how often I came over the house. She had to have known something came between Kennedy and me, but what had Kennedy told her? Did she know about this kiss or anything?

Kennedy led me upstairs to her room. Her bedroom walls were painted a light purple with off-white carpeting littered with three soccer balls. She kicked them out of our way. It was clean and neat, and her bed was made, which I thought was unusual for a seventeen-year-old.

I walked over to her bookshelf that housed her collection of trophies. Two of them from her years on the Merriweather Prep soccer team in the city—one of them being an MVP—and the most recent one was getting into the semifinals this year for soccer.

The shelf on top of the trophies held all her pictures. Pictures that included Jennifer and Melanie, and I even spotted a picture with Liam in it that was at least a year old. There was another of her, Liam, and Gabriel, and I would be lying if I said that I didn't feel completely hurt that she had a four musketeers picture without the fourth musketeer. It was just another reminder how similar we were, with the same childhood memories, yet so different.

And then it hit me: it was as if I was the fourth member of Destiny's Child. I would tell you her name, but no one even knew it. Hardly anyone remembered there used to be four children of destiny.

My first kiss ever was a blessing as much as it was a curse.

"Do you miss New York?" I asked when I saw a photo of her and a few friends on a boat with the skyline in the background.

"I miss my friends," she said. "I miss the city life. But it never felt like home to me or my family."

"So, you were happy to move back?"

"A little. Mostly scared. It kinda sucks moving during high school just as much as it sucked moving in middle school."

Then I spotted an unframed photo hidden behind her New York photos. It was a photo of her and Grant Turner at homecoming. Grant looked super happy just to have Kennedy Reed as his date. But Kennedy didn't look as happy as he did.

"I like how you shove Grant in the back," I said with a laugh.

"Ugh, because that dance was awful, and he was in my room when he gave it to me so I just shoved it there and forgot about it. Give it to me."

I handed her the picture, and she shoved it in the bottom drawer of her nightstand filled with a bunch of other unwanted crap.

"Why was the dance awful?"

"Many reasons."

"Were you upset they didn't play any throwbacks too? Because I was."

She gave me a little smile. "That did play a huge part, but I also didn't want to go to the dance with Grant. He's so boring. He's an awful dancer and super clingy."

I laughed. A lot of girls in school liked Grant Turner. He was tall and fit and had nice blue eyes and flowy blond hair. It was funny that one of the guys all the girls drooled over was boring, an awful dancer, and clingy. It was kind of enlightening, at least for a lower totem pole level like me.

"And," she continued, "Cassie was drunk the whole time, and she's not even a fun drunk. She's mean and loud and combative. I just didn't want to be there."

"So, she's drunk all the time?"

"You're so funny," she deadpanned.

"Where would you have rather been, then?"

"Free," she said, matter-of-factly. "I would have rather been free."

I had no idea what she meant. I stood there for a few moments, trying to grasp what she was trying to tell me in as few words as possible. Her eyes looked away to her off-white carpeting, and her foot found one of the soccer balls, kicking it back and forth between her feet.

"I don't know what that means," I said. "I'm sorry."

She let out a long sigh, still playing with the ball. "I feel like the way I want to live my life isn't the way I'm living it. Like my friends. I'm sorry for being vanilla, but I don't wanna drink every single weekend. Sometimes I just wanna watch TV or some stupid movie, or I don't know, just hang out and talk like normal people. Like, do alcohol and weed have to be present at every function?"

"No, they don't. And that's not being vanilla at all."

"Well, they make me feel like I'm boring."

"Who cares what they think? If your friends make you feel like you're boring because you don't want to do those things, then they're not your friends."

She stopped playing with the ball, and that was when she looked at me again. "I'm so glad that I can go anywhere in the world after this year and leave this crap behind. I get another chance to start over, and I'm going to do it the right way."

"Then do it. You can meet far better people than the ones you're hanging out with now."

"When I moved to the city, Jacob and I didn't really fit in at our school. Everyone acted all rich and snooty, and that was just not me or my family. We got this vibe from everyone at Merriweather that they weren't into us because we weren't into designer clothes, and we weren't from Manhattan, and our parents weren't socialites so that made us even bigger losers than we already were. I only really hung out with the soccer team, and all of them were boy crazy, and there I was still questioning what the hell I was and trying to get myself to not want to kiss you. So, when we moved back to Aspen Grove and all those cool kids swarmed around me for whatever reason, I didn't complain. Because I wanted to be cool. Because I spent the past two years trying to make friends and just trying to be accepted."

It all made sense when she finally explained it to me. I knew exactly what it was like not to fit in, and in middle school, all you wanted to do was blend in and be accepted. I might have done the same thing if a bunch of cool kids wanted to be my friend.

"And I'm so tired of my friends trying to get me to hook up with Grant," she continued. "Like, they're really pushing it, but he sucks at kissing, and I find him extremely boring, and I told them I'm not interested, but Cassie just called me cold and a tease."

I laughed. "Shouldn't have kissed him, then."

She rolled her eyes. "It was, like, two times. Two awful times."

"Who would you rather have gone with? To homecoming, I mean?"

Her eyes looked right at me. "You know that answer already." She kicked her soccer ball over to me and revealed a smirk. I let the ball roll on top of my foot as I stared at her carpet. Processing. I still couldn't believe that this whole time, Kennedy Reed liked me.

"What made you like me?" I said. "How did that even happen?"

She shrugged and took a seat on her bed. I joined her. "I have no idea. In fifth grade, I had a crush on Chris Lamboni. Then one day, I woke up and saw you. Your laugh. Your face. Your hair and how it's both brunette and blond. Your amazing eyes that are blue on some days and then a soft green on other days. And your smile. Your big, glowing, perfect smile. I don't remember a specific moment that made me start liking you. I just started noticing you. All at once."

It hit me all at once—my wanting to be with Kennedy

all the time meant that I had more feelings for her, more than just…what the hell were we? We weren't friends, not even on Facebook. That meant we weren't even friends with benefits. We were just…benefits. Strangers with benefits? Acquaintances with benefits? Old best friends with benefits? Calc classmates with benefits? What the hell would you even call us?

All I knew was that I had a crush on her. No, it was more than a crush. I really liked Kennedy Reed. Because all of Christmas break, I wished Kennedy was beside me, and I spent all that time wondering if she felt the same.

I couldn't be just Kennedy Reed's secret make-out buddy anymore. I was falling. Hard. If her friend breakup with me was as devastating as it was, I couldn't imagine what it would feel like if I allowed myself to like her even more than I already did and have her break my heart again, a different kind of hurt that would be more painful than before.

"What are we even doing?" I said. "With each other? What are we? Just…make-out buddies?"

"I have no idea."

"I need to know what you want out of this. You need to tell me what I should expect so I can prepare. Am I just someone you make out with, or am I something more?"

If Kennedy was any other girl who wanted to hook up with me, I could have easily been a hookup. But nothing about Kennedy made her any other girl to me. No one was able to spin my mind around the way she did. Constantly and consistently.

"I…" she began. "I don't know what we're doing."

"Well, we need to figure it out."

"Right now?"

"Right now. We're not friends anymore. That ended the day you moved to the city. This isn't meaningless to me, and I can't really do meaningless right now. Especially not with you. I feel like if we continue to just be secret make-out buddies, I'm setting myself up to get hurt by you all over again."

"I don't want to hurt you, Quinn. I never wanted to do that."

"Then what are we gonna do? End whatever this is and go back to not talking? Or do we do something more?"

She thought. For what seemed like an eternity. She played with her fingers, and her eyes alternated glances all throughout the room. "I've thought about you for so long," she said softly. "The thought of seeing you in calc and after the last bell is so exciting and something I've never felt with Ian or Dominic. That hidden little entrance of the performing arts center? It's made me feel the freest I've ever felt in my life."

"So, you're in? You want something more?"

"Of course I want something more." My stomach fluttered so fast and hard I thought it was going to fly away from me. "I mean, Quinn, you make me excited for calc. I think that says a lot."

"You make me excited for calc too! Look at us, we're already disgusting together!" We both laughed, and I reached out to grab both of her hands. "So...Kennedy Reed is my girlfriend?"

"So, Quinn Hughes is my girlfriend."

I smiled so wide, and when I did, her mouth mirrored mine.

"Your smile, God, it's everything," she said, studying my lips before her eyes moved up to mine. "And your eyes. They're blue today, just an FYI."

"Stop making me blush like an idiot."

She poked my cheek. "You're blushing like an idiot."

"No!" I said and buried my pathetic face in my hands. "Stop it!"

She pulled my hands away from my face, and when she lowered them, she slipped her fingers into mine.

"You know what I just noticed?" she said.

"Your love for me?"

"Yes, that too. And the scar on your chin." The fingers that didn't hold mine grazed the faint little scar. Her touch was delicate and warm, and I wished her whole hand touched my face like that. "When you flew off your bike like a stuntwoman."

It was a few weeks after we graduated from elementary

school and spent the summer terrified of entering middle school, wondering if we really had to get changed for gym class and take showers in front of our classmates. We were out on a bike ride around the neighborhood when she challenged me to a race down the huge hill on our street. Her house sat right at the bottom of the hill. It was a popular spot for kids to fly down on their bikes in the summers, or in the winters when the roads were so bad that schools closed, kids would haul their sleds up it and enjoy the unsalted hill. Of course, I accepted her challenge, as always, and was determined to win. Speeding down, Kennedy and I maneuvered out of the way of a car passing by us in the opposite direction, driving up the hill. We were going so fast, I lost control, hit the curb, and sailed right off, hitting my chin on the cement. I sobbed, and she abandoned her bike on the sidewalk to walk me back to my house. My hands were covered in blood. My eyes were swollen from sobbing so hard. When my mom said I needed to go to the hospital, Kennedy insisted she come with us. While I was getting twelve stitches, she bought me a golden-brown teddy bear from the gift shop to make me feel better.

I slept with that stuffed animal every day until about nine months after she moved and hadn't texted me.

"That was when I realized I couldn't ever be a stuntwoman," I said. "My dreams were crushed. Worse than the Olympic trials."

Her thumb continued to graze my scar. "Your chin was so bloody. I thought it was going to ruin your face."

"Is that why you came to the hospital with me?"

"Yes! Quinn, you were dripping blood. You landed right on the curb!"

"But you gave me a teddy bear."

She sucked in her lips, seeming proud of herself for making that kind of romantic gesture at such a young age. "I gave you a teddy bear. I wanted you to feel better."

"Did you like me then? When I cut my chin open? Was that teddy bear because you liked me or because I was your best friend?"

"Both. I've liked you since that summer."

My eyes rounded. "For *that* long? How? I'm not even remotely interesting enough for someone to like me for that long."

"Well, I think you are, so shut up. You know that money I spent on that teddy bear was my lemonade stand money? I really wanted these neon blue and yellow Nike cleats. They looked so freakin' cool. Instead, I spent the money on you."

The truth came out six years later. I knew she was saving up all her lemonade stand money for something. Her father's businessman knowledge rubbed off on her, and I knew Mr. Reed was so proud of his daughter's ambition and business strategy. He built her wooden stand and helped her paint it in pastel lime, pink, and yellow. She charged fifty cents for a sixteen-ounce cup of her premium lemonade made with all fresh ingredients. Her stand was the best in town because she offered not one, not two, but three different flavors of lemonade: regular, strawberry lemonade, and cherry limeade. She made bank too. So many people got lemonade from her, especially the lawn care guys.

She gave me lemonade for free, though. Now I knew why.

"I didn't know you spent your lemonade stand money on Honey Bear."

I also had no idea Kennedy Reed liked me that much since the innocent age of eleven. The things we learn.

"Well, now you know."

"Did you ever get the cleats?"

"No. I bought a new Sims game instead."

"This whole time I thought you bought me a bear because you were just a good best friend."

"It was partially because of that but also because I kind of had a crush on you. I liked your eyes and just wanted to see you smile. You have a really nice smile." Her hand rubbed my warm cheek.

"What a romantic eleven-year-old."

"Right? I should charge for dating advice."

"Thank you for Honey Bear, though. I really did love him. I slept with him every night…well…until I realized you weren't going to text me."

"That's understandable."

"But I still have him…somewhere in the house. I should find him."

I reached for her sweatshirt to bring her face to me. As she leaned in, her smile widened, and the red on her cheeks darkened. God, she was so beautiful. My lips needed to touch hers. I grabbed the sides of her sweatshirt to reel her in closer to me. In one fluid motion, she threw a leg over my lap and straddled me, and feeling her pelvis so close to mine forced the softest murmur from me. She made me melt into her bed. Her tongue clashed with mine as both of her hands ran through my hair. I reveled in the movements and tastes from her mouth that sent erotic sensations to my core, and we spent a good two hours making out, undisturbed by her parents. Because we were just reunited gal pals.

Who gave each other swollen yet very satisfied lips.

CHAPTER SEVEN

The only time I was envious of Liam in high school was when he got to spend New Year's with Kennedy.

My girlfriend.

Unfortunately, I couldn't spend the night with my girlfriend. She and Liam carpooled to Cassandra's house, and I drove myself to Tanner's small gathering with our usual crowd...everyone coupled up. Lana and Meghan, Tanner and Erick. And that left me and Riley by default.

This is so going to get awkward tonight.

Since Tanner's sister was in college, she was our one degree from getting our hands on alcohol. Seven six-packs of various beers, a bottle of Absolut Vodka, and a bottle of champagne. The sight was like seeing the sunset in the Grand Canyon, and I was pretty jealous I gave myself a no-bad-habits rule. The party swarmed around the alcohol, except for me. I wasn't about to ruin any chances in my swimming future because I wanted to get buzzed on New Year's when I was seventeen.

Riley poured herself a Solo cup of vodka and orange soda. I was a little shocked she did that, especially when she refused to drink soda. Not just during swim season but in life. She didn't like all the sugar and thought flavored sparkling water was better tasting anyway.

"Are you a soda drinker now?" I said with a playful laugh.

She looked up at me with a straight face. "Are you super straight edge now?"

Yup, she definitely isn't in a good mood tonight. Drink away, Riley. Drink away.

"When I have ever not been straight edge?"

"Two summers ago at Lana's pool party."

"Why does everyone keep bringing that up? I only puked one time in my life. It was needed to repair my broken dreams."

"Well, wanna drink?"

"Nope. I'm not putting any toxins in my body until after world champs."

Riley laughed as she swallowed the first sip of her drink. "Yeah, because one drink is really going to ruin your chances. It's New Year's Eve. Live a little."

"Why aren't you being supportive?"

"I'm not *not* being supportive. I just think it's a little extreme. This one night is not going to mess up a meet seven months from now."

"You can think it's ridiculous as much as you want, but I'm not gonna drink. Thanks for your support, though."

"Yeah, okay."

"I'll leave you alone now. Clearly, you just want to argue."

I left her at the table of alcohol and joined Tanner and Erick. If she was going to judge me for not drinking, I didn't need her by my side anyway.

I texted, *How's your night? I miss you.*

She responded five minutes later with a picture of just her, Liam, and Gabriel. Liam had his arm around her shoulders with a goofy face, and a thumbs-up formed his other hand. Gabriel towered over them in the background as if he'd photobombed at the last minute. But my eyes went straight to Kennedy in a black cocktail dress hugging her athletic body, ending halfway to her knees. She was so incredibly hot and beautiful. Her silky light brown hair. Her natural beauty with just the right amount of makeup. The dress fitting perfectly around her to show off her built arms and amazing toned legs. Her flawless smile with her straight white teeth. Those beautiful light green eyes looking back at me.

She texted, *We miss youuu!*

I replied, *OMG. Why are you so beautiful...and incredibly hot? My brother is so not even worthy to be in the same picture as you. Shoo him away. Gabe can stay.*

"Hughes, phone down," Tanner said. "Live in the present. Come play a game."

Tanner brought out the cards, and a game of Kings ensued. It was inevitable that I would get harassed for being the only one who didn't have a drink in hand, but peer pressure I could handle. The parties that separated Kennedy and me? I couldn't handle that. Half of my mind was in the game of Kings, trying to accomplish my mission of getting Erick and Lana drunk—the two people who were the funniest. Erick broke out in a one-man Broadway show, and Lana dropped a bunch of swear words she never usually said. And the other half of my mind was at Cassandra's party, just wanting to be next to Kennedy for midnight.

The more the night grew, the more I wished I had something to drink. Everyone was tipsy except for me. The couples started getting touchy with each other, leaving me and Riley awkwardly alone on opposite ends of the room.

When the countdown started ticking away at the bottom of the screen, all the couples paired up, leaving me and Riley not sure what to do with ourselves. I daydreamed at the TV, knowing that Kennedy was watching the same thing at her party, wondering who she was going to kiss at midnight. My only guess would be Grant. It was no secret he liked her and would try everything he could for her kiss.

"What's wrong with you?" Riley said when she approached me.

I knew that my sulk wasn't going to help my case of proving to her that I wasn't dating anyone.

"Nothing. I was just…daydreaming."

"About whoever you were texting that made you all smiley?"

"Wouldn't you like to know?"

"I do because I think it's funny how defensive you get when someone asks if you're dating someone. It just really confirms that you're dating someone."

I wasn't falling for it. I knew Riley. She'd given me plenty of signs that she still liked me, and I highly doubted she would have been happy for me if I got into another relationship. Honestly, I would have been a little jealous if she got into one, so I used that to set the bar on her jealousy.

"Look, Riley, I'm sorry if homecoming gave you false hopes about us—"

"Oh, you mean the fact that we slept together, and then you left me and promised me that you'd make it up to me later, and then every time I tried making plans with you, you made up some really bad lie?"

"I'm sorry."

"No, you're not."

"Okay, Riley, I'm not," I said sarcastically, rolling my eyes.

"Know what I think?"

"What's that?"

"I was way too good for you. I would have done anything for you, and you wouldn't have appreciated it or noticed at all."

She downed the rest of her drink and left me for more alcohol. Her comment really stung. A sober woman's thoughts were a drunk woman's words. Even though I knew she was clearly drunk, so her mental filter wasn't in operation at all, the words still hurt. All because she was overstepping her boundaries into a part of my life I didn't want to share with her anymore. Now, I was the bad guy. I already got flak from my friends for breaking up with her for something as stupid as her having too many feelings for me. I didn't want it coming from her too when we had a pretty civil breakup.

With two minutes left, Erick popped the champagne bottle.

Everyone oohed, and he went around the room to fill everyone's empty flute glass. We raised our glasses and heard the crowd on the TV start to count down twenty seconds to midnight.

"Twenty seconds to get your lips ready," he said, making a point to eye both Riley and me.

The two of us exchanged looks from the other sides of the room. We had less than twenty seconds to decide if we were going to be the only ones at the party not to have a New Year's kiss. After her comment, I couldn't have cared less.

We all crowded around the TV, clutching our flutes, starting the countdown from ten. The closer to midnight, the closer the couples get to each other. Riley looked at me. I looked at Riley. It was almost like the year before when we dated, except we were eager to kiss and ring in the New Year together back then. Now, all I wanted to do was make out with my new girlfriend, who was so unbelievably beautiful in her picture. I would have probably cried and cursed the gay gods if I couldn't kiss her in that dress.

"Three, two, one," the party chanted along with the TV. "Happy New Year!"

"Auld Lang Syne" played on the TV as flashes of various couples kissing passionately in Times Square played. Meghan kissed Lana, Erick drunkenly kissed Tanner, and the two began to make out in their own corner. And Riley and I exchanged one last glance.

"Okay, Sister Mary Quinn and Sister Mary Riley," Erick said over Tanner's shoulder. "Go fucking kiss already. Jesus!"

"Yeah, it's not like you guys have never done that before," Lana said.

"It's fine, really," Riley said. "I'm not crying about it."

The whole party looked at me. Again. Because I was the bad guy, and Riley was the poor innocent girl who wore her heart on her sleeve and just deserved love. Like the female version of Ted Mosby and I was just callous Robin.

"What?" I said to everyone.

"What did you do now?" Tanner said.

"I did nothing. She's been in a mood all night. Look at her."

So they did.

"Yeah, no, I'm not playing this game," Riley said. "Who needs another drink?"

Lana and Tanner raised their hands.

I texted Kennedy, *Want to know what we should do? Ditch our parties and be together.*

I didn't need to put up with Riley's jealousy when I could just sneak off with Kennedy.

She replied, *OMG why didn't I think of this before?*

Because we're clearly dumb. My ex-girlfriend is in a bad mood and taking it out on me, and I want to leave. I can be at your house in an hour?

She texted back, *Cassandra is in a bad mood too. Melanie is voming all over the deck. So it's perfect timing for us to bail on our parties. Meet me at my house. 1:00 sharp.*

Where you lead I will follow.

I left Tanner's party forty minutes after she texted me to make it less suspicious. Riley and Lana were the two drunkest at the party, to the point where every word out of Lana's mouth was "fuck," which I thought was hilarious, and all of Riley's words strung together, which wasn't hilarious at all.

By the time I arrived at Kennedy's house promptly at one o'clock, her red Jetta sat in the driveway. I texted her to let me inside, and fortunately for me, she greeted me still in the dress. The first floor was dark, and the only light illuminating the house came from her bedroom upstairs.

"Your family is asleep?" I said as my hands reached for her waist so I could marvel at her body in that sexy dress.

"They just went to bed. I told them I was staying up for you to come over."

"Please, never come out to your parents so we can keep this up. I'm not allowed to have girls sleep over without being forced to leave the door wide open."

"I will stay in the closet forever."

"Good. Now, this dress that you're wearing..."

"I was about to take it off. Do you wanna help me?"

I actually became speechless. I was a teenager who just got into a new relationship with a beautiful girl. So the thought of helping her take off her dress really did things to me—to my mind and everything below my waist.

"I can definitely help."

She wiggled her eyebrows up and down and grabbed my hand, and the two of us ran up the steps to her lit-up room. Right when we stepped inside, she shut the door and locked it, and I pushed her up against it. She backed into it, breathing into me as my lips fell on hers, begging my tongue for entrance. I ran my hands all over her body as my tongue met hers and my hands felt every inch of her in that incredibly sexy black dress. We made out against her door for a few minutes, kissing each other passionately as the whole night brewed more lust and emotions we needed to release.

Then I pulled away and said, "Kissing you is really amazing, but I want to get out of these clothes. Do you mind donating some for me to sleep in?"

"Of course."

She fished out a soccer T-shirt and flannel sweatpants for me to wear. She changed in the bathroom into her PJs, I changed out in her room, and we met each other again in the bathroom so she could hand me her mouthwash bottle while she brushed her teeth.

"I have to admit that seeing you in my clothes is sexy as hell," Kennedy said with a mouthful of foamy toothpaste oozing from her lips. She spat her toothpaste out and washed her mouth with clean water. "Keep the shirt and wear it all the time at school, please."

"I would definitely get looks from your teammates."

"It would be funny."

"Our sleepovers have really changed a lot since last time," I said. "We wore each other's clothes all the time, and now it's suddenly sexual."

"Yeah because we're seventeen and apparently super hormonal, which is pretty accurate. Let's jump in bed now."

As she headed to her bed, she ran her hand from one side of my back to the other. I quickly finished gargling the mouthwash so I could join her.

She jumped on her bed, pulled down her covers, and patted my spot. When I lay right next to her, she cuddled up beside me, nestling her head between my neck and shoulder, draping her arm over my torso. Her bed got a million times more comfortable with her on me. I closed my eyes, breathing in the smell of her room and her hair, feeling our breathing slow down into the same patterns as we fully soaked in the scene of us cuddling with each other for the first time. It was just as amazing as making out with her, except way more intimate. The more we cuddled and breathed in and out together, the more I just wanted to squeeze her and rub her hair.

"Can I ask you a really personal question?" Kennedy said after a few moments of silence.

"No."

She laughed. "Please?"

I let out a long sigh. "I guess."

"How did you come out?"

No one had really asked me that question before. Everyone in my life was there to watch me go through it. I came out so many times, sometimes each coming-out blurred into one story. Being gay, or any part of the queer community, you had to come out to every person in your life who you wanted in your life. I wish I could just send a memo out to the world that I was gay so I could stop coming out, but unfortunately, life doesn't work that way.

So, I told Kennedy about each time I came out. I first told Liam in March of sophomore year when we both found each other staring at this gorgeous college-aged girl at the rec center. He caught me looking at her legs and butt, and I caught him looking at her boobs.

"Were you just checking that girl out?" he asked.

"Um, maybe."

He smiled so wide. "Oh my God. Are you…"

"I think so." I knew 100 percent I was. Because Lana made me excited to dissect dead animals, and every time Meghan slipped me her tongue, I felt electricity spark underneath my underwear. "But don't tell anymore, or I'll punch you in the dick."

"Well, that explains everything. This is so awesome!"

Liam was the easiest. A few days later, he told me that I should probably tell Gabriel, which I knew was going to be awkward because for those two years I suspected that I was gay, I tried everything in my power not to be. I wanted to like boys. I thought Gabriel was the most attractive boy I'd ever seen. During Christmas break sophomore year, Gabriel and I had a Christmas movie night where we watched *A Christmas Story*, *Home Alone*, and *The Grinch*. It was just the two of us on the couch in his basement. We'd been cuddling the whole night, and then halfway through *Home Alone*, he made a move, and we made out for the rest of the movie. It didn't just happen once, but it happened a handful of times in the span of three months when we scheduled movie nights that really turned into make-out nights. Sometimes he tried to go further than making out, but I always shot down the proposition. I liked kissing, and I liked kissing Gabriel, but even as I was kissing him, he didn't give me butterflies or the same rush of electricity below my pants like Meghan did. When we kissed, I pretended that he was a girl like Meghan or Lexa from *The 100* or Alice from *The L Word*, but the smell of his boyish cologne always ruined it for me.

So, Gabriel and I had a movie night again a few days after I told Liam, code for "I want to make out." Right when he leaned in for a kiss halfway through the movie, I pulled away.

"Gabe, I, uh, I need to tell you something."

He frowned. "What?"

"We can't keep doing this. The friends with benefits thing."

"Why not?"

I swallowed the large growth in my throat. "I like you…as a friend. A really good friend and you're really cute, and kissing you is fun, but I don't like you like that. I, um, I…I'm gay."

It was the first time I said the sentence out loud. *I'm gay.* Saying it left a weird taste on my tongue and a wild springing beat in my heart, as if saying those words made it frolic inside my rib cage because I was finally free. I finally put that label on, and it wasn't as scary as I thought it would be. Liberating, if anything.

Gabriel laughed. "Nice joke."

He leaned back in to resume kissing, but I backed away. "No, really. I'm gay. I like girls."

"How? We've been kissing since Christmas—"

"Because I never kissed a boy before, and I thought kissing one would make me realize that I'm not gay, but I am. I'm so sorry. God, I'm an awful person."

And then I cried. What Gabriel should have done was tell me to fuck off for leading him on, but after a few moments of swallowing the information I gave him, he hugged me tightly in his built arms, realizing that my tears confirmed that I was gay and terrified of it.

He was mad at me for leading him on, yes, and I think he thought that he was the one who "turned me gay," but we talked about it again a few weeks later, and he told me he would always be my friend no matter what.

If I thought Gabriel was going to be hard to come out to, I knew my parents would be the largest hurdle I had to jump over. Their generation wasn't really accepting of the new political correctness wave happening in my generation. While Lana, Tanner, and Riley shared with me their successful coming-out stories, Erick and Meghan shared the ones we hear way too much about. Meghan's mom had treated her differently ever since she came out when she was in eighth grade. They barely had any kind of relationship, Meghan said, and that prompted her to live with her dad since he was way more supportive. After Meghan chopped off her hair, bleached it blond, and started dressing more masculine, the only form of communication she had with her mom was on holidays when she and her two younger sisters were forced to spend time with her. No wonder Meghan hated all the holidays.

As for Erick, his home life was even darker. His parents were very Catholic, and when they found out about Tanner shortly after they started dating, Erick said they screamed at him in Spanish for hours. One day, he came home to find all these crosses nailed to his bedroom walls to expel the gayness out of him. They even sent him to a therapist that we later found out used aversion and shock therapy, telling Erick the reason why he spent his evenings with the Hayeses wasn't for the support he wasn't getting at home but because his attraction to Tanner was an addiction. And Erick told us once when he was drunk that his therapist spent one session shocking him to pictures from *Playgirl.* The last half of junior year, we watched our good friend Erick fall into a deep depression. I never thought I would live to see the day that Erick Iglesias didn't have his mischievous smirk on his face, but there was a dark period where he never smiled. Luckily, the school psychologist, Mrs. Gulati, intervened one day at the tail end of junior year when Erick had a mental breakdown in her office. She immediately called in Mr. and Mrs. Iglesias and demanded they find Erick another therapist. They obliged, but Erick was still scarred from his first therapist, and he grew a huge resentment and hatred for his parents. It wasn't a surprise that he was going to hightail it out of Aspen Grove the second we graduated from high school.

Luckily for me, my story was nowhere near as depressing as Meghan and Erick's. It just kind of happened to me a few days before junior year homecoming. I already asked Riley to the dance and planned on telling my parents we were just going to go as "gal pals." The four of us were eating a nice family dinner at the table, and my mom asked us about our homecoming plans.

Liam told them that he was taking Jennifer—his girlfriend at the time—and they were meeting at Kennedy's house for pictures and dinner. Then it was my turn to say my plans.

"I, um, I'm going with Riley Scott," I said, using my fork to line up my peas in a vertical line just so I could avoid giving them eye contact.

"Oh, really?" my mom said, her tone slightly disappointed. "Did Gabriel find a date?"

My mom really wanted Gabriel and me to date. Sorry, Debbie. The most that would ever happen with Gabriel would be his tongue down my mouth and his hand reaching for my jeans that I immediately swatted at like a pesky housefly.

"He did," I answered.

And his date was, like, a huge upgrade from me. He asked his girlfriend at the time, Aimee Byrne, this really beautiful senior with wavy blond hair, bright blue eyes, and 70 percent sexy legs. They started dating a few weeks after I came out to him, and they lasted for nine really intense months. They were all over each other, so it was no surprise when he told me he lost his virginity to her. I told him that my coming out to him was a blessing in disguise because he got Aimee Byrne, one whole year older than us and a total track star babe.

"So, no real date this year?"

I stopped playing with my peas as the tension covered the dinner table like a white tablecloth. From the corner of my eye, I could see Liam watching me, waiting to see if I was going to use this opportunity to come out. I'd come out to him about seven months before and managed to keep it a secret from everyone except him, Gabriel, and my queer friends at school.

This is the time to tell them, I told myself. *Tell them now because you'll come out to the whole school at the dance.*

"I, uh, she's, um, she's a real date."

"Of course, honey, I get that. But, I don't know, every mother just hopes her kids can go to a school dance with someone who they really like, that's all. I just figured you and Gabriel would go again since you guys get along so well. But if you want to go with friends, then go with friends."

I swallowed. Hard. So hard that I could feel the emotions creeping up to my throat and eyes. "I do like her," my voice lowered. "She's not really my friend. She's, um, she's a real date. I asked her to the dance because I like her. Not as a friend."

Silence.

They're going to hate me. I'm such a freak.

"Quinn, do you like girls?" my dad asked.

"Some of them. Not all of them."

My dad laughed. "Same here, hon. Same here."

I finally looked up at him to see his heartwarming smile. And then I looked at my mom, afraid that I would forever crush her dreams of me marrying Gabriel Báez, the cute, chivalrous Puerto Rican boy next door from such a nice family.

"Quinn, how long have you known?" my mom said. Her light brown eyebrows raised in more of a nurturing way than an angry way.

And that was when I broke. "A long time," I said and started to cry. "A really long time."

A few months after Kennedy Reed kissed me.

Mom pushed herself out of her seat and took me into her arms. "Oh, honey, no, why are you crying?" As she wrapped her arms around me, I continued bawling in my palms. I heard my dad's chair screech across the hardwood floors followed by his warm, giant hand on my back.

"Honey, it's okay," Mom said.

"I'm sorry!"

"Sorry for what?"

"I'm sorry that I'm gay, and I don't want to marry Gabriel. I'm sorry!"

"Quinn, put your hands down and look at us," my dad said.

His voice was stern, and anytime his voice was stern, I knew better than to disobey him. So, I did just that, feeling my face turn bright red at the same time my eyes swelled up. Mom and Dad squatted at my eye level.

"Quinn," my dad said so seriously it made me sob harder, just terrified of what his next words would be. "There's nothing you can ever do that would make your mother and I love you less. You shouldn't ever be sorry for who you love, all right?"

"We don't care if you don't want to marry Gabriel, sweetie," Mom said. "I always thought you guys had something special, and that's why I really supported it, but if you don't like him, then you don't like him. I'm just so happy that you're finally going with someone who you really like. That makes me really happy."

"You mean, you're not embarrassed that I'm gay? Because I am. I know for a fact I'm gay. It's not some stupid high school phase."

"Not in the slightest bit. I'd be embarrassed if you were a bully or going around school shouting derogatory terms at people, or maybe if you ended up pregnant, but at least that's not going to happen, right?"

"Not unless a girl I date has magical powers or something."

Mom smiled. "But I'm not embarrassed that you like girls. Everyone loves differently. There are so many ways to love, and we need more love in this world. Whatever form that might be. I am worried that you're going to face some awful criticism in your life because people are assholes, but you're not going to get that from us."

"If anyone gives you any criticism, they'll have to deal with us," Dad said. "And you know that we're protective mama and papa bears."

I wiped my eyes. "I know."

"We love you, hon," my mom said and kissed my head. "Always remember that."

I nodded, and the two swallowed me in their protective mama and papa bear hugs.

"I wanna join. I wanna join," Liam said and squeezed himself in our group hug. "I'm so proud of you, sis."

The four of us hugged in a tight family embrace for at least a good minute. And then afterward, we got frozen yogurt as a family.

"Wow, that's kind of an adorable story," Kennedy said, hugging me tighter. "I'm really glad you had a good experience."

"Yeah, I'm so freakin' lucky. I don't even know what I would have done if my parents were like Erick or Meghan's."

"I didn't know you and Gabriel had something going on, but it all makes sense. As to why Cassandra doesn't like you. She's had a crush on him for the longest time, and she always got jealous when he would say he was hanging out with you and not us."

"Well, at least there's a somewhat logical reason."

"Did you guys ever…you know, do it?"

"No way. He tried a few times to go down my pants, but I always batted his hand away. I just really like kissing, but kissing him, there were no butterflies in my stomach like there were for Meghan and Riley and you."

"Aw, I give you butterflies?"

"Just looking at you gives me butterflies."

She smiled and clung to me tighter. "Good. I'm glad. And you give me butterflies too. Since we were eleven. That was how I knew I liked you. Those stupid butterflies."

I kissed her on the lips and then pulled away when a question popped into my head. "When do you plan on telling your parents?"

I felt her shrug in my embrace. "I don't know. This is all so new to me that I don't think I'm ready yet."

"If you're not ready, don't force it. And I'm sure your parents will be fine. I mean, your mom is a psychiatrist, for crying out loud. I'm sure she gets anxious, depressed queer kids all the time."

"I didn't tell my parents I was dating Ian or Dominic until

after we broke up," she said, which I found odd because she went to homecoming with both of them. "I don't want them knowing my dating life. So, when I feel like they should know, I'll worry about it then."

"Yes, ma'am."

"In the meantime, I would greatly appreciate it if you made out with me."

"I can do that."

I rolled on top of her, and we made out for an hour before the tiredness kicked in and knocked us asleep with her as the best little spoon I could ask for.

Chapter Eight

A new semester brought a new strict schedule. My third-period AP American Lit, seventh-period AP American History, and eighth-period Economics were switched for third-period Environmental Science, seventh-period Digital Photography, and eighth-period Civics with Liam. With my new schedule, my Civics class was right next door to Kennedy's journalism class.

On the first day of the new semester, she caught Liam and me walking to class together and decided to join, inserting herself just like she had when she first introduced herself right before first grade. Liam and I were coloring our driveway with chalk when her family walked over to introduce themselves to their neighbors. Kennedy went right up to us, told us her name, and asked if she could color with us. The rest was history.

"What are you two doing over here?" she asked us with a friendly smile.

"Civics with Mrs. Daughtry. Unfortunately for us, Quinn and I can't pretend we're the other person to spice it up."

"Yeah, we really fucked it up in the womb when we decided to be opposite sexes," I said.

"But at least I have someone I can talk to about hot girls, and you'll only judge me a little bit."

"This is true. I would have died if you were my straight girl twin and I had to hear you talk about cute boys. Gross."

Liam messed up the top of my hair. I smacked his hand away. I'd spent extra time making it look pretty and straight because of the girl who decided to tag along with us.

Kennedy smiled at me before looking at Liam. "Guess I'll be running into you guys now. You're right next to my journalism class."

"Look at that! I gained two new hallway buddies in one day," Liam said.

"My advice for you both, since I had Mrs. Daughtry first semester, take notes. All the notes. She's really into open-book pop quizzes. It's basically a way for her to see how well you take notes and not doze off in class. The worse you do on those pop quizzes, the more she calls on you."

"You hear that, Quinn? Take good notes for me."

"You're hilarious," I said.

Right as the three of us parted ways to our separate classrooms, Kennedy caught my eye and gave me a wink. My cheeks didn't return to their usual pigment until ten minutes into Civics.

She made school exciting. The journey from seventh to eighth period with her…and Liam—but really with her—was always the most exciting part of my day. Every day, those five minutes allowed Liam and me to grow back together. Those five minutes allowed Kennedy and me to reminisce about our lost friendship. Those five minutes helped repair the two broken relationships in my life that meant the world to me.

Those following weeks, I spent at least one night during the weekend at the Reeds' house since that was the only place we could go to without making it a thing. That was when she told me that she would slowly ease into talking to me more so it didn't catch Liam's eye. I thought it was a good plan and was all for it.

So, at school, Kennedy eased in at the perfect pace so the two of us had conversations in front of Liam, and no one thought anything of it. She even made a habit of walking next to me rather than on the other side of Liam like at the beginning of the semester. She walked so closely to me, sometimes our arms would touch, and all those weekend nights together tricked me into thinking I could link arms with her or hold her hand because God, did I really want to hold her hand.

"Kennedy, how much do I have to pay you for your Civics notes from last semester?" Liam asked one early February day. "Because Quinn here is an awful twin and won't let me copy her, and I got a D on the first pop quiz."

"Sounds like a personal problem to me," I said.

"What's up with the Hughes twins cheating? Quinn used to cheat all the time in our sleeping bag races, and now you want to steal my Civics notes."

"Hey!" I said and pinched the back of her arm. She yelped. I laughed. It was kind of sad that was the only way for me to touch her at school, but I also thought it was funny when she squirmed and punched me back in the arm. "I never cheated. You tried to cheat. All. The. Time. One, two, go? Does that ring a bell?"

"It's not my fault you never caught on to my counting. Sounds like a personal problem to me." She nudged me in the arm. "And, Liam, I did warn you about the quizzes."

"But the Articles of Confederation are so boring," he pleaded.

"You know they have *Schoolhouse Rock* on YouTube," I said. "Just watch that."

"Oh my God, *Schoolhouse Rock!*" Kennedy said to me. "Remember how we would always sing those on our walk to school? *We the people*," she started to sing.

"*In order to form a more perfect union*," I sang with her.

"*Establish justice, insure domestic tranquility*," we sang together.

"You guys can stop at any time now. My ears are bleeding," Liam said. "Come on, Ken. Twenty bucks for your notes. Or you give me your notes, and I treat you to a dinner at Ogawa Hibachi this weekend?"

The two of us stopped singing and shot sharp looks at Liam. *Did my brother just ask my girlfriend out on a date?*

Kennedy laughed, thinking it was a joke. But I knew Liam was completely serious. "Yeah, okay, Liam," she said, mocking his proposal. "I'll take the filet mignon and lobster dinner for thirty bucks in exchange for the Civics notes I immediately threw out after my exam." She patted him on the back, and his smile faded just a little bit, along with his ego. "But thanks. I look forward to this luxurious meal."

She playfully grinned at both of us and disappeared into her journalism classroom.

❖

"Look at you and Kennedy chatting away now," Liam said to me that night, creeping into my room as I finished up some homework. "Whoever knew Civics could cure old wounds? Told you she wasn't bad, am I right?"

I got into character. The Quinn from the fall who was still bitter about her broken friendship with Kennedy Reed. I let out a long sigh, pretending to hate so much that Liam was right. "You're right, Liam. She's not too bad."

"So, you think you two are good, then?"

"Maybe. She seems…nice."

"She's incredibly nice. And I'm getting the feeling that she's happy you guys have, like, somewhat rekindled your friendship too. Hey, maybe the four musketeers can get back together!"

"Organize a movie night, and I'm down."

"Okay, but no making out with Gabriel again."

"I don't think that will happen." A pause. "Liam?"

"Yeah?"

"Did you ask Kennedy out on a date? Today? Before Civics?"

Liam didn't say anything at first. His blue-green eyes just stared blankly at me. "I mean…kind of, why?"

"Why?"

"Why did I ask her out? Because she's hot. She has a good personality, she's funny, she's smart, she's nice."

My stomach dropped. My brother had a crush on my girlfriend, and we couldn't even tell him.

"Don't you like Cassandra?"

"Uh, no. Cassandra has nothing but a hot face and hot body. Plus, I would have asked Kennedy to homecoming if Grant didn't beat me to it. That little shit."

God, my brother had a crush on Kennedy. My brother had a crush on my secret girlfriend, and I had absolutely no idea about it.

"Does she...does she know that you like her?"

"Apparently not if she thought my asking her out on a date was a joke." He seemed a little hurt, and his eyes drifted to the floor. "But maybe the moment wasn't right. Maybe I should try again. Not walking to class or making a joke of it. What do you think? You're a girl. You understand girls. What do they like?"

These were similar conversations we had back during our sophomore year after he found out I was gay. He was the first person I told, and if anything, he was excited to have me to go to when he needed advice on girls. He came to me when he wanted to be cute asking Jennifer Stewart to homecoming junior year. *Are flowers too much? If I get flowers, should I get roses, or is that clichéd? You think that she'd be okay with a nice dinner, or should we do something extravagant?* And then, of course, when he wanted to break up with her, I was the first person he went to for advice on how to break up with her but still remain friends.

Little did Jennifer Stewart know that I basically broke up with her.

I guess our hallway walks to Civics mended our cracked relationship just enough for him to come to me for advice again, which hadn't happened since we started arguing more after sophomore year when the Camry entered the scene. I loved our hallway walks. It was pretty obvious that I enjoyed it because of Kennedy, but I also enjoyed bonding with my twin brother, even if it was for only five minutes.

But as grateful and flattered as I was that he trusted me

enough for advice again, it pained me to know that not only did he have a crush on my girlfriend, but nothing he could do would get his crush to go on a date with him.

"Um, I don't know, Liam. Each girl is different."

"You think I should try again? Maybe privately? Maybe just be frank and ask her out on a date. Maybe Valentine's Day?"

No, no, no. She was mine for Valentine's Day. We were a week away, but I didn't think I would have any competition... especially with my brother. I had no plans for Valentine's Day, but I wanted to do something special. Playing tug-of-war with my brother was not really one of my things I wanted to do.

"I know Grant still likes her," Liam continued, "so I should probably do it now. Before anyone else does. What do you think?"

Oh my gosh, everyone stop having a crush on my girlfriend. Like, I know she's the whole package and all, but simmer.

"Do you think she'll say yes?"

He gave me an almost comical look. Liam was an attractive guy. He could get almost any girl he wanted. And he knew this. His eyes laughed at me for even asking the question, but some modesty kicked in his vocal cords and he said, "I think I might have a shot...if I ask."

As much as it made me cringe, I had no doubt that Kennedy liked me. I could tell by the way she gently and methodically kissed me, and hearing about any boy asking her out was hilariously entertaining. Except when that boy was my brother. It didn't make me feel good hoping my brother would get rejected. He was a good guy to girls. He deserved to be with someone who made him happy, and the whole time he asked me what to do about Kennedy, the corners of his mouth were raised. So optimistically. A teenager swept up in a cloud of lust.

"It doesn't hurt to ask," I said, giving up, just wanting this conversation to be over. "But don't get too upset if she says no. You two are really good friends."

"Yeah, but..." He paused, almost as if he was going to

confess something to me but held back. "Yeah, I shouldn't assume anything. I should just ask."

And he did that weekend. I was on my way home from an away meet when he texted me.

> Liam: *I asked Kennedy out. We went to Gabriel's together, and I asked her if she had any plans on Vday.*
> Me: *Yeah...? What did she say?*
> Liam: *She said she didn't have any plans yet. Key word: yet. So I thought that was a sign that she was waiting for plans. So I asked her. And she laughed like she did in the hallway. She didn't think I was serious. Again. I didn't even make a joke about it. I told her I was 100% serious, and she laughed again. Said she only likes me as a friend.*
> Me: *I'm sorry dude. That really sucks.*

I really did feel bad for him. The whole situation sucked.

> Liam: *UGH! I thought maybe she liked me.*
> Me: *Why did you think that?*
> Liam: *Idk. There were vibes. But apparently, she thinks I'm a joke.*

The following week, my parents told Liam and me at dinner about their Valentine's Day plans in the city, and Liam told us he was going to Gabriel's parents' cabin on Whiteface Mountain to go snowboarding with Gabriel and Tom, which meant I would have the house to myself the whole weekend. In a matter of seconds, I formulated my Valentine's Day plans underneath the dinner table while Mom and Dad oohed and ahhed about their hot, steamy city date as if we really wanted to know any more details other than wine and seeing *Hamilton* on Broadway.

Me: *Guess what?*

Kennedy: *What?*

Me: *I have the house to myself this weekend.*

Kennedy: *WHAT?*

Me: *My parents are spending the weekend in the city for Vday. Liam is snowboarding with Tom and Gabriel. Live with me for the weekend. Be my valentine.*

Kennedy: *You sure there's no way they'll come back?*

Me: *Nope. Parents have both days booked with plans that they felt the need to tell us about. TMI! And Liam would die before you take away his snowboard trip. We can make food. Watch movies. Make out a lot...other things...*

Kennedy: *Other things? Like play Mario Party?*

Me: *That's exactly what I was implying! Dibs on Yoshi.*

Kennedy: *Noo. Yoshi was my character!*

Me: *Nope. I already claimed him. You can have Princess Peach.*

Kennedy: *But her laugh creeps me out.*

Me: *We'll do a staircase race. Winner gets Yoshi.*

Kennedy: *Count me in, my Valentine.*

Me: *OMG YAY!*

My parents left me a hundred bucks for food since the fridge and pantry were scarce with it. For once, after practice, I took a shower with actual shampoo, conditioner, and body wash as opposed to just dealing with the chlorine stench on my skin. Of course, this set Madison and Gia off on another round of their new favorite game, "Who's Quinn dating?" while Riley pretended to ignore us three and bolted out of the locker room at record speed. I couldn't smell like pool for my weekend-long date.

Then I went to the store to buy food for a picture-perfect two-day sleepover—chips, salsa, queso, guac, pizza rolls, waffle mix, eggs, bacon, and chicken breasts. Most of the food for Kennedy. I couldn't get too carried away on pizza rolls.

"Oh my God, I'm having so many flashbacks," Kennedy said as she stepped into the foyer, gazing all around the entryway as if she had been transported back to the days of her youth, which I guess in a way, she had. "I'm going to destroy you in this staircase race." She pointed to the wooden staircase.

"Yeah, maybe if you cheat."

"But first rule: no real clothes."

My eyes lit up. "No clothes? This is escalating quickly."

"Well, I meant PJs. But I'm okay with however you interrupted that sentence."

"How about I surprise you?"

Just a minute in, and I already wanted to throw her on my bed and thoroughly kiss her.

I led the way to my bedroom, and we weren't even in my room before she kicked off her jeans, and I couldn't help but watch. She didn't tell me to turn away, and she didn't seem at all insecure about changing in front of me. All the running and soccer ball dribbling over the course of her soccer career had really defined her thighs and calves. She reached for her gray jogger pants and pulled them over my view, tying the laces to keep them in place in the same spot I wanted to run my tongue across. She then slipped out of her shirt and stood there in a black bra, searching for a new shirt in her bag. My mouth became dry at the sight of her perfect chest. Her stomach was just as toned, with the smallest trace of abs. Her collarbone popped out, her chest was muscular, and her arms had no fat on them whatsoever. Her whole body was nothing short of a future Division One athlete. I knew she was in shape since she worked out at the rec center often and was on the varsity soccer team and even played club soccer in the spring. But holy damn, I didn't know she was that toned. She would have fit right in with my international swimming competition.

The best thing about it was that she was my girlfriend. She was all mine.

After she popped her head out of her new shirt, she caught

me practically drooling over her like a pathetic teenage boy. She smirked. I blushed, but my true embarrassment seemed to entertain her.

"My eyes are up here," she said, biting her lip and thoroughly enjoying my eyes scanning her from head to toe.

"Sorry. I couldn't help it."

Even with her black Aspen Grove soccer T-shirt, gray jogger pants, and magenta socks, she was still the prettiest girl in school. Her hair that was straight during school was thrown up in a bun, and her face was free from the very little makeup she wore, and God, she was just pure beauty. The color of her eyes popped out even more, and the whole beautiful tomboy, girl-next-door look she owned in front of me had me feeling completely weak.

"What?" she said.

I smiled. Why? Because she was my girlfriend. How I managed to get someone like her to like me since she was eleven would forever remain a mystery.

"Are you a model?" My hands attached themselves to her waist and lifted her shirt up just a little bit to catch a peek at her wonderfully flat and toned stomach.

She smacked my arm away. "Clean up the drool, sass pants. It's race time. Winner gets Yoshi."

I just wanted to kiss her. Kennedy just wanted to be ten years old and bruise her butt on the wooden steps.

We positioned our sleeping bags methodically and carefully on the top of the steps. The challenge with the stair race was that the staircase was in the shape of an L, so we had to strategize our turn at the end for the ultimate finish. When we were younger, Kennedy and I had that curve down perfectly, as if we were the Tom Brady of staircase races. But with five years of no practice, I wasn't sure I could manage the staircase without a butt bruise or running myself straight into the wall.

"On my count," Kennedy said.

"Oh no, we're not doing this again. You always went on two!"

"And I used to wear my hair in a fishtail braid, but clearly, I've matured, Quinn."

"You're going on three, or you can sleep on the floor."

"Yeah, okay." She chuckled in mockery. "You still have some drool on your mouth. I'm pretty sure no matter what, I'll get the bed."

"Don't be so confident."

"I'll just take off my shirt again."

I swallowed at the same time my cheeks turned warm. "You're going to go on three."

I gave her a suspicious look. She took advantage of her beautiful smile and warm eyes, knowing I'd cave in to her good looks. And I did. So easily.

"Fine," she said. "One."

She stared me down.

"Two," I said.

And then she pushed off. She was halfway down the stairs before I even processed that she cheated. Again. I pushed myself off the top step and both of us ran straight into the wall, never getting the chance to curve the L. But the finish line was the bottom of the stairs, so I crawled on top of her, tumbling down the last three stairs, just to reach my arms out to touch the wooden floors of the foyer. My stomach hurt so badly from crashing and crawling, but I touched first, and victory over the cheater was worth the pain.

"I win!" I shouted. "Karma for cheating!"

She wiggled her way down the last three stairs and then crawled on top of me, her body pinning me to the foyer floor. Her floral-smelling hair dangled in front of my face, and she slowly leaned in and kissed the scar on my chin. Although her lips were tender, my body still quivered just from the touch of her.

"Cheaters don't deserve my kisses," I said.

"Oh really?"

I shook my head. She gave me a mischievous smirk, and I bit my lip. Yes, cheaters deserved my kisses when they had a flawless smile like that.

Everything up until that point was as if we transformed into our childhood selves just for the night. After the sleeping bag race, Kennedy insisted we eat all forty pizza rolls in the bag, just like we used to at our more innocent childhood sleepovers. We played *Mario Party* for a good hour in the dark, and I was even nice enough to let her be Yoshi just so I could say I beat her as Princess Peach (I did, for the record). We even looked back on pictures I dug up in the basement for the ultimate nostalgia, sitting cross-legged on my bed as forgotten memories sprouted in our minds. And yes, Honey Bear made an appearance in the circle too.

When it was three in the morning, we finally decided it was best to turn the lights off and wind down. Both of our inner children went back inside us, and we became our seventeen-year-old selves again, gazing at each other through the darkness in a different way than we used to. Her body snuggled into my side, and her head rested right above my armpit, half of her face buried in my neck. The patterns of our breath slowly synced into solidarity. She threw her arm over me, pulling my body closer to hers, then ran her fingertips up and down my arm so soothingly. After a few moments, her fingers slid up my shirt and delicately grazed my waistline right above my sweatpants. Goose bumps sprouted all over my body, and I tried so hard not to let out the softest moan that crept up in my throat.

"Your stomach feels nice," she said. "Is this what an Olympic trials qualifier's body feels like?"

"I guess so. Just wait until I qualify for the Olympics. Hopefully, I'll have washboard abs, killer biceps, and the most beautiful back muscles you'll ever see."

"Oh God, I'm not sure what to do with myself if you look hotter than you already are."

"Die?"

"Pretty much."

"So, besides me, have you had any other girl crushes? Like, I know I'm the greatest and all, but there has to be someone else in this universe you liked to look at."

"There was one other girl, actually."

I loved how jealous I got. Jealous yet so intrigued by this other girl. She didn't even know what she was missing out on, probably.

"Tell me! Tell me!"

"Well, first girl crush—not including you—was Jordan Lloyd. She was so beautiful. Brown wavy hair, blue eyes, tan skin."

"You have a thing for brunette girls with blue eyes."

She smirked. "I really do. But wanna know a secret?"

"What's that?"

"Your blue eyes are way better. Jordan Lloyd's were straight up dark, but yours pick and choose when they want to be blue and when they want to be green." I beamed. "But anyways, Jordan Lloyd was on my soccer team. A defender, so she was always in front of me. Sometimes I would get distracted and stare at her hair or her legs or…her butt. God, she had amazing legs. Anyway, there was one game, I just stared at her like a creep. She was stretching from side to side as our team was doing something at the other end of the pitch, and I guess I stared too long at her because next thing I knew, the other team was attacking, and I almost gave up a goal. And that's not the most embarrassing part. The most embarrassing part was that she threw her hands up in the air and gave me this 'what the fuck' look. Like, you'd think I would have realized it when I was staring at her butt that maybe I liked girls, but I didn't."

"And she wasn't into you at all?"

"Definitely not after I almost gave up a goal. Plus, she was so straight."

"The straight girls always get you," I said. "Beware of the straight girls. Rule one of being into girls."

"She had a crush on this guy named Nick. *Nick Keyes*." She said it in an annoyed, mocking voice. "But it's okay, though. I think you're a million times more attractive and a better person than Jordan Lloyd, and that's really saying something."

That compliment forced me on top of her. I buried my face in the small of her neck and took my aggression out on her skin. With each kiss on her neck, she ran her hands under my shirt, and when I lightly sucked on her skin, her fingernails clawed farther into my back.

Everything happened so quickly. Of course I'd thought about it when I invited her over. How could you be seventeen, have a whole house to yourself, and have a sleepover with your girlfriend and not wonder if the night wouldn't lead to sex? Before I knew what was even happening, we were both in our bras and underwear. Our clothes were haphazardly tossed all over my floor from all the dry humping that had already ensued, causing my lower half to tingle in intense desires for any part of her body to touch me down there.

I pulled myself away from her lips. "What's happening?"

"I'm not sure, but I don't want it to stop." Her voice was soft and slightly out of breath.

"We can just lie here and talk and cuddle—"

"I don't want to talk and cuddle," she said so confidently that my breath caught in my chest.

"You sure?"

"I mean, I…I just don't know what I'm doing. I'm assuming you've done this before?"

"Three times. But that's it."

"Oh, damn."

"You?"

"Um, just twice, but they were with boys. So, I have no idea what I'm doing with girls. You'll have to guide me."

"I don't really know what I'm doing either. But you don't have to do anything you're uncomfortable doing. We really don't have to do it if you're not ready. I won't be upset—"

"I'm ready. I'm positive. I wanna do it with you."

Her hand pulled my face back to hers so I couldn't change my mind. I took that as a sign to just give what the girl wanted. So, my hand wandered across her back to her bra, and my thumb and pointer finger unhooked it. When I yanked the bra off, all I could do was stare at her and breathe heavily, marveling at all the beauty in front of me. God, she was so beautiful and perfect. My hands glided down her topless body from her neck, to her bare breasts, to her stomach, and down to the base of her body. She let out a gasp when my hand skimmed the fabric of her underwear as her head sank farther into the pillow. My lips needed to be on her, so they kissed her neck, and my tongue traced down her breasts and then to her hips. I could tell she got lost in my world completely by how every touch arched her back. The lower my hand and lips wended down her body, the more control she lost, and when I knew we were both ready, I slid off her purple underwear.

I was so nervous. A million times more nervous than when I lost my virginity to Riley a year before. I had no idea what I was doing then—even more so than now—but this felt so different. Was my throat supposed to be this dry? Was my heart supposed to feel like a brick? Were my breaths supposed to be this ragged? I tried so hard to swallow my nerves, but they just collected in my throat.

When my mouth finally met her center, my kiss sent her back into a full arch. She let out a moan and clutched my bedsheets when I put my fingers inside her. I watched her stomach rise and fall and tremble all at the same time, and I hoped she didn't feel every atom that made up my being shake in unison with her too. Her hand slid into my hair and held my face in the place she wanted my tongue, and when she grabbed a fistful of hair, goose bumps erupted all over my half-naked body. Her other hand twisted my bedsheets, and I craved more of her with each sound that she released. Her body became more flexible, rocking back and forth along my fingers like a wave.

Her breaths sped up. Her moans grew louder until she couldn't hold it in anymore.

As she collected herself after she finished, I retrieved my hand and kissed my way from her hips to her stomach to her chest to her neck, and I kissed her mouth again.

"Get on your back," she said, breathing into me.

"You really don't have to if you're not ready—"

"Shut up and get on your back."

If the sounds she made when I was going down on her weren't enough (they were), I was so ready for her tongue and fingers after that demand. She wrapped her athletic legs around my torso and flipped me over. Everything I did to her she imitated. She sucked on my neck while her hands traced invisible lines up and down my stomach. Her fingers teased me on the fabric of my underwear, and just the teasing made me melt into my bed. Her soft lips kissed my waistline, prepping me for when she glided my underwear down my legs.

Just like I did when I first saw her naked body, her silhouette towered over me, and all I heard was her light breathing. At first, I worried she didn't like what she saw. Did my naked body and boobs freak her out? Were my nipples too big or too small for her liking? Did she finally realize seeing my body that she wasn't into girls? Crap, could I get a blanket to cover up?

But just as my mind started racing, her hand rested on my stomach and felt the pathetic excuse for abs that barely showed through my skin.

"Are you a model?" she said softly but jokingly.

I smiled as she curled her fingers upward so her fingertips drew endless spirals all over my stomach. I closed my eyes and inhaled deeply and nervously. I felt so exposed. My naked body just out there in the open, feeling the gentle air of the house brushing against my skin, igniting goose bumps everywhere with the help of Kennedy's hands. My naked body, the nerves traveling through me, and my strong desire for her mouth; I'd never felt more vulnerable than I did at that moment. I felt as if

I was giving my whole being to her, and that was terrifying to know that this girl could easily break me in two if she wanted to. But when she bent over and finally put her lips on my waistline, I exhaled the breath I'd been holding in and realized I trusted her with everything like I'd never trusted anyone before. Her touch felt so right and calming and magical. It made me feel so whole and safe and alive.

When I felt her warm mouth on me, I sucked in my breath as my throat caught a moan. I got lost in her world the same way I got lost in the woods, so suddenly and carelessly. Nothing else existed to me. We were the only two people in the house, all of Earth, in the whole universe, and we were connected. Her mouth, her fingers, our emotions. I grabbed a pillow and clutched it over my face, muting the cries that I held inside. My hands tightened around the pillow the more she kept going, the deeper she went inside me, and the faster her tongue flicked in circles on me, until finally, I released my grip when she made me finish.

We kissed each other delicately to sleep afterward, stroking each other's hair, face, and bare skin. She nuzzled her face into my neck, and I felt her body loosen in my arms as she drifted to sleep.

❖

The next morning, I woke up spooning her. I could tell she was still asleep from her heavy yet soft breathing. I still couldn't believe it. She was in my bed, bundled up under my covers and in my arms, snuggled so close to me. I needed to pee so badly, but I didn't want to move. I wanted to fully enjoy her body right up against me. She faced away, but her hair was right under my nose. I used my fingertips to softly rub her arm, burying my face in her back, taking a deep inhale of the mixture of smells emanating from her shirt, a combination of her and fabric softener.

Why are you so perfect?

She let out a sleepy grunt, and her body did a full stretch.

She then slowly turned over with squinty eyes, and when she saw me, she smiled.

Waking up to see that award-winning smile and those bright eyes was hands-down better than the best sunset photographed and flaunted on Tumblr. And boy, did Tumblr have some amazing pictures of nature, cats, and really attractive women cuddling, kissing, and grinding on each other.

"Good morning, beautiful," I said and ran my fingers through her knotty hair.

"You're a creep," she said in her dream-drenched voice.

I laughed and kissed her on the forehead. Her face smelled like sleep and the exfoliating cream she used before we went to bed, and the smell of it made me kiss her forehead again.

"Want some breakfast?" I asked. She nodded. "The menu this morning is waffles, scrambled eggs with—"

"Bacon bits?"

I smiled. "With bacon bits. I remember our sleepovers."

"Those were quite different than the one we just had."

"Just slightly different."

I planted my hand on the spot next to her to hoist myself out of bed to make her the best Valentine's breakfast she'd ever had, but both of her arms wrapped around me. She yanked me in, and I fell right on top of her. Her chest served as a nice cushion. She let out a small grunt when I landed.

"Am I not allowed to leave?" I said.

She bit her lip and nodded. "Kiss me," she said softly.

My whole body tingled. She could say it over and over again, and every time, my body would have that same intense tingle.

"But you have morning breath," I said.

"I said kiss me, not put your tongue inside me," she said more harshly—yet still charming.

"But I'm hungry," I teased.

She then wrapped both of her legs around me, pinning my pelvis to hers. I could have just about died at that point. Her leg grip was strong; I couldn't move even if I tried. Those hamstrings and calves I saw the night before, dear God.

"Now you're stuck until you give me what I want," she said.

My body didn't even feel real, it was so overcome with desire. I kissed her—my mouth closed to hide the morning breath—but I kissed her so hard yet soft that I didn't care about the breakfast of champions I was going to make her. I just wanted her. I kissed her lips over and over because just kissing her with a closed mouth wasn't enough.

She pulled away abruptly and said, "Breakfast can wait a little bit, can't it?" I nodded, probably way too fast to be cool about it. "I don't think my body has gotten over last night."

"Oh really?"

If I didn't get on Team USA for Rio, at least I had that talent in the bag.

"God no. It was amazing. Every part of it. I want more."

"You were pretty amazing too. You sure you never hooked up with Jordan Lloyd?"

"Not even in my dreams. But forget about her. She's so freshman year. Whatever you did last night, you should do it again. Right now."

Anything she demanded, I would give her.

We ran to my bathroom, brushed our teeth so poorly our dentists would have lectured us at our next appointment, and went back to bed to do it all over again.

She was my favorite kind of morning.

After breakfast, we took a shower together. One time, Riley and I fooled around in the locker room showers during a morning practice hardly anyone went to because of a snowstorm, but we were both in our bathing suits, and no orgasms were involved. Just making out and wandering hands above bathing suits, enough to feel pleasure but also enough to scare us into thinking someone would catch us in the act. I'd never taken a shower with anyone completely naked before, but if I had the house to myself with my girlfriend, why would we take two separate showers and waste water, especially when there was an awful drought in California? I needed to practice conserving before moving out there, so I decided to start then and there on that Valentine's Day.

We must have been in there for at least a half hour; most of the time we argued about whose turn it was to stand in the warm water. When we weren't arguing, we let our hands run up and down each other's wet bodies. We lathered each other up with soap just so we could touch each other again. We sang along to the music that played from my phone and styled each other's soapy hair into mohawks and pixie cuts.

When we got changed, I took my singing phone and chose a specific song for Kennedy, who had her hair flipped over, tying it into a damp messy bun. The song began to play.

"What are you doing?" she said and looked at my extended hand.

"Wanting to dance with you," I said. "Give you the dance you wanted at homecoming."

That comment colored her face pink. The song playing out of my phone was "XO" by Beyoncé. It had popped up on my Spotify multiple times since Kennedy and I started becoming a thing, and every time I heard it, I thought of her. Honestly, it'd been on repeat ever since our first kiss in November.

Her smile was so big when she wrapped her arms around my neck, and I placed mine on her hips.

"This song makes me think of you every time it comes up," I said.

"I've never even heard this song, but I like how you always think of me when it plays."

"You never heard of this song? It's Beyoncé!"

"I don't listen to Beyoncé, but I'll start listening to this song."

"You don't listen to Beyoncé? You're dead to me."

That was when she kissed me, her hand on my neck holding

my face in place. She knew how to work me perfectly. She knew when she threatened me with taking her shirt off or kissing me to make up for a severe flaw I found out she had. She knew what she was doing because it worked every time.

"Am I still dead to you?" she said when she pulled away.

"No, definitely not. Under one condition."

"What's that."

"There's a rule to this song, you know."

"Oh really? And what rule is that?"

"Every time Beyoncé says that you gotta kiss me, you have to kiss me."

"Oh God. Cruel and unusual punishment."

Just then, Beyoncé sang the lyric, and Kennedy responded like the rule follower she was, kissing me softly and perfectly on the lips. We danced for the rest of the song, kissing each other when Beyoncé told us too.

This can't get more perfect, I thought all throughout our dance.

We spent the afternoon watching Disney movies just like we did when we were younger when the rain or cold trapped us inside. Back then, we built forts out of blankets in my basement and cushioned the ground with practically all the pillows in the house. My dad helped us drape the fort perfectly over the TV so that it enclosed us. Now Kennedy and I bundled underneath blankets on the living room couch, cuddling close to each other, my arm around the side of her and her head resting between my shoulder and chest. Outside, snow flurries fell from the gray skies, and occasionally, the two of us would drift our eyes from the TV to the window. The scene we created was nothing short of perfect. Lighthearted movies, blankets, snow, hot chocolate, and Kennedy wrapped in my arms.

We watched *The Lion King*. Cried. Hard. *Beauty and the Beast*. Sang. Hard. *Fox and the Hound*—

"What the fuck?" Kennedy yelled as the *Fox and the Hound*

credits rolled. She wiped her eyes. "How is this a story about friendship? How does Netflix label this as a feel-good movie? They aren't even friends! There's no way for them to be friends!"

"Well, yeah. Copper was trained to hunt Tod."

"They promised they would be friends forever, though!"

"Yeah, well, they were full of shit."

Heartbroken redness sucked out the color in her eyes. She used her soccer shirt to wipe her cheeks as I tried hard not to laugh at her.

"Kennedy, we used to watch this movie all the time. How do you not remember the end?"

"I do remember the end!" Her voice cracked. "I remember the waterfall, and I thought they became friends and worked it out."

"No! One is a hunting dog, and the other is a fox. How the hell can they be best friends? Not being friends is their fate."

"This movie is an awful movie about friendship! All these Disney movies are tragic. No wonder people need therapy. I need therapy after this."

I paused to think of a solution. One we could both enjoy. "Have you ever seen *The L Word*?"

"Hmm, no. What's that?"

"Oh my God! If you're going to kiss girls, you need to do it the right way."

If there were still a bunch of people throughout the world who believed the homosexual agenda was actually a thing, well, I was going to be a part of it and spread it. Whatever Kennedy needed to help her fully understand her sexuality, I volunteered as tribute. And the first step to spreading the lesbian agenda was pure art known as *The L Word*.

Step Two: Tumblr ships.

Step Three: *The 100* because Clexa.

Okay, mostly Lexa.

Needless to say, after the pilot, all the sex scenes and the sexual tension from the TV found its way cuddled up underneath the blankets with us. Kennedy started it all by kissing and sucking on my neck. I'd like to think it was the ladies of *The L Word* who inspired her to kiss me. Thoroughly. As if my neck had never been kissed. At just the right time, she tossed me back on the couch and straddled me. Barely any time passed before we both yanked each other's shirts off as if they were the worst things to ever be. Feeling her bare skin against me brought the same comfort a warm blanket did on a cold night.

For not being out, she wasn't shy at all with me. She showed the most confidence when we were secluded from the outside world. I didn't fight back. I allowed her lips to wander down to my bra and then my stomach. I allowed her hands to slowly slip underneath the inside of my pants and her fingers to run across my smooth skin. I allowed her waist to grind up against me, and I allowed myself to bask in all the wonderfully numbing feelings that took over my body when she did all of that.

I thought there would have been more instruction involved, but I didn't have to coach Kennedy in anything. She just knew. Maybe she was just a natural, but I liked to think that our chemistry was so strong, she was just intuitive. She knew the exact spots to kiss, the exact spots to touch, and the perfect times to be tender and the perfect times to be rough. Her right hand crept underneath my underwear until her fingers found their way inside me. I let out a gasp and buried my whole face in the pillow I was lying on. Every touch and kiss made my fingers clutch the pillow harder. My heart picked up speed. My body relaxed. My breaths shortened. My moans became louder. My wanting her became so much stronger. She was pushing me over the edge, so quickly, so very close—

"Oh my God!" Liam yelled.

My heart felt like a semi-truck rolled over it. Kennedy and I threw ourselves off the couch in a not-so-subtle motion, like bricks collapsing one by one after being bulldozed by a wrecking ball. She tumbled first; I fell on top of her. She let out a grunt. I let out a cry when I bumped my head on the coffee table, and I yanked the blanket off the couch to hide our half-naked bodies. Liam's thumps and trips echoed in the foyer, and his hard footsteps sprinted up the wooden steps before silence overcame the house after a loud bedroom door slam.

We were caught. Right in the act. By my brother.

Chapter Nine

For what seemed like forever, Kennedy and I hid our faces in blankets and pillows and calmed down our breathing. We'd kept each other a secret for three and a half months, and then my brother had magically appeared to find his friend—his crush—with her hands down his sister's underwear, who was at most six seconds away from an orgasm.

I could have started crying at that moment. Never in my life had I ever been so humiliated and so exposed. But I swallowed the tumor in my throat when I heard sniffling coming from Kennedy. She had more to lose than me, and I had to suck back that lump in my throat for her.

"Hey, you okay?" I said, finally sliding the blanket from my burning face. Uttering these words was so hard when all I wanted to do was crawl into a hole with her and never come back out.

"I can't believe he saw us," she muttered into the pillow, too ashamed to show her face. "He saw us. God!"

"I know—"

"Oh my God, I'm so embarrassed. He doesn't even know, Quinn." She finally showed me her face, red and puffy from sobbing. "He saw me in my bra. He saw me on you. In you."

I winced at the thought.

The more she cried, the more I wanted to join her. As the reality of the situation set in, my body disintegrated into complete, utter embarrassment. If my relationship with my brother was already strained from the pressures of high school, finding his closeted crush having sex with his sister on the couch would take months—maybe even years—to just forget about and act as if nothing happened at all.

"I gotta go talk to him. I gotta do it now before it gets even more awkward."

The last thing I wanted to do was look Liam in the eye after that. But we had to address it, and the longer we avoided it, the more awkward it would be. And as horribly embarrassing as it was, I knew that Liam wouldn't utter a word to anyone about it.

I threw on my clothes and took the longest walk of shame up to his room. Loud rap music blared through his locked door, probably to untangle the vivid picture scarred in his mind.

When I knocked on the door, there was no answer. I knocked again. And when I still didn't get an answer, I pounded on the door.

"Liam, let me in!" I yelled.

The door whipped open, and a wave of rap music took over my eardrums. Liam instantly turned around without giving me any eye contact. He sat at his desk and dove back into his computer screen, pretending to look at Facebook.

"We need to talk."

"No."

"We need to."

He continued to scroll down his Facebook newsfeed, so I slammed his laptop shut, and Facebook and the blaring rap music shut off.

"What the hell!"

He finally looked at me, but I could already see that he was scarred.

"Let me explain—"

"What the fuck was that, Quinn?"

"You were supposed to be at Gabriel's cabin!"

"Before Whiteface Mountain got a blizzard warning and we

left so we wouldn't be trapped. Trust me, I'd rather be trapped up there than finding you two fucking each other."

"I wish that would have happened too."

"Is this what you do when you have the house to yourself? Kennedy Reed fingers you?"

I shuddered at the sound of him saying "fingers." Gross.

"Liam—"

"I told you I liked her. I went to you for advice on how to go on a date with her for this exact day, and you go behind my back and fuck her instead!"

"Liam—"

"No wonder she rejected me. You wanted her to reject me. You probably told her to reject me just so you guys could hook up."

"That's not what happened at all—"

"That's so fucked up. I trusted you!"

"If you give me a second to speak—"

"She can't be gay. She dated Ian and Dominic. She just kissed..." He paused. "She's kissed lots of boys."

"That really doesn't mean anything. I've even kissed a boy."

"I didn't even know she was gay."

"She's not gay. Well, I don't really know. She's still figuring it out."

"It's a good thing you're allowing her to experiment on you. How generous."

"Okay, stop with the biphobic comments. She can like girls and boys. Stop being a dick."

"Oh, I'm a dick? You're hooking up with the girl I like!"

I rolled my eyes. "Okay, so she's my girlfriend. And she's been my girlfriend since right before New Year's, long before I knew you liked her."

"Since New Year's? Oh my God! It doesn't even make sense!"

"It does, though. She's liked me since, like, fifth grade."

"Fifth grade!"

"The reason why she's ignored me all these years is because she kissed me the night before she moved to the city. When we were thirteen."

"So, like, this whole time the three of us were walking to eighth period, you two were a thing?" I nodded. "Oh my God!"

"I'm sorry you're finding out this way, but I really, really like her, and I don't want something like this to fuck everything up. I know you're upset, but she's still figuring herself out. Don't go around telling anyone. If you care about her like you say you do, you won't tell a soul about what you just saw. It has to be on her terms."

He could barely look me in the eye, and that was when I finally got a sense of how much he liked her. Liam had crushes all the time. He dated girls and then got bored with them a few months later. I thought Kennedy was just next in line for him to crush on before he discovered the next girl. He went through crushes faster than he went through favorite rap songs, and I wanted him to understand that that wasn't me at all. I lusted hard after Lana and Meghan, I really liked Riley at one point, but my feelings for Kennedy were on a whole other level. I was absolutely crazy about her.

She made me want senior year to slow down, but she sped it up more than I ever wanted to. I'd dreamed of California ever since I was a freshman. I already had a playlist of every single California song created over the last hundred years to ease my excitement for the big move in August. But now that Kennedy was in my life, I wondered if I'd made a mistake. Maybe I needed to apply to colleges near Syracuse where she'd just got accepted to. I'd spent most of my high school career just wanting it to end, wanting to leave the shallowness that was my school behind and live in a place more open and freer...like California.

And then in the near end of my adolescent struggle, through the shifting tides of discovering who I was, through the haze of my self-doubt and insecurities, through the wavering ground of successes and mistakes of growing up, there she was, the only thing calming my world down.

"You hated her just a couple months ago," Liam said.

"Yeah, well, I don't anymore. I really like her. She makes me want to stay in New York for college—"

"You gotta be fucking kidding me."

"What?"

"You've been with her for three months, and you want to abandon your dream school for her? That's stupid. That's really fucking stupid."

"You want a silly little crush to ruin our relationship even more? Because that's what you're doing—"

"A three-month relationship shouldn't change who you want to be. You've dreamed about Berkeley since freshman year, and now you want to what? Go to Syracuse to be with her?"

"A little crush shouldn't change how you treat my relationship with her. Your popularity shouldn't change how you treat me around your friends like I'm so beneath you. Like, you can't even tell Tom or Cassandra to fuck off when they harass me about the Olympics. The Camry shouldn't change our relationship. But all of those things did change, didn't they? Don't start lecturing me on what things are worth changing. You're the king of letting little things in life change who you are."

"Cool. Get out of my room now."

He turned back around and opened his computer up. His computer resumed its rap music angst, and I knew nothing I said or did would make him listen to me. So I went back downstairs to check on Kennedy. She was clothed, curled up in a ball on the couch, cocooned in the blankets, her eyes still red and swollen, and her body quivering in between breaths.

"Hey," I said and tucked a tendril of hair behind her ear. My heart sank just feeling how terrified and embarrassed she was. "I talked to him. Asked him not to tell anyone. He still has a lot to process, but I think once he does, he'll be okay with it. I hope.

He does like you, after all, so maybe he'll never be okay with it. Who knows?"

"I'm so embarrassed."

"I think we all are. But it's going to be fine," I said. "I promise, everything's going to be fine."

"You don't understand, Quinn. He's my friend. All my friends are friends with him. I hang out with him all the time. Now every time he sees me, it's going to be so awkward. Our friends are going to pick up on that."

"Have you given any thought about telling someone? Your brother? Your parents?"

"All the time." She finally sat up, wiping her eyes with her hands. I joined her on the couch and grabbed a hold of her trembling hands. "You know, maybe this is a sign. Maybe I need to stop hiding—stop hiding you. How have you been okay with me hiding you when you're out?"

"Well, I mean, it's been kind of hard, but it needs to be on your pace, and I like you and care about you, so it's something I'm willing to compromise. For now, at least. I understand it's hard, and it takes time, and no one can rush you…or should rush you."

Kennedy and I were so brand new, I was trying to get over the fact she was my girlfriend. If a couple months had passed and my feelings just continued to grow, I would want her to start coming out to a few people, but I knew what it was like coming out. It was scary. You didn't want to lose friends or have your family disown you—not as if I thought any of that would happen to her, but it was a fear you couldn't shake. People surprised you in good ways and bad.

I kissed the back of her hand. "You come out when you feel like the timing is right. Or come out slowly, one person at a time. Just know that whenever you decide to tell anyone, you won't have to do it alone. I'll be here for you. Every step of the way."

She grabbed on to my hand tighter and rested her cheek on my shoulder. "I know you will."

❖

The Valentine's Day Encounter™ strained our walk to Civics. On Monday, Liam walked ahead of us, causing Kennedy and me not to say much either. On Tuesday, he made up a pathetic excuse that he had to go to the bathroom. On Wednesday and Thursday, I found him already in the Civics classroom, probably taking the roundabout way to Mrs. Daughtry's class.

His processing was a lot more intense than I thought it was going to be.

"You need to talk to him," Kennedy said to me outside our classroom on Thursday. "Clearly, he's not okay with it. He used to talk to me all the time, and now he can't even sit by me at lunch. Not a word. Not one text."

"He's pissed because I'm dating you and he's not. He'll come around."

"He's my friend, Quinn. I don't want him mad at me."

"If he's mad at anyone, it's me. Not you. Trust me. You're too pretty to be mad at," I teased and butt bumped her.

"Quinn, this isn't funny. I'm being serious—"

"What's going on here?" Cassandra said in her usual snippy tone, popping out of nowhere. Probably from the pits of hell.

Kennedy's face turned beet red, as surprised by her friend's sudden and random appearance as me. "I, uh, nothing. Just needed to, uh, ask Quinn about the calc homework."

Really? Calc homework? My girlfriend couldn't have come up with a better lie than that? Like, say, I don't know, I was just talking to Quinn because she's a decent human being, and we have things to talk about now?

"So, um, why are you over here?" Kennedy asked.

"I need to stop at my locker. I have a physical in a half hour." She looked at me as if I was vermin. "Glad I was over here, though. I guess I missed the memo that we're now asking Quinn about calc homework."

I waited for Kennedy to pipe up and say something. *Shut up, Cassie. That was uncalled for, Cassie. Stop looking at her like she's actual filth scrubbed off the floor, Cassie. Take the stick out of your tight asshole, Cassie.* Something along those lines. Some kind of sentence that not only defended her girlfriend but defended a human being from her bully of a best friend. But she didn't utter a single word. She just looked at the ground, letting her friend treat me like the Aspen Grove pariah she truly believed I was.

I felt like such an idiot, especially when Cassandra scanned me from head to toe, looking for imperfections to use against me to make me feel smaller than I already did. Kennedy allowed it by standing there doing absolutely nothing. And if she couldn't find anything, I expected a gay or an Olympic joke.

Before Cassandra could belittle me again, and since Kennedy had no plans to say anything to prevent whatever thought brewed inside her best friend's mind, I took matters into my own hands.

"Might wanna ask me more about calc since I have an A minus in the class and you got a sixteen on your ACTs," I said.

Her smirk immediately washed away, and her infamous snarl seeped through.

"Quinn!" Kennedy said, her tone telling me that I was the inappropriate one.

She can speak! What a miracle! Bless the heavens and gods above us!

"Might wanna try a little harder in swimming," Cassandra said. "Because you're never gonna get that Olympic medal."

"Yeah, I'm sorry, but I can't take anything you say seriously when you can't even get into college."

"Are you fucking serious right now?"

I beamed at how my words really contoured Cassandra's resting bitch face. She was finally getting a taste of her own medicine, and I loved that I was giving it to her on a silver platter.

"Fine," I said. "Nice talking to you guys, as always."

"Quinn," Kennedy said, and this time, I could tell she wanted to redeem herself.

"Who cares about her? We're not even friends with her."

Again, my girlfriend said nothing back.

It was a nice reminder of how much our worlds were different, how much I was blinded by high school lust and love. How could we share one world outside school and share the most intimate parts of our lives and souls with each other, then at school, act like nothing more than mere acquaintances at best? Just two people who only talked about calc homework.

❖

Her text read, *Hey you still up?*

It was ten thirty, and yes, I was still up, lying in my bed in the darkness with my headphones playing my angry playlist, currently filling my ears with "The Kill" by Thirty Seconds to Mars, maybe a little too loudly. It didn't help I was PMSing either. It was the perfect kind of music for my mood.

But no, I didn't text her back. I hated how I reacted to that whole situation, but I couldn't text Kennedy. I knew that if I did, it would just be mean, and I didn't want to be mean to her because I knew I would instantly regret it. I didn't have a problem with keeping our relationship a secret. I had a problem because she couldn't even defend me to her friends or admit to them that she spoke to me on a platonic level. Talking to me didn't mean she was a lesbian. If she couldn't admit to her friends that we occasionally talked because the two of us would walk with Liam to eighth period, then there was still something about me that she was humiliated by. Was it because I wasn't popular? Was it because I was an out lesbian, and she secretly thought talking to an out lesbian meant that would label her as one too? Because it was contagious?

I ignored her text because a part of me blamed her for still hiding so deep in her closet that she couldn't defend me in public. In the darkness that I allowed to swallow me, I found the grudge I carried on my back for four years.

Even when she took a seat in front of me in calc the next day, her text message was still left unanswered. So she sent me another one, and my phone vibrated in my book bag.

She texted, *Quinn?*

I looked at my phone before the bell rang to start the class, but I didn't even swipe the message open. Instead, I put it back in my bag, knowing she could hear the whole thing. Right after I put my phone in my bag, it vibrated again, but I didn't check it until I sat at my lunch table.

Followed by, *Are you ignoring me?*

Didn't respond. I didn't know what to tell her, but I sensed it was a good idea to avoid any conversation with her until my anger simmered down just enough to not push her away even more.

I hoped that the weekend would help. To try to forget about it for a few hours, I went to Madison's swim team party after our last dual meet. I didn't check my phone at all and realized how much I really had missed out on with my swim team because I was chasing after Kennedy. It was a great distraction, even if Riley's presence was slightly awkward and discomforting given our last exchange together.

But as much fun as I had bonding with my teammates— playing Madison's homemade Guess Who game with pictures of every boy on the team and breaking up into groups to TP the boys' houses one last time before the season ended—when I came back home, I remembered that I couldn't just text my girlfriend about the wonderful night I'd just had.

Well, I could text her and be mature, I thought. *Or my silence can make a stronger statement. Let's go with that.*

Have you ever been so angry at someone but desperately wanted to talk to them at the same time? That was how I felt that night. I tried so hard to swallow the anger. Ignoring her for a whole day was enough—and pathetic and immature, yet I couldn't muster up the words to say something. And then, when I knew for sure I wasn't able to text her that night either, I created our first ever fight. I was scared and angry at myself that I couldn't just confront her about it in a reasonable way.

The whole weekend passed without a text from her. I think she got the hint.

On Monday, she came into calc, and her presence wasn't stealthy. I didn't need to be eyeing the door in order to know when she came in. A wind of apples and flowers wafted over me as she took a seat, and she threw her hand on top of my calc book. I flinched and as a reflex, glanced up at her. Those beautiful eyes had morphed into fern-colored daggers.

"Why are you ignoring me?" she whispered loudly.

I looked around the classroom to see if anyone noticed Kennedy Reed talking to Quinn Hughes—more specifically, Cassandra. But people were either still on their way in, doing their homework, chatting, or on their phones. For just a small moment, our hidden bubble floated into forbidden territory: school.

"Are you talking to me because Cassandra isn't here yet?"

"What the hell are you talking about?"

"You can't stand up to your friend when she's being a bitch to me? Am I really that embarrassing a human that you can't do that?"

Jennifer and Cassandra walked in, their eyes on Kennedy with her hand planted on my calc book and her head leaned in toward mine. Cassandra's eyebrows scrunched. Jennifer acted as if she didn't see it, nor did she care, and when the three friends exchanged awkward glances, Kennedy moved her arm and faced the front.

The bell rang. Mr. Carmichael walked in and closed the door.

"My point exactly," I whispered to her.

At lunch…

Meet me in our spot after the last bell. Please! her text said. *K.*

After the last bell, I opened the door to the PAC. Kennedy stood in the corner in the usual darkness. The door closed behind me, and once it sealed shut and our world was locked and hidden, she unleashed everything.

"What the fuck did I do, Quinn?" she said pretty loudly. If anyone was trying to make out in the PAC, they would have definitely heard her. "Why are you ignoring me like a child?"

"Like a child? You think I'm being a child? How about you stand up to your friend when she's being a bitch to your girlfriend."

"I'm sorry, Quinn—"

"Are you, though? I mean, you told me to knock it off when I made my comment to her, but you couldn't say anything to her?"

"Your comments were blatantly mean—"

"And hers weren't?"

"She's very self-conscious about her ACT score and getting into college."

"Oh, I'm sorry. Forget the fact she rubs the Olympic trials in my face. But you're right, I should be more considerate about her insecurities about her ACT score."

"I didn't mean that."

"I don't understand how I'm so embarrassing that you can't even tell Cassandra to shut up or say that we talk or are friends."

"What? Quinn, I'm not embarrassed by you."

"Then why didn't you tell Cassandra to fuck off? It's really not that hard to stand up for me. Saying that we're friends doesn't make you look like a fucking lesbian. You even shove a fake platonic friendship in the closet with you."

"Shove in the closet? Quinn, if you just texted me back, I would have told you that I told Jennifer about us." My eyes brimmed with tears. My heart thumped. "Yeah, we had dinner on Friday, and she asked why Liam was being weird, so I told her everything. I told her our whole entire story, and she didn't care. If I was ashamed of you, I wouldn't have done that—I wouldn't have come out to Jennifer. If you weren't ignoring me, you would have known all of this."

"You…you told Jennifer?"

"Yes! Because I like you," she said, moving her hand on my cheek, wiping away the tears staining my face. My head tilted into her warm palm. "I care about you so much. This, what we have, is amazing. It makes me feel amazing and free and everything I've ever wanted to feel."

"Then act like it! You letting Cassandra treat me like that really doesn't convince me that you feel happy and free with me. More like embarrassed."

"I'm not embarrassed by you. I'm sorry. What she did wasn't right, and it's my fault for not saying anything. I'm really sorry that I didn't, okay? This isn't easy for me, and I'm going to make a lot of mistakes. But I'm trying. I'm really fucking trying. I've liked you since I was eleven." I smiled as my little cries stuttered in my throat. Her thumbs wiped a new round of tears from my cheek. "You mean everything to me. I mean that. It's just that I'm so far into this whole facade that I don't know how to get out, so I keep going along with it because that's all I know how to do. But I'm done playing along with it. I promise. Please believe me."

"I believe you."

I did; I truly did.

She kissed the scar on my chin before pressing her forehead against mine. "I know I haven't been a good girlfriend, but that stops today, okay?"

"Okay."

"Can you kiss me now?"

God, yes.

❖

I couldn't believe how late I was to practice. Forty minutes late. Because I was arguing and then making out with a girl. It was probably the flakiest moment of my seventeen years of existing, and I was already so embarrassed by it. States was in two weeks. We were tapering. For non-swimmers, that means it was the worst time of the swim season to be forty minutes late. Especially since I was a co-captain. Also, being the best swimmer on the team and going to the world championships was a blessing and curse. Leanne held me to a higher standard than Madison or the other upperclassmen because my swimming abilities forced me into a leadership position. Because of all of this, Leanne was going to rip me a new one, I just knew it.

By the time I ran onto the pool deck, the team was already finished warming up and starting their first real set. Leanne was in the middle of explaining the set when she saw me walking as fast as I could for Hot Lifeguard not to yell at me. And she was there on the lifeguard stand, her eyes following me sprint-walking down the pool deck, still looking so hot. Leanne had never looked at me with such disappointment before. After shooting daggers at me, she turned back to the team in the pool and finished explaining the set. My face immediately started to burn, and I rushed to the locker room to get changed.

As I walked over to lane one—my practice lane—I tilted my head downward, shoving my messy bun into my green swim cap and wrapping my goggles around my head. I didn't want to look Leanne in the eye because I knew I was in so much trouble. All I wanted to do was sweep by her, hop in my lane, and disappear into the water.

But that didn't happen.

"Quinn," she said sternly. "Let's talk over here."

No, not in front of Hot Lifeguard.

I hated getting in trouble so much. I hated letting people down. How could I have let myself be so reckless?

She positioned herself in her spot on the pool deck, yards away from Hot Lifeguard's stand, and took a deep breath. "Quinn, we need to talk." I didn't say anything. My brain had no response because I knew there was no excuse for coming in forty minutes late to practice when we were two weeks from states. So I just stared at her blankly, waiting for her to continue with her lecture. When she got the hint that I had nothing to say after that, she said, "You're forty minutes late to practice. *Forty.* You missed warm-ups and the first set. States is in two weeks. We're tapering. This is it for the swim season."

I thought I'd only missed warm-ups. Knowing I missed the first set made me realize how much trouble I was about to be in.

"This isn't acceptable. Not from other teammates and especially not from the captain and someone who's going to the world championships. You set an example for the underclassmen that you might not realize. They like you. You're a good leader. You're a good person. And seeing the captain and someone so accomplished come late makes them think they can get away with it too. You know the other people going to world champs are working their asses off right now. They're not blowing off practice."

"I…I wasn't trying to blow off practice!"

"Then why were you late?"

I paused. Why was I late? I couldn't tell her the truth. She wouldn't accept the complications of secret high school relationships. "I…I lost track of time."

"Doing what? How do you lose track of time by that much?"

"I, um, I was in an argument with a friend, and we were talking about it, and it took longer than I expected. I'm really sorry. It was really careless."

"That's something that can be dealt with after practice."

"I know. I realize that. I just lost track of time. I'm sorry."

"You know my rule for unexcused absences."

"I do."

I felt like a dog with her tail between her legs.

"You know that also applies to you?"

More tears flooded my eyes. "I do."

I'd only seen it happen to the same offenders, the ones who weren't as fast who didn't really care as much as the top swimmers on the team. Leanne made them do five minutes of wall sits, and for the record, one minute was pretty brutal. I'd only seen Gia do it once two years ago. It was kind of a rarity because Leanne did a good job scaring the shit out of us. We knew better than to show up late for warm-ups.

Apparently, I forgot.

"Ten minutes. Go on."

"Ten?"

"Five isn't a challenge for you. Ten. Do it or walk out the door."

Legs at a ninety-degree angle, back straight, head and palms flat against the wall. By the fifth minute, my legs started to shake. My team had each taken a glance over at me to check in with me, and they didn't need to take their goggles off for me to notice their shocked eyes. The few times I opened my eyes, Hot Lifeguard watched me, and when our eyes met, she quickly looked away.

I couldn't tell you what was harder: wall sits for ten straight minutes at a perfect ninety-degree angle or holding back the cries lodged in my throat.

Once I jumped in and began to swim, I cried and let my goggles collect the tears. It's what the swimming world calls croggling. Nobody can see through the slick, shiny reflection of the goggles. I was safe behind them, and I just cried as I swam through the monotonous motions of the practice sets.

In the locker room afterward, no one spoke to me. I couldn't tell at first if it was because I gave everyone the clear indication that I was not okay or because everyone was mad at me. Either way, I got changed in silence and bolted out of the locker room so I could cry in my car.

As I headed across the pool deck, I pulled out my phone to send Kennedy a quick text.

Got in trouble for being late today at practice. Like really badly. Had to do wall sits for 10 min in front of my whole team which was embarrassing AF and I can't stop crying about it. So, I don't think we should be meeting up at the PAC anymore. I need to focus on states and training because apparently, I'm doing a really good job fucking it all up.

I took my anger out on the front doors to the pool, and they slammed back.

"Quinn!"

When I turned, I saw Riley jogging over to me. She was seriously the last person I wanted to deal with. Since the February air was so cold, and my hair was wet and frozen, the last thing I needed after getting in trouble was to get sick right before states. So I continued to my car so the heat could save myself from any sickness.

"What, you're not even gonna talk to me?" she said.

"It's cold. If you wanna talk to me, then let's do it in my car."

When we both got in, I blasted the heat and directed the vents to my face. After I plugged my phone into my car charger, I reached my hands in front of the heaters to warm them up—and also to stall.

"What's going on?" Riley said. "You haven't been you for the last few months."

"Nothing's wrong except I pissed off Leanne."

"Why were you late to practice? We were supposed to enjoy our senior year all together, and you've only hung out with us twice. Why are you avoiding us?"

"I'm avoiding *you* specifically, but I'm not avoiding the team. I'm not trying to, at least."

"Then what's going on?"

Adrenaline rushed through me because I knew what I was going to do. When I turned to Riley and I saw her concerned look, I knew I couldn't stop the words from coming out of my mouth. I had to tell someone on the team so they knew I still cared greatly about the team and states and medaling at the world champs, even though my recent actions said otherwise. If I was going to tell anyone on the team about Kennedy, it was going to be Riley. Sure, she was my ex-girlfriend, and we hadn't been exactly close for the past few months, but despite our history, she knew what it was like to keep a relationship hidden. She would understand.

"You're right," I said. "This whole time, you were right. I'm dating someone. And I really, really like her. And I've let myself get distracted, and it's my fault. It's all my fault."

"Who is she?" Riley asked, and no matter how she tried to keep her face from revealing her hurt, her voice said it all.

"She's not out."

Her frown intensified. "Does she go to Aspen Grove?" I nodded. "And she's not out?" I shook my head. All the out kids we knew at our school were in our circle of friends, so to hear that someone who wasn't in our clan was one of us was like hearing there had been gold loot hidden somewhere in the school this whole time that we'd never known about "Is she a senior?" I nodded. "Do I know her?" I nodded again. "Well, damn, who the hell is she?"

"I've been with her," I said. "When I come to practice late, it's because I'm with her. The only time I get to talk to her privately in school is when we have ten minutes after the last bell. That's when we sneak off and well, make out."

She let out a laugh but not in a way as if she was amused. "A secret spot? Like the gym locker room?"

"No, not the gym locker room."

"The swim team shower? Man, any girl you make out with at school shouldn't feel too special. Apparently, it's your move."

"Fuck off, Riley."

A moment passed for us to get over the zinger.

Riley sighed. "I'm sorry. Continue."

"You done with your crap? Because I'm really not in the mood for it."

"I'm done. Please continue."

Of course she wanted me to continue. She was finally getting the answer to who I was dating.

"Today, well, this girl and I talked about this argument we've been having, and it took longer than I thought. I lost track of time. And I feel awful about it. I really do."

Riley continued to collect all the words I said. After a few moments, she said, "How long has this been going on?"

"Since November."

"November! Wow. Well…that explains everything."

"I'm sorry I'm telling you this. You asked and—"

"No, Quinn. It's fine, I think. I mean, you've been so distant; any hope of us getting back together I had from homecoming is long gone. I just wanted to make sure that everything was okay with you, so as much as it kinda makes me jealous, I'm just glad it's not anything worse."

"I'm fine. I'm just…well…"

"In love?"

I wanted to smile. It felt so nice for someone other than me or Kennedy to acknowledge that I was crazy about her. Love was a strong word and a strong feeling. I wasn't sure if I truly was in love with her, but however I felt, it was the strongest feeling I'd ever had about someone. Maybe I did love her to an extent, the full extent of seventeen-year-old love. But I'd known her almost my whole life. For four years, our kiss had floated in my memory and ignited my whole self-journey in discovering my sexuality. We hadn't just dated for four months. We'd known each other since we were seven. And I loved her. Not just as a person but her entire being, and I wanted the whole world to know.

"Yeah," I said and stared out of the windshield at the small snowflakes collecting on the hood. "Maybe you can call it that."

"Does anyone know?"

"Her best friend and Liam."

Her eyes grew. "Liam?"

"Yeah, he kind of caught us."

"Caught you? Doing what?" Then she got it. "Oh…you…you guys have already done that?" I nodded, and she sank her in seat, directing her gaze on the accumulating snowflakes too. She had to know that time was going to come. We weren't going to be each other's only ones forever.

Then my phone vibrated. Both Riley and I glanced down at the phone, seeing the exact same thing light up my phone screen.

Her text read, *As in we can't see each other until AFTER states?*

I didn't feel like a whole person when I saw Riley's reaction. Her mouth hung open. Her eyes were the widest I'd ever seen them. And so much of me wanted to go back in time and shove my phone in my bag so the secret could stay there. So I could shove myself back in Kennedy's closet, for her sake. For our sake. God, her closet made me feel almost too at home.

The secret was out.

"Kennedy Reed? You're in love with Kennedy Reed?"

CHAPTER TEN

R iley!" I said way too defensively. "You can't tell anyone. She's not out—"

"I didn't even know she liked girls! I didn't even know you guys talked."

"Well, we do. We used to be best friends before she moved."

The windows started to fog up. I put on the defroster, and Riley continued to act as if the world was ending. It was then that I got a sense of how upset she was that I was seeing someone else. That I'd slept with someone else. That I was probably in love with someone else.

She rubbed her face in disbelief, shaking her head and running her hands down her face.

"God, I'm so dumb. So, so dumb."

"What? Why are you dumb?"

"For ever thinking I could get you back."

When I heard her sniff, my stomach muscles tightened. The only other time I made her cry was when we broke up, and even that was painful to watch.

"I'm sorry," I said.

"I'm sorry too," she said. "That Kennedy needs to hide you. That the only place you two can be open and free is some secret spot at school. If she realized how lucky she is to have you, she wouldn't be hiding you."

"Lucky to have me? Riley, you just told me you were too good for me at New Year's. Fucking make up your mind about me already."

"Okay, Quinn." She gathered up her bag. "If you're truly happy with her, then I'm glad." She opened the door, and a gust of chilly air flew into the car as she got out. "Just know that I would never hide you. Not for a second."

She slammed the door shut.

From the rearview mirror, I watched her get into her car directly behind me. The back lights turned on, and gas puffed out of the exhaust. I couldn't leave the parking lot after that conversation—after all the conversations I had in one day that made me feel like the lowest of the low. And from watching Riley's car sit there behind me, I sensed she felt the exact same way.

❖

In the days following, Riley couldn't talk to me or look me in the eye. It was especially awkward since we were on the same relay team getting ready to compete at states. I upheld my promise and made it to all my practices right on time. I explained to Kennedy about Leanne's confrontation and how I really needed to focus on swimming for the next two weeks. She seemed to understand and even encouraged my focus.

But I avoided telling her that Riley found out about us. That was something I couldn't deal with. Not on top of Riley and Liam ignoring me and my proving to Leanne that I still really cared about swimming. I thought I was already living and breathing swimming, but apparently, I'd done a good job allowing myself to get distracted by Kennedy, Liam, Cassandra, and Riley. For two weeks, I was going to forget it all and do whatever I needed to do to kick ass at states.

It wasn't until Wednesday the following week—the day

before we left for states—that Madison and Gia finally sensed the thick tension that hung between Riley and me.

"So, I know Leanne just lectured us about how she wants lights out at ten at the hotel both nights but...I think we should sneak into Alex and Steven's room anyways," Madison said as all four of us changed out of our suits. She had a huge crush on Alex and was determined that our two-night stay at the Holiday Inn near Ithaca College was going to be her first kiss with him. Real sexy times.

"Yes, I second this!" said Gia, who conveniently had a crush on Steven. Steven was definitely less interested in her than Alex was in Madison, but I don't think he complained too much about getting female attention. "Give these two lovebirds some quality time." Gia waggled her eyebrows up and down at Riley and me.

We both shot them a look, like God-please-don't-do-that-to-us look. Riley had moved to the opposite corner just so she didn't have to change right next to me. I think the fact that we couldn't be on the same side of the locker room spoke volumes.

"Whoa, I thought you two wouldn't mind," Madison said.

"Why does everyone assume we want to get back together?" Riley said. "Just because we get along—sometimes—doesn't mean we want alone time. It doesn't mean we want to share a bed either. We're broken up for a really good reason."

"Wow, Riley, tell us how you really feel," I said.

"Someone should," she said. "I wouldn't wanna lead you on or anything."

Madison and Gia alternated glances back and forth to us. I just rolled my eyes and buttoned my jeans.

"I feel like that was an undertone," Madison said, "and that Gia and I should really let you guys hash this out."

"Please don't," I said.

"Can I just say that whatever it is needs to be resolved by Friday at nine a.m.?" Madison said. "Because that's our prelim for the relay, and I really don't wanna miss out on finals because of whatever you two are bickering about."

"I think someone is leading someone on," Gia said to Madison.

Then both of them looked at me.

"Why are we assuming it's me?" I said.

"Because you're a tease," Gia said.

"And assertive," Madison said.

"And Riley was madly in love with you."

"Um, actually I wasn't," Riley said sharply and slung her duffle bag over her clothed body. "You guys keep acting like I kissed every inch of the ground Quinn's ever walked on."

"Because you kind of did," Gia said.

She really did, hence the whole breaking up with her because she was too much. At least Gia could admit it, even though I felt as if she took Riley's side of the breakup. Everyone did, actually. The only person out of all of our mutual friends who was Team Quinn was me.

"No, I didn't," Riley said defensively. "And stop thinking that. It's insulting."

Gia threw her hands in the air to surrender.

If I was going to call Riley out on her bullshit, I sure as hell wasn't going to do it in my bra and jeans. She would probably like that too much. So, I threw my crewneck sweatshirt on, and once my head popped out of the hole, I decided to fully engage in the conversation.

"What have I done in the last few months that has led Riley on? Huh? Anything? Weren't you just accusing me of not hanging out with you? How could I have led you on if I wasn't hanging out with you?"

Madison and Gia looked at Riley, who was halfway out of the locker room. She turned around to give me a hurt and defeated look. "Fuck you, Quinn."

"It's a legit question!" I said. "If this is going to be turned around on me, then tell me what I did to lead you on so I can stop it. I'm tired of always being the bad guy in this relationship."

"Well, honestly, you're not doing a good job right now being the good guy," Gia said. Just when I thought she was on my side, she jumped right back to Riley's.

"We never talked about getting back together. We haven't kissed since homecoming. So, why am I the bad guy because I've moved on? That's not my fault."

"You know what, Quinn," Riley said, "please don't come to me when your heart gets broken, and it will get broken, by the sound of it. I really don't give two shits if it does, so have fun in your closet."

She walked out. Riley was one of the sweetest girls I'd ever met, but man, when you were on her bad side, her words could cut diamonds. I think I was the only one on her shit list, so she had all the time and energy to really sharpen the blades on her words. Maybe I deserved it, but she had no right to be mad at me for having a girlfriend. That wasn't fair at all.

"Fix it," Madison said to me. "I really don't wanna miss out on a chance to do awesome at states because of whatever has gotten up both of your asses. If we suck or don't even make it to the final heat, I'm blaming you two."

The tension between me and Riley didn't have any impact on our relay. I purposely tuned her out, and Madison insisted she and I share a bed in the hotel room so they could keep us separated.

If anything, ignoring Riley enhanced my performance. Our relay took first overall. And that wasn't even the best part. Not only did I make the finals in my 200 and 500-yard freestyle, but I beat my state record in the 500-free by half a second in the prelims, I beat my school record in the 200 by a second in the finals, and then I beat my newest 500-free record in the finals by two seconds. I beat three school records in less than a day and even got a new state record in the 500.

Oh, and I won every single one of my events. So that was icing on the cake.

My times surpassed my goal times for the end of the season. I was so proud of myself, especially given my pretty crappy past couple of weeks. I'd triumphed—much to my surprise. I proved to myself that I could still come back after veering a little off track from my strict schedule. *World champs, I'm ready for you, and I'm ready for a medal.*

After my races, I talked to a few reporters from all over the state, even a reporter from *Swimming World*, the *Sports Illustrated* of swimming. What I just did at states put me on cloud nine. I felt invincible. I felt as if I could achieve anything. I didn't even care if Riley was the only one who didn't congratulate me on my accomplishments. Nothing could bring me down.

When I came home from Ithaca College, the happiness inside almost blew out of me when I spotted Kennedy's red Jetta parked in our driveway. Liam's bedroom was lit up behind the closed curtains. I had no idea why she was over at my house with him— who had given her the silent treatment ever since the Valentine's Day Encounter™—but she'd texted me two hours before, asking what time I was going to be home, so I just assumed she wanted to see me.

Murmurs from his room carried down the hallway as I crept up the stairs, hoping the reason why Kennedy was over was so she and Liam could mend their broken friendship. Liam's door was open, and when I popped my head in, I found Kennedy in his computer chair and Liam tossing a stress ball up and down while lying on his bed. Kennedy's face lit up. Her smile was so contagious.

"Oh hey, swimming prodigy," she said.

"What are you doing here?"

"I have my reasons. One of them is in your room; the other is right here." She pointed to Liam. He saluted.

"Is he done being an ass?"

"For the most part," she said. "We had a very much-needed chat. Right, Liam?"

"Yeah. She practically dragged it out of me." He tossed the ball to her. I wanted to spit up just a little bit because I knew that was his way of flirting, but like the top-notch goalkeeper she was, she snatched the ball in her right palm before it could hit her face, and she chucked it at his knee.

"Now, go to your room," she told me.

"Am I being disciplined?"

Liam coughed a gagging noise. Kennedy just giggled and smacked his foot.

"More like being rewarded." She batted her eyebrows.

Just to make Liam uncomfortable for my own entertainment, I continued, "It's not much of a reward if you're not in there."

Liam chucked the stress ball at me. It hit my knee. "Oh my God, just go to your room, or I'm gonna call Mom and Dad and ruin their bar night because you brought a girl over."

I knew his threat was a joke. I could sense fake anger in his voice.

So, I followed what I was told to do. When I flipped the lights on to my room, I found a bouquet of flowers in a glass vase—white lilies, baby pink roses, and lavender statice. Next to the vase was a Swensons to-go bag and large milkshake cup, scenting my room with a fried chicken sandwich and a large French fry, the very order I'd been craving since the night we talked at Swensons.

She really knew the way to my heart.

"Kennedy Renee Reed!" I shouted for her to come in my room as I buried my hand in the to-go bag, shoving a handful of French fries in my mouth. I think after breaking three school records in a weekend and pretty much signing myself to the finals in the world champs, shoving a large handful of fatty, salted fries in my mouth was the perfect award.

"Yes?"

Still chomping on the fries, I went over to her standing in my doorway and squeezed her. She was my other award. The million-dollar check to the golden trophy.

"Flowers and Swensons? This is so romantic," I said and kissed her cheek.

"Well, you deserve all of it. Fat indulgences to celebrate swimming being over and all your records. And flowers because I thought they were pretty, and you're kinda pretty, and I'm so proud of you."

I swallowed the fries and yanked on her shirt to pull her in for an actual kiss. "Thank you," I said. "Really. You didn't have to do this."

"I know, but I wanted to. Plus, it's pretty hot that you broke your state record."

"Oh yeah? Can you show me?"

She bit her lip, so I pushed her onto my bed, climbed on top of her, and kissed her. I snuck my hands up her shirt, feeling how my touch ignited the goose bumps on her skin. I loved so much knowing that I had the power to do that. She grabbed hold of the back of my hair, and when I nibbled on her bottom lip, she let out a soft moan, and I felt her mouth forming a grin.

"Oh my God, I'm dialing Mom's number right now," Liam shouted from the hallway as he headed downstairs, a slight teasing tone ringing in his voice.

"But I can't help it," I said softly to Kennedy. "Your lips are like crack."

She wiggled her neatly shaped eyebrows up and down, and we repositioned ourselves so we could sit incredibly close to each other while sharing Swensons.

"You know what we really need to do?" she said as she stole some fries from the bag.

"Make out?"

She smiled. "I would like to resume that, yes, but I was thinking more of, like, a date."

"A date?" My eyes widened. "Out in public?"

I felt as if I could explode in happiness. Was Kennedy finally ready to flaunt our love in public? Telling Jennifer had to be a sign. Reconciling with Liam had to be another. Of course I wanted to go on a date with her.

"No, sheltered in your room. Of course out in public. I wanna date you."

"What about people finding out?"

"Well, I figured maybe we can go somewhere outside Aspen Grove. That might be a good step for me, I think. I already told my best friend; Liam seems to be okay with it now, and I really just wanna spend time with you that's not trapped in my room. Going out in a neutral zone is just another step to being more honest and open about someone who I'm super crazy about."

My cheeks warmed up. "You're super crazy about me?"

"Is it really not obvious? I spent my lemonade money on you!"

I washed my mouth with a large gulp of the chocolate malt and pulled her cheek to my lips. "It's obvious. I'm pretty crazy about you too. And this date idea? The most genius idea you've ever come up with!"

"I know! Why can't that be considered my final exam?"

"I would love to date you. I think I know the perfect spot."

"Really? Let's do it next Saturday!"

"Okay, but I'm keeping it a surprise."

"I'll dress nicely. Be prepared for any scenario."

I gave her a soft kiss on the lips. "You always look nice, even when you're not trying."

What she didn't know was that she only needed to say, "I wanna date you," and within thirty seconds, I already constructed the perfect date night to sweep her off her feet, and I couldn't wait.

CHAPTER ELEVEN

It was official. I got a full ride to Berkeley. A full ride. To my dream school. In California. I cried when I signed my national letter of intent. So did my mom. There was a lot of happy crying in the Hugheses' household that week.

My family took me out to celebrate at my favorite fondue restaurant, which just happened to be the place I was going to take Kennedy on our date on Saturday. I even made reservations before my parents paid the bill to make sure we got the table right by the mini waterfall—because if I wasn't old enough to order the best wine the restaurant had to offer, I was going to make sure I could make up for it with a white tablecloth restaurant and a freaking waterfall next to our booth.

Liam even surprised me by ordering a California state flag for my dorm room and joked how I can be a basic non-California girl. The gesture was so sweet, given the last few months. But it was nice to see the good parts of my brother finally appear again.

Even though I had a lot to be excited about, nothing compared to my plans for the weekend. I decided to throw a party. I told my parents that I wanted to have people over for a little party, and I hardly ever attended/hosted parties; I think they were beyond thrilled that I was going to be a normal teenager for once. Because they trusted me (way more than Liam), they decided to give me the house while they went out with their friends for a much-needed adult dinner date.

And then the next day, I would sweep Kennedy off her feet with *our* date.

It was going to be an awesome weekend.

I invited the usual people to the party on Friday: Madison, Gia, Meghan, Lana, Tanner, Erick, and even Riley, though I didn't really expect her to show up. I even invited Gabriel since it had been a while since I hung out with him. He greeted me with the biggest hug when he walked through the front door, spinning me around a few times before putting me back down.

"You're truly amazing, my queen," he said with a bow. "I'm not worthy to be in your presence."

"Yeah, I've known this for a while, but I wasn't going to say anything."

The plan was to eat a bunch of junk food, play some board games, and have a good time. Luckily, Tanner and Erick read my mind and did bring over alcohol, four six-packs of various beers, and my own six-pack of Guinness with a red bow on it. Okay, that little detail I didn't mention to my parents, but I knew my friends. We didn't go hard like Liam's, and we were all going to be responsible, knowing that my parents were going to come home around one o'clock. I thought I was allowed to treat myself to a few beers. Getting a full Division I scholarship and getting three school records and a state record deserved a small celebration with close friends…and a few beers. Nothing too crazy. And everyone I invited knew not to get too crazy. It was just a low-key, chill night. That was all.

Thank you, Tanner's sister, for buying us the alcohol!

For the first twenty minutes, we blasted music through the Bluetooth speakers. Erick prepped the Candy Land drinking game and insisted we play. I didn't know Candy Land could be made into a drinking game, but leave it to Erick to find a way. Lana and Meghan vouched that the game was totally worth it. We all opened our first beers as Liam started a fifteen-minute power hour to songs about California. After those fifteen minutes, I already felt the beer, and suddenly, I became the target of multiple rounds of teasing since I was the first to surrender my body and mind to the alcohol.

It was nice to peacefully coexist with a wide range of people in various high school cliques. But like all good things, it came to a screeching end.

Right when I opened my third bottle of Guinness, the doorbell rang. The only person who I expected it to be was Riley, but even then, I would have been shocked if she showed up. She really wasn't my biggest fan at the moment. Then I noticed a shadow when I headed to the door. Liam. He swerved around me, looking a little happy from the fifteen-minute power hour, and opened the door. Tom, Cassandra, and Jennifer each held their own alcohol and celebrated when Liam motioned them to come inside.

"Gabe! You, me, beer pong, now," Tom called to Gabriel in the living room behind us.

Leave it to Liam to take advantage of my parents' trust for me and ruin it with his partying friends.

"Um, what's this?" I said to Liam.

Why did he have to ruin his week of friendliness with his friends crashing the party? Most importantly, Cassandra, Satan's daughter.

"We'll be in the basement," he said. "Tom, our party's in the basement."

But Tom had already found his best friend chatting up Madison and Gia in the living room.

"That's not a proper way to treat your guests," Cassandra said so subtly.

"You're not my guest," I said.

Right as she opened her mouth to say more—because she always had to say more—Jennifer placed both of her hands on her friend's shoulders. "She won't be saying any more mean things to you—whose house we're in. Right, Cassie?"

Cassie sharpened her glare at me, giving me one last nonverbal threat to get her "last word" in. She didn't scare me. Not in the slightest.

"Oh, scary," I said, and Jennifer pushed her friend farther into my house. Then I turned to Liam and his wide, smiling mouth. "What the actual fuck?" I attempted to yell through my clenched jaw.

"Oh please. You think you can be the only one to have people over while Mom and Dad are gone? We'll be in the basement. Completely out of your hair. It'll still be chill."

"Liam, this is the one time I wanted to have people over for a good time. Mom and Dad trust us—they trusted me."

"Yo, Liam," Tom shouted from the living room. "Fix us up a beer pong table, would ya?"

Right as Liam headed downstairs to get a table to serve as the beer pong table, the doorbell rang. Again. My heart pounded just thinking of anyone who could have been on the other side of the door. It could have been Riley; it could have been the rest of Aspen Grove's finest partiers. But what stood on the other side of the front door was something I never thought I would see in all of my years on Earth.

Melanie, Kennedy, and Riley. Together. Side by side. Looking at each other as if they were aliens. The girl who always ended up naked at parties, my girlfriend, who I didn't invite, and my ex-girlfriend, who knew about the girlfriend but the girlfriend didn't know that she knew.

I was thankful, in that moment, I'd just had fifteen shots of beer in fifteen minutes before I had to deal with the situation that I knew wasn't going to end well.

"Oh fuck," I said, the words slipping out like a wet bar of soap.

"Party's here!" Melanie said and invited herself in, flashing her large bottle of Grey Goose like it was the ticket inside.

That left me with Kennedy and Riley. Both knew each other and all the history we had. And all that history came pouring down on me like a ton of bricks. I had no idea what to say. The two tried to avoid giving each other any eye contact, and I had no idea how to even address the ten points that probably needed to be addressed at the moment. So, I just stepped aside and let them into the house. Riley gave me a glare as she continued inside.

"Your ex-love seems like she needs a few drinks," Kennedy said with a laugh as she stepped in, leaning really close to me when she said it, close enough for me to smell the peppermint gum with each word that left her mouth.

God, I needed to kiss her right then and there but controlled the urge when I heard Tom's annoying cackle from the living room, reminding me that both of our worlds were already coexisting with each other in the same room, and the last thing everyone needed to know was that our kisses were secretly the bridge that connected the two.

"I've felt that way about her for the past month or so. I'm surprised she even showed up."

Kennedy grinned. "She's probably still in love with you."

"That's probably an accurate statement."

"I can't really blame her. You're pretty hot and well-achieved for an almost eighteen-year-old. Speaking of well-achieved..."

In the hand not holding her Captain Morgan rum, she handed me a red envelope. "I got this for you, future Olympian," she said. She slyly let her fingers trail my waistline as she headed into the house, and the feeling she left me with ignited my whole body and warmed my cheeks.

I stared at her handwriting for a few moments, my name partnered with the outline of the heart. Inside the envelope was a card that said in different fonts for each word: "you're awesome, fantastic, a shining star, the sh*t, a boss, super de duper." Inside the card, the last bullet point said: "simply the best" with a paragraph of her perfect handwriting taking over the rest of the card.

Quinn,

> *There are no words to describe how proud I am of you for all your accomplishments. For your full ride scholarship, for your state records, and for the success I know you'll have at the world championships. Watching you achieve these goals these past few months has been so inspiring. I'm so excited for you and what the future has in store for you. I know you'll continue to kick ass at everything you put your mind to. You're an amazing person, and I'm so lucky to have you as my girlfriend.*
>
> *Love,*
> *Kennedy*

My goal of the night: sneak away with Kennedy to show her how much I appreciated her and her support.

The boys were already in the beer pong game, and the party circled the table. Tom and Gabriel versus Liam and Tanner. Tanner stood there with a lazy posture as if he would rather be anywhere than at the table with his football teammates, and Erick snickered behind him as if it was the greatest thing he'd ever witnessed.

"With all those muscles, I expected you to do better," Erick said to Tom after Tom missed his first throw.

"I'd like to see you do this, then," Tom said.

"Nah, I'm DJing, and I'd rather look at you, Mr. Tight End."

Meghan, Lana, Gabriel, and Liam roared with laughter.

"Shut the fuck up, Iglesias. You're not funny."

"Loosen up, Tom," Tanner said, "and he is funny, and you're not gonna talk to him like that."

"Then tame your boy toy."

"How about you fuck off?"

Oh great, the worlds are already fighting. Fuck me now.

Gabriel smacked Tom in the stomach. "Stop being a shit, Felix. Now, let's win this."

Erick winked. Tom frowned as he rubbed the pain from Gabriel's smack out of his stomach.

I crept over to the fridge to get the third Guinness I hadn't had a chance to drink yet and also hoped my presence in the kitchen would get Kennedy's attention so I had a reason to talk to her because God, she looked so beautiful. Her hair was perfectly straight, messily parted down the right side, and I wanted to ruffle it with my fingers. Her eyes were outlined in a sweeping line of black mascara and eyeliner, and don't even get me started on those skinny jeans rounding out her butt and legs and the off-white tank top flaunting her sculpted arms and collarbone.

"Oh, so you're drinking now?" Riley said as she crept behind me, gesturing to my Guinness.

"I think I deserve it. Are you talking to me again, or are you still being an asshole?"

"If you're still being an asshole, I'm still being an asshole."

"Well, cheers to that." I raised my bottle to the nonexistent drink in her hand and took a sip. "With this attitude, I'm surprised you even came."

Just as her mouth opened to respond, Kennedy stepped in our circle. "Do you guys wanna shot?"

Kennedy held her bottle of her Captain Morgan up to Riley and me. The rum was already down a fourth of the bottle, and she had a wide grin on her face. Her glance alternated between the two of us, and I noticed the assessing look in Riley's eyes, probably viewing Kennedy in a whole different way after finding out that we were together.

"She needs one," I pointed to Riley, and it was her turn for the embarrassment to color her face. I hid my smile by drinking my beer.

"Well, then let's fix you up a shot."

Kennedy headed back to the kitchen island where Cassandra, Jennifer, and Melanie circled around. Riley shot me a what-the-fuck-did-you-just-do look. I motioned her to the island, and when the two of us joined, Kennedy came up right next to me, and her breeze of apples and flowers tickled my arm. I didn't expect her to be so close to me in front of her friends, but there she was. Not as if any of her friends would have noticed. Melanie swayed her hips to the music like the drunken mess she already was, Cassandra typed away on her phone, and Jennifer watched Kennedy pour the rum in each shot glass, but she didn't count. She already knew about us. And Riley watched us like a hawk.

"Here ya go," Kennedy said and passed the shot glasses to all of us. She saved the last one for me, and when she slid me mine, her fingers purposely went out of their way to touch my fingertips.

Gabriel appeared between Melanie and Cassandra and pushed himself into the circle. He took Melanie's shot from her. I might have been imagining it, but knowing that Cassandra had the biggest crush on Gabriel, I thought I noticed her cheeks turn the lightest shade of pink when his shoulders touched hers.

"Are we doing a round of shots?" Gabriel asked.

"Hey, that's my shot!" Melanie said.

"We were just about to do a round. Gotta congratulate Quinn," Kennedy said and raised her glass. "Cheers to our senior year and to everything you've accomplished, Quinn."

"What did she accomplish?" Melanie asked. She sounded genuinely curious.

"Three school records, a state record, and a full ride to Berkeley; oh, and going to Russia for the world championships in July," Kennedy said. I wanted to unleash the smile that was growing underneath my skin, but I held it in. It felt so good hearing my girlfriend brag about me to her friends, especially Cassandra. Hearing the list of accomplishments detailed her permanent scowl even more.

"How do *you* know all of this?" Cassandra asked with a tone and a raised brow.

"Because she told me. It's called talking, Cassie."

"The real question is: who doesn't know all of this?" Gabriel said. "To my queen!"

That comment made Cassandra throw daggers at me with her eyes.

"Cheers, Quinn," Kennedy said, and just as her friends concentrated on downing their shots, she flashed me a wink.

After I finished my shot, Gabriel came over to me and gave me his usual bear hug, picking me up and spinning me around as fast as he could. Just to annoy Cassandra, I wrapped my legs around his waist, and his spins grew faster. He smelled like the wonderful mix of his house, cologne, and freshly consumed beer and rum. When he put me down, he ruffled the top of my hair as I teetered from the spinning.

Riley sandwiched herself between Lana and Meghan, who were still watching the loud and intense game of beer pong. Cassandra's defined scowl was directed at me, and the alcohol already making me cheery encouraged me to give her a wink. That really did it because she flipped me off and joined the boys at the beer pong table. Melanie followed Gabriel, and Jennifer followed Cassandra, leaving Kennedy and me alone in the kitchen.

"Want another shot?" she said quietly as if the open floor plan of my kitchen and living room had no effect on her. Her friends could have turned around at any time to see her talking to me as I gave her a flirtatious smirk and major heart eyes. It felt as if the two of us had been plucked out of this world and put in another because nothing else existed around us. "I have to admit, seeing you drink is a rare sight. I feel like I need to soak this all in."

"Lucky for you, I'm such a pathetic lightweight and well on my way there. And yes, I want another shot. But no more after that. Can't get too crazy when my parents trust me with the house."

"I like that you're a good girl."

She wiggled her eyebrows and granted my wish of another

shot. We gave each other solid eye contact, pounded the shots back, and let the awful taste of straight-up Captain Morgan contort our faces. We both laughed.

"All this alcohol is making me feel a little warm," I said. "I think you should take off my clothes upstairs."

Her eyes widened. "Wow. Someone gets really blunt when they're drunk."

"I'm going to disappear to my room now. The second I disappear, count to sixty, and then I'll reward you for your superb counting skills."

She was right on time. Sixty seconds later, my bedroom door slowly opened. Beauty tangled up in Kennedy came waltzing in my room. She quietly and delicately closed the door. But as conservative as she was sneaking into my room, all the things I wanted to do to her fell on the opposite side of the spectrum.

My waist pinned her against the door, and I pressed in the lock when my hands slid underneath that sexy tank top she wore. My lips latched on to the neck I'd been eyeing all night, and my aggressiveness sucked out the softest but sexiest murmur from her. As our rum-soaked tongues got reacquainted with each other, my right hand unbuttoned her pants and skated down her smooth skin until it reached its destination, and when I pressed her center, Kennedy's nails dug into my back. Her body loosened, and I used my waist to secure hers in place so she didn't tumble to the floor. We only had a few moments to take each other in before it started looking suspicious, and I was determined to get her off. And I did so in record time.

If I thought her body was relaxed when my mouth first sucked on her neck, then that was nothing. With her cries muffled into my neck, I caught her trembling body when she landed back on Earth after her visit from whatever planet I was able to send her to.

"Oh my God," she breathed softly into my ear. "Oh my God."

Oh my God was right. Her quivering, limp body relying on

mine to stabilize her and the remnants of her moans dancing on my earlobe sent an intoxicating warmth through my body.

"I think we need to head back downstairs," I said as I retrieved my fingers from her.

"God, no. It's my turn."

"How about we make a deal. You can save it for tomorrow night when we have our hot, steamy date. I drive, I pay, only if we can claim your house as our safe space."

"Deal."

"Now go back downstairs. I'll meet you down there in a second."

After I washed up and rejoined the party, I found Jennifer and Kennedy taking over the spot Tanner and Liam once claimed. It was no surprise the two lost to Tom and Gabriel. Riley helped herself to Tanner's Bud Light in the fridge. I only joined her in the kitchen so I could treat myself to another beer to celebrate my growing list of accomplishments.

"You two were gone quite a bit," Riley said. Her voice was suspicious.

"Wasn't that long," I said. I knew she purposely tried to call me out on my and Kennedy's mutual disappearance, so I gave her a wink to let her know I gave zero fucks if she knew what we were up to.

Because she wasn't my girlfriend. I wasn't doing anything wrong. And her ongoing jealousy annoyed the crap out of me.

When I joined the party huddled in the family room, Erick, Tanner, Lana, and Meghan were deep in a conversation, guessing what number each person at the party was on the Kinsey Scale, and I began mentally preparing for my reaction when they got to Kennedy. *Just act cool. Drink your beer. Or maybe get another one. Excuse yourself to the bathroom. Go interrupt Liam's flirting with Madison and Gia.*

"Melanie will totally sleep with a girl in college," Meghan said with confidence. "Total spaghetti girl. She'd have her own fuck girl for a month or two in between guys. Maybe a sorority sister. And then forever live on the dark side of sexuality. The hetero side."

"I don't see it," Lana said. "She's way too straight. I think she'd make out with a girl when she was plastered and then wake up the next morning pretending like she didn't know anything about it."

"Or that would be her excuse for all her make-outs with girls," Riley said. "I see her making out with a bunch of them but sleeping with one? No. She's totally grossed out by vagina."

"I agree," Erick said to Riley. "Same with Jennifer and Cassandra. Jennifer was all about that Liam di—"

"Don't even finish that sentence," I said.

"And Cassandra has too much up her ass. Both are a hard zero. Madison Olivares, on the other hand, I wonder." He tapped his beer against his cheek in deep thought.

"Nope, super straight," I said. "I had a giant crush on her my sophomore year and was heartbroken when she started dating Corey Griffith."

Cassandra went out to her car to grab more alcohol she had hidden in her trunk, and when she left, the stuffy air followed her outside. The beer pong game was now down to one cup for each team. In between turns, I caught Kennedy's glances at me, and every time we caught each other, our cheeks mirrored the red blushing across our faces. The glances turned into winks we tossed each other from across the room. My hope was to get her to cave and blush. I totally won that game.

With the alcohol kicking in full swing, enough for me to say I was legitimately drunk, I wanted to give her eye contact to coax her to the best hiding spot in my house so I could have her again. Unfortunately for me, she was way too invested in that beer pong game to get that the constant glances were trying to get her to have sex with me.

"What about Kennedy Reed?" Lana asked the group.

Oh crap. Remain calm. Act like you don't know anything.

Everyone studied Kennedy from head to toe. Her eyes were

back in the game, focusing too much on Tom and Gabriel's cup to see that half of the party was gawking at her, looking for something gay to pick out so we could analyze where she slept on the Kinsey Scale. She aimed the beer pong at the one lone red Solo cup on Tom and Gabriel's side.

"A one," Tanner said. "Only because she's way too nice to tell a girl 'no, I really don't wanna make out with you.'"

"Seriously?" Erick said. "I'd give her at least a two or a three. She has the whole ChapStick lesbian vibe going on."

Clearly, she was anything but a zero. The noises she'd made in my ear informed me of that just a half hour before.

"You're all wrong," Meghan said. "She's a four."

The group exchanged surprised looks. Riley and I continued sipping on our drinks, and I tried to be as invisible as I could. Maybe I was too hard on Meghan's gaydar. Maybe every assumption she ever made was right, and there were a lot more queer people in Aspen Grove than I thought.

"Oh my God, Meg, not everyone is gay," Lana said. "I can't find anything that screams anything higher than a one."

"Are you kidding me? Babe, your gaydar is awful. Everything about Kennedy Reed is gay."

"How?" Tanner said. "I don't buy it."

"One, she has short fingernails. It's the first thing I notice on hot girls—"

"Because you want all of them to be gay," Lana said.

"Two, her arms. They're, like, perfect arms."

"Because she plays soccer."

"Then why are they better than Cassandra, Jennifer, and Melanie's? All of us ladies know that girls like arms, so we make sure we do our daily bicep curls. Which leads me to three, I see her working out at the rec center every day. She definitely does more arm workouts than leg workouts, and she's always wearing cutoff shirts. How does that scream straight? No straight girl wears cutoff shirts. They wear racerback tank tops."

She had a good point. When Kennedy watched my 500 on the track, she was definitely wearing a cutoff shirt.

"Four, she wasn't even into Grant Turner at all like any straight girl would be. She looked super miserable at homecoming, if anyone noticed. And five, earlier, I overheard Cassandra and Melanie say she hasn't been on a single date since Dominic Powell last year. Someone that hot would have been on at least one date…unless she's into women, which she is. She's a four."

I hoped by taking another sip of Guinness that the cold beer would cool down the fire erupting on my cheeks as my friends picked apart my surreptitious girlfriend. My coordination teetered like a seesaw, and my whole body felt warm and satisfied. That was it. I was cutting myself off. Not a chance in hell I would be that girl puking at her own party. Plus, the night was still young, and I didn't want to steal the toilet away from Melanie Krugel when she needed it. From her lazy, red eyes and wobbling knees, I'd say at her current pace, she'd be there in about two hours max.

Then Cassandra rejoined the party, but something was missing from her. Her pouty face. Instead, she stood in the entryway connecting the foyer and the living room, her face loosened in hurt and confusion. Her eyebrows rose, her eyes soft on me before falling on Kennedy. It took me just a moment to realize why she looked so concerned and shocked.

In one hand, her new Absolut Vodka bottle. The other hand, the red envelope.

I choked on my beer in mid swallow. It was the first time I'd ever seen her scowl uncoiled. She just stood there as all the words Kennedy wrote on that card soaked in her mind. My eyes completely froze on her. My body felt as if my veins had been filled with cement. I had no idea what to do for damage control. Casually stroll over to Cassandra and talk to her privately as if the card was no big deal? Or do what I really wanted to do and make a scene? Who the hell reads a card that doesn't even belong to them? Of course, Cassandra Jones. Because she was the worst human being in all of Aspen Grove.

A pong ball flew over my way and rolled underneath the couch. As Tom and Gabriel searched the nearby ground for the ball, Kennedy caught Cassandra's gaze in the entryway. Her eyes followed down to the card. Everyone else carried on drinking, chatting about the Kinsey Scale, and Gabriel came over to dig his hand underneath the couch where I stood. Cassandra, Kennedy, and I all glanced at each other, waiting to see who was going to make the first move.

I jumped out of my spot, and once she saw me darting over to Cassandra, Kennedy ditched her spot at the beer pong table. Together, we pushed Cassandra to the foyer where the card should have been.

"What the hell are you doing?" I yelled through my clenched jaw. "You think you can just come into my house and go through all my stuff?"

It was as if she wasn't the Cassandra Jones that I had known for four years. She just stood there and let me push her into the wall without any resistance. Her dark eyebrows rose farther up her forehead, shocked, horrified, and concerned all at the same time. A part of me expected to be shoved back, but her whole body was limp.

"It was on the ground," she said, completely defeated. It was the softest tone I'd ever heard come out of her. "I just picked it up and—"

I snatched the card out of her hand. "Read it? You thought because it fell on the floor that gave you reading rights?"

She looked at Kennedy. "You two are…together?"

The little streak of red that highlighted Kennedy's face when she overcame embarrassment infected her whole face in dark red. I didn't know I was worth a whole face colored in dark red embarrassment.

"Cassie, I—"

"You're dating a girl? You're…you're gay?"

"No. Cassie, I—"

"Out of all the girls you could date, you're dating...*her?*"

"Can we go outside and raise our voices out there?" I said.

Call me crazy, but with Kennedy's new promise to be more open with us, I thought she would tell Cassandra the truth no matter how much she feared her best friend would retaliate. The closet door was propped open for her to waltz outside and own our relationship. Tell Cassandra that she was dating me, how it wasn't a big deal, how Liam and Jennifer didn't think it was a big deal, and what would have been a really awkward confrontation would dissolve into nothing.

But that didn't happen at all.

Instead, the three of us found the whole party gawking at us in the entryway, staring at us like you would imagine if discovering that the most popular girl at school was dating a girl. Lana, Meghan, Erick, and Tanner found more amusement in it than we did, and I knew the smirk Meghan tried to hide was because she was absolutely right this whole time.

When my eyes fell on Kennedy, I could feel the embarrassment ripping her apart. I would have scooped her up in my arms and told her it was going to be okay if I could, but that was just adding alcohol to the fire.

"Dude, your sister is dating Kennedy?" Tom said to Liam. "Man, she must have a twin thing."

"Shut the fuck up, Tom," Liam snapped.

What the hell did that mean? After his comment, Kennedy looked even more mortified, as if she witnessed her life crumble right in front of her. I saw it too. The world we built together dissolving.

"What?" I said. My heart thudded. "What does that mean? What is he talking about?"

"She doesn't know about homecoming or New Year's?" Tom slurred, and I wasn't sure if he realized everything he was spilling out.

"I swear to God, Tom," Liam said and shoved Tom against

the wall. Before he could lunge forward, Liam already grabbed his shirt in his fist.

"I dare you to shove me again," Tom said.

"Learn to shut your mouth, you idiot."

Gabriel quickly sandwiched himself in between them.

Kennedy's eyes darkened on me, and I couldn't tell if it was because her pupils sank deeper into the pools of tears or guilt. Everything started to collapse. My confidence. My relationship. My heart. I felt as if my lungs were being used as a stress ball.

Kennedy scurried out the front door, and I bolted after her, using the remaining strength my body had left.

"Kennedy!" I shouted and broke out in a full sprint to catch her running down my driveway. "Kennedy! Stop!"

I grabbed her shoulders and turned her around. She threw her face into her palms.

"What the hell?" I tugged at her wrists so she would stop hiding her face. She was going to look me in the eye and tell me if what Tom said was either true or false. She tried to move away, but I gripped her wrists tighter. "You hooked up with my brother? You fucking hooked up with my brother?"

She tried peeling my hands off her to no avail. "Stop it," she cried. "You're hurting me."

I let go of her. What was happening to me? I experienced such an overwhelming sense of anger that I didn't even feel like a real person. Anger and heartbreak were a lethal combination. I didn't mean to hurt her. Jesus, I would never want to do that. She even looked at me as if I terrified her, and I wasn't sure if it was because of the truth she held in or if it was because of my reaction. Maybe it was a little bit of both. I was scared of myself too, if that meant anything. I didn't like it at all. I felt like a monster.

"Oh my God," I muttered, and I felt as if I was going to puke. "Oh. My. God. You slept with my brother?"

"It was one time, Quinn! At homecoming. At Cassie's. It was before anything started happening with you—"

"Jesus! What about New Year's?"

"It was a tiny peck, I swear. We were just standing there, and I really didn't wanna kiss Grant so…"

"You kissed your girlfriend's twin brother, the one you already slept with, and then just added to the secrets you were keeping from me?"

"It didn't mean anything! Just a stupid little peck. Nothing with him meant anything!"

"You kissed him on New Year's? After you slept with him too? You slept with him, became my girlfriend, kissed him on New Year's, and then spent the night with me?"

"Quinn, all of this happened before you and I were something. All of this happened before I fell in love with you."

"Fell in love?"

"Yes!"

It burned. My chest. My eyes. My whole body. So badly. The emotion swaddled me to the point it made it hard to breathe. Not even the perfect March air could loosen the grip. What was even worse was the girl who I cared about more than anyone else in my life stood in front of me feeling the exact same burning and agonizing pain I felt.

"I…I can't stop picturing you with him," I said, my voice starting to shake. The image of them together wouldn't leave me alone. *Fucking leave me alone!*

"Don't do that—"

"You really couldn't have just told me? That's all you would have had to do. 'Hey, I hooked up with Liam once, but that was before us, and it didn't mean anything.' And then you kissed him at New Year's and then just added that to all the things you were hiding from me? That wouldn't have been a big deal if you weren't lying to me."

"I wasn't sure how you would react."

"Yeah, so lying about it is way better. Smart one."

"Quinn, it didn't mean anything. I was drunk and thought I wanted it, but when it was happening—"

"I really don't wanna hear details of you sleeping with my brother."

"I don't want that to mess this up. I don't want it to mess this amazing thing up." She cried harder. "Please, Quinn. I know I messed up, but I'm so sorry."

My brain told me to kiss her. *Forget about what happened before you guys talked and just kiss her.* But my heart hurt so badly. From Liam, from the Outing™. My heart wanted to find a compromise with my brain, but it wasn't sure how. I couldn't get past the lying, the secrets kept from me. Kennedy and I were supposed to have our own secrets with each other. She didn't need the same secrets with my brother.

"We need to go back in there," I said. "The only way for us to take back this outing so it can be in our control is just going in there and owning it. I think maybe if I have some space for a few days, I can get over the Liam thing, but I can't keep hiding all the feelings I have for you. I want to act like your girlfriend at school, not watch you give some lame lie to your friends about why you're talking to me. The only silver lining in this is that Cassandra just propped open the door for us to come out. I told you that you wouldn't have to do this alone, so let's do this together."

All she did was shake her head. She glanced at the neighbor's driveway, more tears stained her eyes, and her lips didn't produce any answer to my non-rhetorical question.

I didn't think it could hurt even more, but God, her silence ripped me in two.

"What? What are you doing?" I said. "You're shaking your head to that? They already know, Kennedy! All we have to do is just take it back and act like it's not a big deal!"

"It is a big deal," she said. "It's a big deal to me."

"It's a big deal to me not to go back in the closet. I can't go back in there, Kennedy. I just can't. If you truly love me like you claim you do, then you'll do this. You'll fight for us. You'll stop lying to everyone. I'm willing to fight for us because I'm crazy about you. Let's do it together."

She just stood there in silence, looking utterly helpless. Since she'd moved back to Aspen Grove, she never felt so far away from me. *The person you try to be is a stronger presence in the room than the person who you really are.* Kennedy would rather be closeted and unhappy than the person who she really was— the girl who I fell for. The girl standing in front of me wasn't my Kennedy. She was Kennedy Reed, Ms. Popular, Ms. Co-Captain of the soccer team, and Cassandra Jones's best friend, a label that wasn't at all flattering. Saying that she loved me was just empty words to make up for the guilt she felt. That wasn't love. Not in my book.

"No," she said so softly, I must have misheard it. She just told me she loved me so she couldn't have just told me no. That wouldn't make any sense.

"What"

"I said no."

Her words felt like a punch straight to my stomach. "No?"

"This was supposed to be *my* decision. *My* control. *My* words. None of that was mine. I had no voice in that. That's not coming out. That's being exposed."

"That's why we go back in there and take our control back. I'll be with you!"

"I can't."

I took a few steps back. I really just wanted to fall on my driveway, curl up in a ball, and sob. The girl I cared so much about refused to go to her friends and say she was proud of me— proud of us.

"I'm done," I muttered, and the sound of my own words yanked my body apart even more.

"What? Just like that?"

"I have no idea what I have to do to be worthy of existing to you. You're running away from us, from me. I'm not going to be your dirty little secret anymore. Not when we can easily take this all back in our control and fix it and be happy. But I guess you don't want that, do you?"

The most painful part of the night wasn't finding Cassandra holding that card in her hand. It wasn't the whole party watching our confrontation from the living room. It wasn't finding out that Kennedy had slept with my brother and never told me about it. And it wasn't even me telling Kennedy that I was done with her. The most painful part of that night was watching her stand so still in front of me that I never thought she would leave that spot again.

I had no words for her. The hurt choked my lungs. A tear broke free from my eyes after holding back for so long. My hands trembled as I opened the front door to find everyone still in their spot. All eyes were on me, but I couldn't even see them. I just stumbled up the stairs and let myself completely break when I plopped on my bed.

Underneath the sobs that collected in my damp pillow, I faintly heard Liam shooing everyone out of the house, telling everyone that the party was over. Minutes later, there was a knock on my door, and I heard it slowly open. That someone who came into the room sat by my bed and put their hand on my back. From the softness of her touch, I knew it was Riley, and I cried even harder knowing how much I'd hurt her and how she still stayed behind.

No matter how much I pushed her away, she never ran away from me.

I wept for the rest of the night, and she held me the way I wished Kennedy could hold me, so tightly that no one could try to take me away from her.

The whole week, I'd only been able to think about Saturday and the wonderful date we would have. The whole week I had this grand plan to sweep her off her feet without any restraints holding us back. I would have never guessed that both of us would instead fall on our faces.

Chapter Twelve

The morning sun shimmered through my curtains and onto my face, triggering my headache to thump inside my brain. I wanted to believe that the whole party was just a horrible dream, but when I turned and found Riley in the fetal position, I knew something awful must have happened for us to actually share a bed. The tension that followed us over the past few months appeared in the form of a few respectable inches separating us. But apparently, it wasn't enough tension to force her out of my house like the rest of the party.

In my bathroom, I assessed the damage to my face from crying myself to sleep. My blond-brown hair stuck out as if I'd been electrocuted. My eyes were dark blue with flecks of red. They looked as if they were ready to close shut for good, and small red dots of burst blood vessels freckled the bags hanging under my eyes.

I soaked my face in cold water for a few minutes to make my eyes feel whole again.

When I came back to bed, Riley started waking up slowly. I checked my phone, hoping for a text from Kennedy that said she was sorry and how she'd owned up to our relationship proudly to her friends before the night ended.

But no text like that existed.

I got texts from all my other friends, checking in to see if I was okay and letting me know that if I needed them, they would be there, but nothing from the one person who I wanted to hear from the most.

"How you doing?" Riley said groggily.

I thought I'd cried everything out of me. I never cried that hard before in my life, not even when I failed to make the London Olympics. But when Riley asked how I was doing and I relived the night all over again, there were still emotions left inside I needed to cry out.

"Hungover and gutted. I feel absolutely gutted," I said and crawled back into bed, using the covers to wipe up the residual tears.

"Do you wanna talk about it?"

That was one thing we didn't get around to doing after the party came to an abrupt halt. So, I told her everything, and when I reminded myself of that date I was supposed to have, I cried even harder. In an alternate universe, I would have woken up, celebrated the sun shining on my face, stared at the clothes in my closet to find the perfect outfit to capture Kennedy's eyes, fixed my hair the best I could, and picked up the hottest date I'm pretty sure I could have found.

I shouldn't have been crying to Riley with a hangover, dreading the phone call I had to make to cancel my dinner reservations that would only make the breakup official.

"You were right," I said, still blubbering. "You were right this whole time. I feel so stupid. So fucking stupid."

She hugged me tighter, and I buried my wet face in her shoulder. "You're not stupid. You trusted her. She gave you all the reasons to trust her, and that doesn't make you stupid."

"If she says she loves me, why does she have to hide it? What is so bad about me that makes me such an embarrassing person to date?"

"Nothing, Quinn. Absolutely nothing." She held me out so I could look straight into her eyes. "You're a good person. You're smart, you're caring, you're funny, you're sympathetic. You're everything someone needs in a girlfriend, and if she's ashamed of that, then she doesn't deserve you at all. Don't let her make you think otherwise."

Her words didn't mean anything to me at that moment because it didn't matter how bad Kennedy made me feel, she was the only one I wanted to see and the only one I wanted to hold. But Riley stayed with me for that whole day. She even went out to the store to buy me Gatorade, my favorite cashew-milk cookies & cream ice cream, and tortilla chips and guacamole to cheer me up.

But of course, she ran into my parents. That must have been awkward because by the time my parents came home, everyone had been gone for almost two hours, and I was asleep with Riley in my bed. Riley told me when she came back that my parents didn't know she was at the house, and she admitted to them that something happened between me and Liam, and I was really upset about it.

"I'm sorry, Quinn, I had to tell them," she said when she joined me back on the bed. "I told them I was only here to comfort you because they gave me a look like they were plotting to lecture you about sneaking girls into your room."

Great, an upcoming lecture about that. Again.

"It's okay. They were going to find out eventually."

"I told them you needed space, and I was taking care of it. You thirsty? I got you three bottles of lemon-lime Gatorade. Your favorite."

Of course, I guzzled about a fourth of it in one gulp. I was dehydrated from being hungover and crying out the remaining water left in my system.

"You're too good to me," I said. "You're right about another thing: I really don't deserve you."

"Quinn, I'm so sorry I said that to you. I was drunk and angry that you were hardly talking to me for no reason at all. I wanted to say something to make you pissed, but I didn't mean it. Please, don't believe what I said."

"I've been so mean to you."

"I've been mean to you too. But let's squash it, okay? Let's forget about our drama and eat chips and guac and cashew-milk ice cream and binge watch some *Gilmore Girls*. Preferably the one where Dean breaks up with Rory, and Lorelai encourages her to wallow."

"I'm ready to wallow now."

"Good, and I'm ready to eat this food."

❖

Even though high school swimming was over, I still had to wake up at the butt crack of dawn for my club practice, and my Camry rights during the week were still intact. It was a nice little rule made by Mom and Dad with a little extra oomph for another round of "Fuck you, Liam."

I don't remember how I got myself to my club team's pool for morning practice. Somehow, I mindlessly drove to the pool without really being aware of the turns, the stop lights, and the speed limits, which was a great way to get myself killed. At dryland practice, I told Leanne I wanted to use heavier weights than I usually lifted. I had all this angry energy boiling inside me, and the more energy I had to use to lift the heavier weights, the more the anger would seep out of me. That was my theory at least. Dryland helped release all my anger. Almost in a therapeutic way. It was like having Mr. T in front of me, yelling at me to punch him in the hand to let everything out that I've been bottling up. With my hands clutched tightly around those twenty-five-pound dumbbells, I used every ounce of strength to push out the toxic energy in the form of shoulder presses. My cable push-pulls went up another ten pounds, and I told Leanne I wanted to do a few more extra sets of star planks so unleashing the anger could burn my whole body. She looked at me as if I officially had gone crazy. Maybe I had. What person in their right mind voluntarily added two extra sets of star planks?

Answer: people who lost their minds.

Then after dryland, I got in the pool for an hour, and the pool brought me comfort like my mom opening her arms for an embrace. The water cradled my body so delicately, as if it told me it was all right to cry. No one would notice the emotion leaking out of me because it'd just flow right into the pool. So, I croggled the whole time, but I refused to let crying slow me down. I figured the more I pushed myself through the water, the more all the toxic emotions in me would drain, and maybe I could start feeling whole again.

In the school hallways, I still felt like a zombie. Not because I woke up at four thirty for dryland and swim practice, but on top of being exhausted, my brain was deactivated, and everything inside me was dead. I felt as if part of me shriveled into nothing, and the worst part about this whole thing was having to go to calc with my ex-girlfriend sitting two inches in front of me, the best friend who outed her, and Liam's friend who outed him.

I seriously debated skipping calc just to avoid it one more day, but I was too afraid that my A- would drop or that Mr. Carmichael or the school nurses would call USA Swimming, and they would strip me from my spot on the national team. So I went and held my breath until the bell rang, and Kennedy's seat remained vacant. She'd chickened out, and I let out a relieved sigh, knowing that I'd saved myself from what could have been an extremely awkward encounter at the nurse's office. I had another day to mentally prepare to be in her presence; at the same time, I was completely worried that she felt the exact same way as I did. Gutted.

I let the pool cradle me again for three hours after school and braced myself for the dinner I knew my parents were making and how I would be forced to be in the same room as Liam for the first time since Friday. Neither of us could look each other in the eye, and Mom and Dad finally had enough with the awkward tension permeating their house. About ten minutes in, when the silence and our brief responses to their questions about our day and weekend overpowered the table, Dad lowered his utensils and unlocked Pandora's box.

"Okay, so can one of you please tell me what happened on Friday?" Dad said.

Neither Liam or I could look at Mom and Dad from our dinner plates. Quite honestly, I didn't believe I should have spoken. Liam could tell them what happened because if it wasn't for him, all the things that went wrong on Friday wouldn't have happened at all.

"Nothing?" Dad said. Silence grew. "You know that I'm forbidding both of you from leaving this table until the issue or issues are addressed."

"Ask Liam," I said with still no eye contact.

"Oh, shut up, Quinn."

Eye contact back on.

"I didn't do anything wrong. In any case. There's nothing for me to own up to, and you know that."

He glanced back down at his untouched plate of steak smothered in steak sauce, mashed potatoes, and green beans, but all three foods were mixed together from him playing with it.

"Own up to what?" Mom said.

"Actually," Liam said and looked me straight in my eyes, "you do have something to own up to. How about you tell Mom and Dad what you've been doing for the past couple months. Or should I say *who* you've been doing."

"You mean, the one you slept with at homecoming?"

"You mean, the one you slept with on the couch on Valentine's Day weekend?"

I could have just lunged across that table and strangled him with my bare hands until he turned a light shade of pink. My parents' faces looked as if they felt ready to vomit and then pick up religion again. I could have easily joined them...well, minus the religion part. The Christian God would have hated me more than Cassandra Jones.

When Liam noticed their shocked looks, he sat there with

the smallest trace of a smirk, as if he won my breakup, as if he was glad he had something on me so Mom and Dad didn't think I was this innocent kid like they thought I was.

"Well, I'm going to open that bottle of scotch," Dad said and slipped out of his seat to the small bar right behind him. "Didn't really expect all this information at once."

"Um, can we backtrack a little?" Mom said, way too innocently after the truth bombs of her children's sexcapades just lit up the dinner table. "You did what on Valentine's Day weekend?"

"Little Miss Innocent snuck her secret girlfriend to the house while we were all gone—"

"Goddamn it, Liam!" I yelled and slammed my hand on the dinner table. "You fucking piece of shit!"

He was pissed because they trusted me with the house on Friday and not him. He was pissed that I spent Valentine's Day with Kennedy. Pissed that I got to kiss her. Pissed that he lost a girl to someone who was embarrassing and lower on the high school totem pole than he was.

"Hey!" Dad snapped. "That's your brother!"

"Quinn," Mom said softly, "you have a girlfriend?"

"I *had* a girlfriend," I cried. He didn't even care what transpired over the weekend. Not only did I lose my girlfriend, I lost more of my brother, who should have been more sympathetic than he was. He should have been on my team, not the enemy. "And then his friends outed her to everyone. I *had* a girlfriend because she refused to own up to our relationship together." I wiped my face. "I'm so sorry, Liam, that you've gone through high school never being in a relationship longer than three months and never knowing what it's like to care about someone more than yourself. And you wonder why she doesn't like you? Look at yourself. You're trying to win my breakup. And guess what? You won. You won my breakup, so go ask her out even though she's gonna say no to you. Again. Because you're a piece of shit. Now go fuck yourself like you usually do every night."

I threw my utensils on my plate and stormed upstairs.

About an hour later, there was a knock on my door. I didn't lock it because I knew the words I said to Liam served as their own lock, and I knew my parents would check on me later when I had time to calm down. And that was what happened.

"Quinn, honey," Mom said as she took a seat next to me on the bed and placed her warm hand on my quivering back. "What's going on?"

"We just want to make sure you're all right," Dad said as he kept his distance at the foot of my bed. He always became uncomfortable any time I cried. Typical dad move but I didn't blame him. "It sounds like a lot happened that we didn't even know were…well…a thing."

"I'm not all right."

Mom rubbed my back for a few moments as I collected the strength to turn around and tell my parents the truth.

"What happened, sweetie?"

"Kennedy Reed was my girlfriend," I said in between convulsions. "We've been a thing since November. And I really, really liked her. And apparently, Liam did too, and he hooked up with her, and she didn't even tell me about it. And her friend outed her to the whole party, and I told her we should tell everyone we were together, but she didn't want to. She's embarrassed by me. She's always been embarrassed by me."

Mom pulled me into her, the same way she did when I came home crying the first day of sophomore year when Kennedy ignored me. Her smell was comforting. It was a mixture of her designer perfume, the smell of our house, and her natural scent. I buried my face deeper in her chest as if her smell would ease all my troubles. "Oh, honey, I'm so sorry."

The best thing about the conversation was that my parents never took the time to say, *Since when did you started talking to Kennedy Reed? I didn't know Kennedy liked girls. Quinn, you slept with her in this house? On our couch?* They just consoled me, knowing that although I hid a big part of my life from them, made plenty of mistakes, and disobeyed their trust, they saw past that and instead saw their daughter in pieces over her first heartbreak.

"Quinn, honey," Mom said. She ran her fingers delicately through my hair. "You need to remember that Kennedy isn't out yet. Everyone is different. And it might not necessarily mean she's embarrassed by you; she still might be embarrassed of herself and hasn't learned to love herself for who she is. If she's not comfortable with herself, how is she going to be comfortable with people knowing about you?"

"But she could have told me about Liam. She didn't have to hide everything from me. How can I trust her when she slept with him and didn't tell me about it, and she doesn't even want people knowing about me?"

"Hon, there's a lot going on right now, and I know it hurts, especially when there are things between both Kennedy and your brother. But give it a couple days to fizzle down. Who knows, maybe Kennedy will realize how much she needs you. Just give it some time. I think everyone needs some time right now."

Give it some time. But the real question was, after all the trust I lost, did I want Kennedy back?

❖

She came back that Wednesday. At least what was left of her. When she sat in her seat, she took the air in the room with her. The smell of her body wash and shampoo put me in the same spell it did when her hair bunched up in my face as I held her in my arms. Suddenly, we returend to the world we used to live in. No acknowledgments when she collected my homework. No smile. No blushing. No nothing. This time, she felt further away from me than she ever had before.

Thursday, she came into class surprisingly early. No sooner had I taken my seat then she came into the room, swept by me, and approached Mr. Carmichael at his desk.

"Hi, Mr. Carmichael. I have a question," I heard her say.

"Yes, Miss Reed?"

"I was wondering if I could move my desk. Maybe switch with someone in the front? I've been having problems seeing."

Kennedy Reed, the Queen of Lies.

"Of course."

Half of me was relieved that she wasn't sitting directly in front of me, then the other half of me reminded myself that she was moving because of me. Because she didn't want to be anywhere near me. Because she was maybe 100 percent over me?

"Miss Stewart," Mr. Carmichael said to Jennifer as she walked in. "Do you mind switching seats with Miss Reed so she's able to be closer to the board?"

Jennifer studied Kennedy for a split second, knowing full well her best friend had pretty stellar vision. Kennedy gave her an eye that pleaded with her to do it.

"Yeah, sure," Jennifer said, deciding to acquiesce to her friend's game in order to protect her from me. "Should I just take her seat?"

"Yes please."

Kennedy didn't waste any time taking Jennifer's seat, leaving Jennifer confused and wide-eyed as she slipped into the seat in front of me. She looked at me with her perfectly shaped, creased eyebrows, shrugged, and faced the front of the class.

Kennedy became a mirage. I could see her—everywhere—but she wasn't real. I couldn't have her. And I had to sit with that feeling for forty-three minutes.

Every day.

As if I couldn't be less whole. Just like I predicted when we first started becoming something, having even more history and having her forget me all over again hurt even worse than before. In calc and lunch, she didn't look at me. At lunch, she sat on the opposite end of Liam, Tom, and Cassandra. She never once looked up from her food. She was always in a daze, and I don't think I noticed her take a bite of her lunch in the first two weeks.

Between seventh and eighth period, I'm pretty sure she found an alternative way to her room because I never saw her. I had to walk to eighth period completely alone.

Both my brother and my ex-girlfriend found alternative routes just to stay clear of me.

After lunch that Friday, Gabriel caught up with me at my locker.

"Hey, how are you doing?" he said as I swapped out my books from my book bag. I shrugged. That was the only reply I could give him. "I'm so sorry, Quinn. I really hate seeing you like this."

"It's not your fault."

"Kennedy's absolutely miserable too. I wish I knew what to do to make you both feel better. I didn't even know you two were a thing, but it seems like you guys really liked each other if both of you look completely miserable."

"Yeah, well, I was too much of an embarrassment for us to stay together. It's why the four musketeers can never be a thing again, right? The three of you are all popular, and I'm just that loser who swims every hour of the day."

"That's not it at all."

"Then what is it? This is the second time I've been written off by her."

"Remember how scared you were when you first came out? You were terrified when you told me, at least."

"That's because we'd been making out for, like, three months, and I was worried you were going to be mad at me."

"You were scared telling your parents. You were scared going to homecoming with Riley Scott. She's terrified too. You of all people should know how she feels right now."

"Okay, then, coming out aside, she fucked my brother and lied about it." I paused. "Did you know about them? Liam and Kennedy?" The way he just looked at me told me my answer. "Great. So, everyone knew about their hookup? I feel like a complete idiot."

"Yeah, everyone did know about their hookup, and everyone but Liam knew that she wasn't interested in him. At all. We all told him to give it up, that it was never going to happen. But I think he saw it as a challenge."

I slammed my locker door shut, using all the anger seething inside me. "Oh, that's nice. Liam was trying to use my ex-girlfriend as a conquest. I knew it."

"Does it matter? She never liked him. Or Grant. And we were so confused as to why Kennedy seemed so happy all of a sudden compared to earlier this year where she kinda of drank too much; like, on Melanie levels. I couldn't figure out why she went from being miserable and drinking a lot to suddenly being so happy and…well…not drinking a lot. But it all makes sense now. It's because of you. Not Liam or Grant. *You*. Listen, I'm free tonight if you wanna talk or do something to get your mind off things. We haven't hung out in forever."

I gave him the smallest smile, which took a maximum amount of effort to give. "I really appreciate that, Gabe. But I have practice."

"I know. I meant after."

"I kinda really don't wanna do anything. I'm sorry."

"It's okay. If you change your mind, you have my number."

Was this what a heartbreak felt like? Waking up every morning feeling as if you slept with a boulder on your chest? Feeling as if trying to get through the day was like trying to push yourself through a wall of bricks? Did a heartbreak make you so numb to everything that you didn't want to search for any happiness at all? You would rather lie in bed and wish time would speed up around you to where you felt 1 percent whole again just to function?

In the fall, Mrs. Roux taught our French Four class a phrase that was untranslatable into the English language. *La douleur exquise*. It's the immense pain of wanting someone you can't have. I didn't understand what that word truly meant until days after the party, when I found myself still sobbing in my bed and that boulder strangling my lungs every day. If all those feelings I described were what it meant to suffer a heartbreak, then the only words that fit into the hole that Kennedy punched out of me were *la douleur exquise*.

CHAPTER THIRTEEN

Swimming saved me. It saved me during the dark moments of my adolescence when I realized I was different from most people. Different because of my sexuality. Different because my goals for the year involved swimming instead of getting into a relationship. Different from my brother, who rose up the totem pole at Aspen Grove while I was just sort of there—either liked only because I competed on an international level or hated because what high school kid gave up most of their social life for unrealistic dreams and goals? What a weirdo.

It saved me again when all I wanted to do was think about my first heartbreak, sulk in my bed, and cry to a breakup playlist I created on Spotify. I could have spent my whole spring break listening to that melodramatic playlist I made for myself while gorging on the cashew-milk cookies & cream ice cream I craved, but I didn't. I had medals to win and Olympic trials to qualify for. While my friends traveled to places like Florida, Hilton Head, or the mountains for a relaxing, fun-filled spring break, I lived and breathed the pool and chlorine. I pushed my anger out in dryland. Croggling wasn't even a thing anymore by the time spring break came around. Even Leanne noticed a difference and told me that whatever was going on with me was turning me into a beast at practice. Her words, verbatim, and hearing her calling me "a beast at practice" with an entertained grin on her face was like my spring break reward. Did that mean I was bouncing back from getting my heart broken? Did that mean I'd successfully convinced Leanne that I still obsessed over winning a medal at the world champs?

Having her see how much heart and soul I poured into practice made me feel as if I was getting back on the right track to a world champs medal. After punishing me with wall sits a few months back, calling me a beast at practice was my little beacon of light whenever I felt like crap.

At least there was a small sliver of light.

❖

The first weekend after spring break, I reached out to Gabriel to finally hang out. Swimming had really helped me. Leanne's compliments lifted me out of my rut. At least I was rocking some aspect of my life, so I was ready to face the world again and be social.

I couldn't remember the last time the two of us hung out in his basement. Maybe once last summer? Definitely not at all once senior year started, and he was busy chasing after Melanie and I was busy training for the world champs or with Kennedy in secrecy. He ordered a pizza for himself and an enormous Greek salad for me, showed me a huge collection of comedies that had "no love storyline or any of that stupid crap," as he said. He offered me a rum and Coke—rum he kept secretly stashed in his room—but I felt super pathetic because the rum he had was Captain Morgan, and I knew that was Kennedy's favorite. I stuck to water, of course. Being healthy physically, mentally, and emotionally was meaning more every day the world champs grew closer.

Gabriel suggested we watch the dumbest, funniest movie in his collection, and that meant *Superbad*. Both of us had seen it at least fifty times, so we did a lot of talking in between. Our plans for prom (he was going with Melanie, I was riding solo), our plans for the summer (train, train, and then train some more), did I reconcile with Liam yet (hard no), and was I planning on hooking up with Riley at prom (that wouldn't have been smart at all). And then he tried convincing me to finally ask out Hot Lifeguard since she'd been giving me smiles before and after practice ever since the fall. Not going to lie, his convincing made me seriously think about it. Something casual and completely meaningless would be perfect.

As I walked up my driveway coming home from Gabriel's, I noticed my phone light up in my hands. It was two texts from Kennedy. My throat tightened as I procrastinated on opening the message. I had such a good night with Gabriel that I didn't want it ruined by whatever Kennedy had to tell me. But my curiosity forced me to open it as my stomach slowly dropped.

Her first text read, *Can we please talk?*

Followed by her second text sent twenty minutes later, the one that lit up my phone screen: *It's important.*

I swallowed as my fingers took over and started typing a response. My brain and heart were so tired of constantly producing emotions in my body like a twenty-four-hour factory that they finally just let my fingers take control.

I replied, *What's there left to even say?*

How much I miss you.

That text was a punch to the gut. Maybe like five punches to the gut. A long breath came out of me as I took a seat on the concrete front porch. The night was warmer than an average late April night in upstate New York. The air smelled as if summer was just around the corner, and even the night bugs chirped in the darkness, and the whole scene engulfing me smelled and sounded like summer. Which meant happiness was near, right? What a great way to ruin the happiness and the glimmer into the looming summer with a text message from my ex-girlfriend— who I hadn't spoken to in a month. We hadn't talked, smiled, or made eye contact since that night. It was as if we were invisible to each other. And here she was, reaching out to me right as I started to finally accept what happened, telling me how much she missed me. It was amazing how much the stitched-up wounds quickly spiraled open from just one text from her.

I knew if I was going to engage in this conversation—despite making so much progress since our breakup—I was going to need all the fresh air my lungs could hold. So, I took a few deep breaths to calm myself down.

I had no idea what to say back. Of course I missed her. I missed her like crazy. There wasn't a day that passed that I didn't think about her, about kissing her, hugging her, or wishing so much that I could bury my face in her chest as we cuddled and I deeply inhaled the wonderful and comforting smell of her shirt.

As I stared at her text message, wondering if I should text her or not, I watched the typing bubble appear and disappear, triggering my heart to race every time those three little dots popped up on my screen. I watched it for a good two minutes, going through every possible thing that she could tell me. How much she hated me. How much she regretted our relationship. How I was just an experiment to her bi-curiosity, and she really was in love with Liam. How she was going to prom with Liam. How she never wanted to talk to me again.

It was amazing how three little dots engulfed in a texting bubble could trigger your anxiety to run a full marathon.

And then, finally, came her long text.

I sucked in a breath of the warm, summer-smelling air and braced for the worst.

Her novel-length text read, *I told my parents and my brother about us over spring break. They asked me why I've been so upset. So, I told them everything. We dated. I stopped talking to you because I kissed you the night before we moved. How I've liked you since, and I tried running from it. How I've been so miserable without you. Long story short: my parents are really shocked, but I think they took it well. Jacob doesn't care either.*

They said that they just want me to be happy and find someone who makes me happy, and I told them you make me happy. They told me that I needed to tell you that. So, this is me telling you that. No one has made me feel the way you do. Not a single person.

Holy fucking crap, I thought. *She's out.*

I read the text over and over again so every word could marinate in my mind. Forget about all the crap that scurried through my head just a moment ago from the texting bubble. It was everything I would have never guessed that she would say. She told her family everything? And from the sounds of it, literally everything? My body felt pinned to the concrete patio, and those night bugs I'd listened to on my walk home? Yeah, they didn't really exist anymore.

I must have typed ten different responses, changing my mind, backspacing, and writing something new. I guess it was her turn to deal with the anxiety of the appearing and disappearing texting bubble.

Ultimately, I went with, *Wow. That's really amazing, Kennedy. Seriously. I hope you're proud of yourself for coming out to your family. I sure am.*

I am proud of myself. It's like a huge weight has been lifted off my shoulders, and I feel like I'm not hiding this part of myself anymore. It feels amazing. So, all the important people in my life know. I'm not afraid anymore. I want you to give me a second chance. I miss you SO much. We can be open and free this time.

I started crying. Not because I was happy, but because what I wanted her to do still didn't change the betrayal and hurt that lived inside me. Why was my heart still broken? I wanted so badly to run over to her house and tell her how proud I was of her because I was so incredibly proud of her for coming out to her family. She did more than I even asked her to, but why didn't I feel different? I wanted to feel differently. So badly. But I still couldn't shake off the gut-wrenching feeling she left me with when she gave me a hard, flat "no" in my driveway. I still couldn't get the image of her sleeping with Liam out of my head. We were together for five months, and the whole time, she kept the fact about sleeping with my twin brother right next to her in the closet.

But the reality of all of it was that it was too late. The damage had already been done, as much as I wanted it to be fixed. Kennedy couldn't undo the pain she'd caused. The first person who I was head over heels for shoved me into the darkest parts of her life too many times for me to just open my arms back up for her.

Fighting through the stinging in my eyes, I let my fingers respond as my lungs constricted. *Kennedy, you lied to me. Our whole relationship, you kept this big secret from me. Apparently, you didn't trust me enough to tell me about you and Liam, and you didn't even trust me enough to own our relationship together when everyone already knew about it.*

She texted, *Quinn, I'm sorry. I already said that I was sorry. I can't take it back, and I wish more than anything that I could.*

I replied, *I believe that you're sorry, but I can't just forget about it and jump back into this relationship feeling 100% healed because I'm not. I still get angry just thinking about the lying and imagining you with Liam. I haven't even worked things out with him yet. Plus, we're leaving for college on opposite sides of the country in four months. I'm all in world champs training, and I'm doing really amazing at that. I can't backtrack knowing that we'll have an expiration date in August when I move to Berkeley and you move to Syracuse. How would that even work?*

The text bubble appeared and disappeared at least five times. *I can't believe I just told her no,* I thought. *I can't go through this all over again.*

Another round of *la douleur exquise* coming right up.

She responded, *I don't know how it would work...*

I bit down on my lip so hard when I wrote out my next text, *I'm so sorry, Kennedy. Please believe me.*

How the hell could Kennedy and I have an expiration date? How the hell could Kennedy and I expire, because all the feelings I had for her felt way too real to be dead. How could something so real and amazing like this not work out, especially when there were tons of people in shitty relationships they shouldn't have been in. How could we not fucking work out?

The stitches I gave myself unraveled, and my chest burned just rereading my text and watching her texting bubble stutter again on my screen.

Don't take my no for an answer, I thought. *Give me an answer. There has to be an answer. Find a way to be together. I'm so sorry.*

She texted, *I believe you.*

I guess there really is no answer to how this could possibly work, I replied.

With that, the conversation died instantly, and I cried myself to my room.

Erick had sent me a playlist of all the songs I needed to listen to in order to mend my broken heart. He was one of those people with about two thousand songs on his iPod (yes, he still had an iPod, an iPod Classic, to be exact) and he knew exactly how to cater his playlist to speak to me. "Everytime" by Britney. "Broken-Hearted Girl" by Beyoncé. "All Too Well" by Taylor Swift. "The Harold Song" by Kesha. "Someone Like You" by Adele. "Already Gone" by Kelly Clarkson. "All I Want" by Kodaline. And every single song Damien Rice ever wrote because he was the king of making people ugly cry over their heartbreaks. "I Remember" by him made me do exactly that for about an hour straight.

Somehow, through the crying and music, I heard a knock on my bedroom door. I shut myself up, quickly wiped my face, and pulled the headphones out of my ears. Liam softly called my name from the other side.

Just what I need: more drama.

"What?" I said.

The door opened cautiously; a ray of light from his room illuminated his face. In the shadows, I noticed his sympathetic and worried look.

"Hey. I, um, I just wanted to see how you're doing. I haven't checked in at all, and I've realized that's pretty shitty of me."

"How does it look like I'm doing?"

"I can't really see anything, but I can only imagine you're not doing well."

He could have turned away at that point. He didn't have to waste any time checking in on me at all. But he did, and instead of locking himself in his room to blare his rap music like he'd been doing the past six weeks, he broke through the wall we built and crept into my room. As much as I wanted him to leave me alone, I also wanted him to stay because honestly, I really missed my brother. I really needed him right now.

"Do you wanna talk about it?"

When he took a seat by my feet, I just cried. He scooted closer to me but still kept his distance. He rubbed my knee, which I think was his way of giving me a hug, though I wouldn't have shooed him away if he offered me one.

"She just told me she came out to her family and begged to get back together," I said as I cried. "And I had to turn her down. I can't forget about how she hid you from me or how she said no to me on our driveway. I wanna forget about all of it because I want her so much, but I don't know how we can ever work out when college and world champs are in four months. How can something that made me feel so good not work out?"

"I don't know. It's just at a really crappy time." He let out a long sigh. "I...I don't know what to say. I can't even imagine what you're going through right now, and I'm so sorry for being such a dick about it. I should have told you about me and Kennedy. I didn't know it was something to tell you until I found out you two were dating, and I was just so mad and jealous that you guys were together to even think about telling you about some drunken hookup before you two were something. When Kennedy came over when you were at states, we talked about it—telling you—and we thought it would be best to wait until everything was all right between the three of us before we dropped another bomb. It probably wasn't the right thing to do either, but I honestly had no idea what to do. I'm sorry."

Knowing that they talked about their hookup and how they were going to purposely hide it from me made the flowers and the Swensons she got me that night instantly rot in my memory. It meant so much less knowing I walked in a second after the conversation hushed from the sound of my footsteps.

But as the knowledge of their conversation tainted the wonderful memory I had, Liam did sound genuinely sorry, and the look he continued to give me when his hand consoled my knee was the most genuine I'd seen him in years.

"It's okay," I said. "I mean, it's not, but I forgive you. I'm sorry too."

"And I shouldn't have said all those things in front of Mom and Dad either."

"Same."

"I know I've been a piece of shit to you for the last couple years, but I want you to know that I'm on your side, and I'll always be on your side, and I don't want you to think you have to go through this alone anymore. I want you back. I miss happy, sassy, funny Quinn."

Another round of waterworks. This time, I reached my arms out to him to let him know how much I needed his hug. He latched his arms around me and held my head into his shoulder, allowing me to cry into his shirt.

I didn't realize how much I missed him until his arms hugged me back so tightly. We just sat there in the darkness, hugging as if we'd never hugged before. I sobbed into his chest, and he rubbed my back. I cried even harder the more he consoled me and the more he showed me how much he was on my side. I hoped that reconciling with Liam would push me in the right direction to get over this awful heartbreak because half of my broken heart was from my strained relationship with the first best friend I ever had in my life: my twin brother.

CHAPTER FOURTEEN

Our summers working at country clubs, babysitting, lifeguarding, waitressing, and teaching swim lessons paid off in a magical, twenty-passenger, white Escalade limo sitting in my driveway for prom.

What a beauty she was.

All the girls came to my house that prom afternoon to do each other's hair. We'd practically spent our whole life savings on that ridiculous Escalade limo, so we resorted to a more economical route for our hairdos. Madison and Gia were in charge of that and spent four hours straightening, curling, and styling, while we sipped on Red Bull and blasted music from the Bluetooth speakers. They did everyone's hair except for Meghan, who politely told them that she refused to let any straight girl style her grungy pixie cut. There was no way she was going to have an ounce of straightness on her, she said.

"Quinn had a crush on me sophomore year," Madison said. "That has to count for something?"

"It depends," Meghan said. "What were your thoughts when you found out?"

"I was excited. She's pretty hot."

"Are you kidding me?" I said as if my whole life had been a lie. "Why didn't you tell me this earlier? Ugh!"

"Because I was too busy getting Corey Griffith to like me."

I waved off her comment. "Corey Griffith is a dweeb. I'm way better than Corey Griffith."

"I can attest to this," Riley added.

"See! Thank you!"

"Well, I know this now," Madison said. "I didn't back then."

"I'm glad all is right in the Quinn/Riley department again," Gia said. "I guess that just shows how much better Quinn is than Corey Griffith. Riley can still attest to her greatness."

I playfully flipped my hair back to Madison. "Gia even knows. You missed out, girl."

"Well, damn. There's always hope tonight, right?"

I winked at her. "You bet, beautiful."

Meghan eyed Madison skeptically. "Okay, you get *one* curl. Use it wisely." Meghan turned back over to Riley, Lana, and me. "I knew she was at least a one on the Kinsey scale."

Inside the country club was like something from a fairy tale. A giant chandelier hung over the middle of the dance floor. The lighting was dim, and blue and purple streams of lights climbed up the white walls. White rope lights spiraled up the white columns throughout the ballroom, and the tables hid underneath white tablecloths decked out in formal table settings.

Our group found our table placements and slowly maneuvered around all the other Aspen Grove juniors and seniors in their rented tuxes and shimmering formal dresses. Somehow, we managed to get a prime table, two rows away from the dance floor and three rows away from the table of water and party punch. We weren't sure how we got that lucky since we weren't on the top tier of Aspen Grove High's totem pole, but none of us complained.

As we took a seat at our table, across the ballroom, students still trickled in as the catering staff began passing out the first course salads, which I eyed like a hawk because I'd starved myself all day to gorge on the delicious food I knew we were going to get. But then, like magnets, my eyes fell right on her when she entered the ballroom. I suddenly forgot all the salads dancing around the tables. My heart swelled up to a brick thumping in my chest. Just the sight of her made it difficult to breathe. If that New Year's cocktail dress made me feel things, then Kennedy in that prom dress made me feel as if a Fourth of July finale went off in my stomach. Her skin glowed in the blue and purple lighting, her makeup enhanced her perfect cheekbones and jawline, and her hair was done so elegantly in a curly updo. And that dress she wore. A sleeveless, full-length dress: her top in sparkling silver, the bottom a royal blue. She looked like absolute royalty. Actually, she looked better than Kate Middleton, and that was really saying something if my opinion meant anything.

Her beauty sucked me right in. I didn't even notice the waitstaff passing out the food because my eyes and brain were engulfed in all that was Kennedy Reed.

I watched every inch as she strode into the ballroom with her group. Liam told me that her date was Jennifer, and Jennifer even gave her a promposal on the soccer field. Soccer balls that spelled out "Prom bitch?" I was glad that she was in good hands and that Jennifer tried to give her best friend a prom worth remembering while all this other turmoil in her life went on around her.

The group looked around the ballroom for their seats with their table cards in hand. I was almost positive that her straying eyes weren't that dedicated to finding their table. Those eyes were searching for something she wanted more than just her seat, and the thought of her trying to find me shot nerves in my gut. I had to force myself to look away, and in an instant, I lost the group to the countless tables that made up the ballroom.

I was able to breathe again.

A Caesar salad for the appetizer. Parmesan crusted chicken breast with vegetables and roasted rosemary potatoes for the entrée. A vanilla bean crème brûlée for dessert. And I wasn't sure how I was supposed to stay inside my dress for the rest of the night with a bloated gut. Luckily, we were just two rows away from the dance floor, and Erick only gave everyone ten minutes to rest their stomachs before he demanded everyone's attendance right in front of the DJ booth.

"You guys let me know when you want me to flash my Andrew Jackson to the DJ for some *Circus* songs," he shouted to us over the music. "I'm not about to go through another dance without listening to at least one Britney classic."

"Can you not refer to paying the DJ as 'flashing your Andrew Jackson'?" I said. "It kinda creeps me out."

"Fine, but if Tanner and I win prom kings, you better believe I'm demanding what song I'm gonna dance to."

"Yeah? And what's that?" Lana asked.

"'Dirrty' by Christina," he said with confidence.

"He insisted we memorize the choreography from the music video," Tanner said. "He made me practice ever since we made it in the top three."

"We're gonna shut down all the heterosexuality in here," Erick said. "Just you wait."

I had to put invisible blinders on my eyes because I knew that they would constantly look for Kennedy. And they did, for the first few songs we danced to. Riley and I shared a couple of dances. With my little teasing game with Madison, she initiated a few dances with me, and I didn't complain at all that a hot straight girl was grinding up on me. Even if it was facetiously. I liked that attention. At one point, Gabriel found me on the dance floor and told me over the thumping music that Melanie was being dramatic and he needed a breather. So, he found me and became my number one dancing partner: one of the most popular and attractive guys at Aspen Grove grinding behind one of the out and proud lesbians. The irony wasn't lost on me. But he was an amazing dancer, and man, did he smell wonderful. *So yes, Gabriel, grind up on me just so I can smell your cologne.* It even intrigued Meghan, who tapped him on the shoulder to ask what he was wearing. He sniffed her neck, said she smelled amazing, asked her where she got her tux because he loved it, and a bromance was formed right in the middle of our queer friend group. Magical.

An hour had gone by, and the heat in the ballroom jumped from room temperature to Miami level from sweaty, hormonal seventeen- and eighteen-year-olds. The DJ announced for the finalist couples to come to the front of the dance floor, and the crowd formed a semicircle. Tanner and Erick received the most applause, so it was no surprise when the DJ announced them as prom king and king, and everyone cheered and whistled. They were both given king crowns, and after the photographer snapped a picture of the victorious couple, Erick slid his twenty-dollar bill to the DJ and mouthed something to him.

"Guys, I think he just showed the DJ his Andrew Jackson," I told our group.

"Oh, this is about to get so gay." Meghan clapped. "I'm so fucking excited. 20Gayteen is in the house!"

Then, the sounds of Christina Aguilera from the early 2000s came on, and Tanner and Erick got into their rehearsed positions. The music played, and Erick's hips undulated slowly and provocatively to the beat of the song. A few whistles came from the crowd. The semicircle that formed around them became tighter as everyone inched up to watch them like a really good street performance. Tanner ditched his cool, laid-back yet reserved quarterback attitude, and I was pretty sure that really captured everyone's attention to see what they had up their sleeves. Erick Iglesias acting like this was no surprise. But Tanner Hayes? A year and a half with Erick had rubbed off on him.

Their routine was flawless, and with every rehearsed move they made, the crowd applauded and danced with them. Tanner slipped off his tie when the chorus came around, and when the second verse came, Erick threw an invisible rope to Gabriel and pulled him in. Gabriel surprised us all when he waltzed into their circle and joined them in dancing absolutely ridiculously, trying to imitate Erick's dancing. By the second round of the chorus, the space created for the couple turned into a sweaty, happy mosh pit with quite a few people joining us for the remainder of the song.

The gay kids always lived in the shadows during my years at Aspen Grove High, just like every day in the real world. I was so happy and amazed that my senior year ended with Erick and Tanner winning prom kings, probably the first time ever a gay couple won the meaningless title in the school's history. Meaningless to straight couples, but it meant everything for the student body to vote for the gay couple. The juniors and seniors that made up the crowd erupted in applause, not boos, at their crowning. Their dance routine was celebrated, not made fun of. And the rest of the crowd grew from our little gay mosh pit and filled out the whole dance floor. In those moments, during that Christina Aguilera song, the hundreds of sixteen-, seventeen-, and eighteen-year-olds of Aspen Grove High School celebrated the fact that we were all humans and forgot about the labeled boxes we each lived in every day. After all the comments from people like Cassandra Jones trying to make me feel awful about who I liked, the crowd at prom made me feel so accepted and loved. Erick always had a smirk on his face, usually followed by a joke or something sarcastic. But this smile was different. I saw the world that Erick and Tanner shared. Their smiles were genuine, and their gazes locked, and just for that moment, the pain and unhappiness Erick had experienced from his parents and therapist really didn't matter because for once, he was accepted for who he was, and he looked as if he felt the acceptance as much as I did. The smile on his face as the whole school danced happily and carefree around us while he held his high school sweetheart in his arms was the purest smile I'd ever seen on him.

It was my favorite moment of all of high school.

Now that Erick and Tanner had taken over the front of the dance floor with their gay mosh pit, we danced mere feet away from Liam's group of friends. They were always up front because obviously, they had to have all the attention on them, I only assumed. My curious eyes searched for Kennedy's classy updo and instantly spotted her dancing with Jennifer and Melanie. I couldn't get over how pretty she was, and I genuinely felt happy that she was smiling and seeming to enjoy the dance with her two best girlfriends. But as much as I enjoyed seeing her flawless smile over the shoulders of our friends, I couldn't help but feel envious of Erick and Tanner, swept up in their cloud of high school love. God, how much I wanted to have my own version of what they were currently experiencing.

Instead of my own cloud, a few yards and a handful of people separated me from the person who I really wanted to share that prom moment with. In a few months, we'd both go off to college, meet someone new and exciting, get the same rush of excitement in our stomachs every time that person smiled or texted us, and we'd completely forget about the people we crushed on in high school. It pained me to imagine her with someone other than me. She was the gold medal I'd been working for all through high school, and I'd never realized it. I couldn't end high school on the note we left off on. Rejected, heartbroken, and avoiding each other more than we avoided each other before. If I couldn't get the gold medal, and the best I'd be able to do was win silver, which in my head was getting to dance with her to our song at prom, I was going to do everything I could to make that happen.

My friends freaked out when the DJ played one of Erick's requested songs. It was Robyn's "Dancing on My Own," which I knew was going to be the theme song to my summer when we all came back home from our first year of college, assuming that Kennedy found someone new in her life. And if it was a girl, God, someone just stab me. It would be less painful.

Hearing the song squeezed my stomach as I ditched my friends jumping up and down and shouting the lyrics. I walked up to the DJ, my throat dried up from nerves. His large headphones were wrapped around his neck as he studied his Mac laptop. Then he glanced at me as if he was annoyed that yet another high schooler was telling him what songs to play and ruining his creative process.

"Hi," I yelled over the Robyn song blaring from the speakers. "What do I need to do to request a song?"

"Just request one."

"How long will it take to play it?"

"Well, one of the prom kings gave me a whole playlist he wanted me to play in exchange for a twenty, so probably after that."

I rolled my eyes. *Fucking damn it, Erick.*

"This one's important."

"That's what the prom king specifically said about 'If U Seek Amy.'"

"Okay, but this is for high school love."

"Is that a thing, though?"

Well, this DJ's an asshole.

"Can you please play 'XO' by Beyoncé? Sometime soon? Everyone out there wants a slow song. They've been waiting for it all night, and I've just been designated to be a representative of the dance floor. I'm a friend of the prom king, and he told me to tell you to add it to the list. Sometime soon."

He glanced down at a handwritten list on a piece of notepad paper. I couldn't believe Erick actually preplanned this list as if he had written out his speech like an Oscar nominee. "Only Beyoncé song I have by the prom king is 'Crazy in Love.'"

"That's a mistake. He actually wants 'XO.' Do you want me to get him? He's difficult, that one—"

He raised his hand. "No, that's fine. I'll squeeze it in, I guess."

"It would really mean a lot to some people out there if you played 'XO.'"

"I'll see what I can do."

As I slipped on back into my friend circle, I caught Kennedy glancing at me, and that made my stomach coil into tighter knots.

Her eyes were on me, and instead of immediately falling back on to Jennifer, she gave me a half-smile instead.

Please don't reject me, I kept saying over and over again as I tried my hardest not to look back at her group.

Five party songs from Erick's playlist later, the mood did a one-eighty turn. The familiar synthesizers softly hummed the intro to my requested song.

My heart sunk. Oh my God, I just fully committed to this irrational idea of dancing with Kennedy Reed in front of everyone at prom.

Just like clockwork, my anxious stomach ache revved up.

"Oh my God, is this Beyoncé?" Erick exclaimed.

This was it. I had to march over there in the midst of Tom Felix, Jennifer Stewart, Melanie Krugel, and fucking Cassandra Jones and ask their friend—who had my heart completely—to dance with me. If she rejected me, I think I would have been even more embarrassed than when Liam walked in on us or Cassandra found that card. Because this was the last chance to reconcile any last bit of hope we had at keeping each other in our lives. Asking her to dance in front of her douchey friends made me so vulnerable. I'd sworn to myself after Cassandra Jones's party at the beginning of the year that I would never step into their world again. One party was enough. But my high school love was in there, and I wanted her so badly. Risking my dignity and setting myself up for possible humiliation was worth the risk if that meant I got to dance with her and hold her in my arms.

If she even wanted to dance with me. I mean, I did reject her a few weeks ago when she let her guard down. Ball was in her court to return the favor.

Beyoncé's beautiful voice echoed in the ballroom in the opening lyrics, and the sound of the song and the memories that braided with it went straight to my eyes and gut. I had no control over my body. I just kind of floated over to that group, ignoring everyone else that surrounded her. My eyes were just on her beautiful ones. No one else. If I focused on Tom or Cassandra, on top of my stomachache and nerves crawling up my throat, I probably would have just barfed on the dance floor. Yum.

Jennifer noticed me first. Without even the slightest pause, she grinned and pushed her best friend over to me. Kennedy stumbled in her high heels, and I caught her from tripping right on her face. That got all her friends' attention. Both Tom and Cassandra glared at me as if I had no reason breathing the same air as them. The nerves burned my cheeks, and the touch of her hands forced my arm hair to stand up as if it was begging for an encore of our relationship. I think Kennedy felt it too because her eyes fell on my hands still holding her steady as the touch of her sent shocks running through my body.

"You good?" I said.

She steadied herself back on her feet. "Embarrassed but good."

"Do you wanna dance? I mean, our song *is* playing."

"Well, then, that means we have to dance now," she said with a small smile.

As I took her hand and moved us a couple feet away from her friends, I caught that whole group eyeing me down in every single way possible: Jennifer offering us both a heartwarming smile. Gabriel and Melanie both lifting their eyebrows up and down. Tom and Cassandra rolling their eyes and whispering something to each other. Liam with his wide grin and Grant with the most emotionless, boring face.

I positioned us so we didn't have to watch them gawking.

Her eyes are on me. That's all the matters right now. Forget about the rest.

How meticulously I placed my hands on her waist, as if they had assigned seating, killed me. With the history we had, I shouldn't have had to act so controlled and conservative around her. When she wrapped her arms so loosely around my neck, I could feel the uncertainty she had about touching me too, as if there was only one way to position our hands on each other to tame the fire sparking between us. But yet, despite that, she still had the ability to cause my stomach to fly up to my mouth. Two months had gone by since we last touched each other, and just the touch of her soft skin on mine sent those electric currents through my whole body. Her floral shampoo and her eyes on me swept me up into a wonderful familiarity I wished I could let myself fully bask in; the feeling of surrendering myself to her all rushed back to me.

"You look really beautiful," I said. "Like, really, really beautiful."

Her cheeks reddened. "You do too."

A wave of peppermint gum brushed underneath my nose. How much I wanted to kiss her fresh lips.

Just as my eyes fell to her lips, as I inhaled her peppermint breath, Beyoncé sang the lyric we used to kiss to, and my stomach shifted upside down. We held each other's eyes, remembering a time in my bedroom when we celebrated as that lyric hummed through my phone speakers. How we kissed every time the lyric came up because that was the unwritten rule, and here we were at prom, disobeying our song and Beyoncé. My eyes brimmed with tears as the song continued without a kiss.

"I'm so sorry, Ken," I said, feeling my nerves shake in my throat, "about our text conversation a couple weeks ago. It killed me so much to say no. It really did. I'm so sorry."

She nodded with pursed lips and raised eyebrows. If she started crying, I think my whole body would just crack open with her.

"I understand why you did it…I think."

I miss you so much. You don't even know.

"I always thought we would go to prom together. I thought about it all the time when we were together and all the ways I'd ask you."

"How would you have asked me?"

I looked up at the ceiling as I tried to gather every detail in my head. "Well, I was going to torture you with a scavenger hunt."

"Oh really?" she said with intrigue in her voice. "Explain."

"Well, okay, so it was gonna be a scavenger hunt with all of the significant places of our past. It was gonna start with a note in your locker that led you to our make-out spot in the PAC. Just a little note propped up against the corner. No one would even see it. And then that would have led you to a note hidden under a rock right by the tree at the bottom of the hill where I cut open my chin. And then I never really quite figured out the next one, but I wanted something at your old house. And then it would end with me in your room with a Swensons bag with a large fry, fried chicken sandwich, and a chocolate malt in your room with 'prom?' written on the aluminum foil of the sandwich. Something stupid like that."

Her nostrils flared while her arms around my neck tugged me a little harder. As the chorus came around, I saw the sadness in her eyes, and it wasn't until I saw that look and went through the scavenger hunt in my head that I wished so badly that it would have happened.

"It doesn't sound stupid at all," she said very softly. Her gaze fell to the ground for a brief moment. "I would have really loved that. I would have said yes."

Why couldn't she be my prom date? Why can't we work this out?

Instead of having every single prom song to dance with each other, we only got this one, knowing full well we had about two more minutes of this memory left. The conservative space between us never felt so large and exposed. Although I'd just filled my stomach with a delicious three-course meal, it never felt so empty. My heart dropped to the pit of my stomach, and the lump sucked up all the moisture in my mouth. The vague sight of us going to prom together made me pull her closer until we erased that stupid conservative space between us, and our stomachs pressed together. She tightened her grip. I rested my cheek against hers and tried so hard for the *la douleur exquise* stinging my eyes not to seep down in between our cheeks. I could almost taste her lips that weren't mine to taste. The way her hand held the back of my head so securely in her palm made me wonder if she was hoping I would kiss her. God, did I want to kiss her and taste her lips and her peppermint gum and kiss her until we woke up from this horrible nightmare we'd been living in for the past two months. We'd be in matching prom dresses with corsages we spent way too much time at the florist picking out for one another.

I closed my eyes and pretended my body wasn't contaminated with *la douleur exquise*.

"Kennedy?" I said.

"Yeah?"

"I really miss you."

I didn't open my eyes. I was too scared. Scared because her eyes were my kryptonite, and seeing them soak in the same pain and hurt as moments before would just intensify the stomachache slowly simmering inside me.

"I really miss you too."

Her thumb resting on my shoulder started gently caressing the column of my neck. Just one graze and I felt my face melting into hers.

My eyes opened, and through the stinging that only intensified as our song and memory neared, I noticed all the other couples around us watching our dance closely. My friend group. Her friend group. Other friend groups. All eyes were on Kennedy Reed holding Quinn Hughes as if she never wanted to let go: our cheeks stuck together, our eyes both fighting back tears. But despite our audience, her thumb didn't stop moving. Did she even know that everyone around us was watching her graze my neck? Did she know that some of them were whispering to each other with intrigued smiles as if some juicy drama was unfolding right in front of them? Did she care? Did I care?

"Kennedy?"

"Mm-hmm?"

"Everyone's staring at us."

"I know."

Her tone was content and confident, as if she'd finally inhaled spring air after months of cold darkness. It was almost as if she wanted our little crowd to know the history that danced alongside us. So I relaxed my body farther into hers, and we found ourselves in an accidental embrace of consoling each other. When the kissing lyric played again, we hugged each other tighter in the absence of what would have been a wonderful kiss. For the last minute of the song, we danced in silence, knowing that in just a few more moments, the dance would be nothing but a memory, and we would have to let each other go all over again.

Kiss her. Kiss her now. She'll kiss you back.

"Kennedy?"

"Mm-hmm?"

My heart raced. "I…I think I might love you a little bit."

Her thumb finally stopped tracing invisible lines on my neck. She pulled her cheek from mine so that her eyes were only a few inches away from me. Her hands clasped on to my face as if it meant everything to her. "I think I might love you a lot."

The ending of "XO" fizzled and sped up to an upbeat bass as a way to transition the romance that filled the air back to sweat and energy.

Just like that, the moment ended. We landed hard back to our reality of poppy EDM songs surrounded by all the juniors and seniors at our school. Their eyes were still on us. She removed her hands from my face, and after a second without her touch, my body screamed for her to come back to me. How could that dance end so quickly? Why did the DJ only play half the song? How many Andrew Jacksons did I need to make Erick flash the DJ just for him to play "XO" on repeat until we spun ourselves back to a time when we were together again?

Her heartbreak still glistened in her eyes just like mine. She leaned in, and for a second, I thought she was leaning in for a kiss on the lips, and God, I would have let her kiss me. Just one kiss. One kiss to seal and validate the powerful words we just revealed to each other. But instead, she gave me a long and soft kiss on the cheek.

"Thanks for the dance, Quinn. I hope you have a good rest of your night."

And she disappeared into the mosh pit of dancing, jumping, grinding teenagers.

"Why didn't you kiss her?" Gia shouted when the group swarmed around me. "You had that whole song to kiss her! Her face was on yours! She was waiting for it!"

"Yeah, Quinn," Meghan said, "She gave you heart eyes the whole time. I really expected better from you."

"Okay," Riley chimed in, annoyed. "Everyone, calm down and let her process all of this."

"Here," Erick said and reached into his tux coat pocket to hand me the flask that he apparently had the whole night. "I think you probably want this."

At that point, I didn't care if I probably shouldn't have consumed whatever mystery alcohol was in the flask. I needed just one little shot as my body attempted to hold every brittle piece of me together. The muscles in my throat tugged toward my stomach, and my chest was heavy. The first time I ever told someone I loved them, I couldn't even kiss them. A girl told me that she loved me, and we couldn't even celebrate with a kiss.

Why did saying "I love you" hurt so much? It shouldn't have hurt so much.

I snatched the flask from Erick, and I took a gulp of the really nasty alcohol. The warm, powerful burn that ignited in my mouth was just what I needed to kill the *la douleur exquise* that poisoned me. If death had a taste, it tasted like whatever kind of bottom-shelf crap was in Erick's flask.

"You need better taste in alcohol," I said when I handed him his Death Flask. "I need to get some air now."

The night was warm, though much cooler than the middle of the dance floor, and the sweet smell of summer faintly perfumed the air. The air was just the right temperature to cool down my face. The smell of summer was just enough to soothe everything I felt inside me.

"Hey," Riley said and took a seat on the bench beside me. "Wanna talk about it?"

I wiped my eyes. "I just told her that I loved her. And she told me the same thing."

Riley drew in a breath. "Oh wow."

"And I couldn't even kiss her. I never thought the first time I told someone I loved them would make me feel so empty and heartbroken."

She rubbed my back. "I'm so sorry, Quinn. I really am."

I wiped my eyes again. "I wanted to kiss her so much, but I knew if I did, it would have made it worse."

"I completely agree."

"I really thought about taking her back. A couple weeks ago when she told me she came out to her family. God, did I want to take her back, but the truth is, I just need time to myself. I need to focus on the world champs and enjoying my summer with my best friends. Not falling in love or anything that comes with hooking up with someone."

"I'll make sure you have that summer."

"I need to be selfish right now. I need to go to Russia feeling the healthiest mentally, emotionally, and physically. I really want a medal, and I really want to qualify for the trials."

"Keep your eye on the prize. You still have four months to get there. Now, come on, let's go back inside and dance. Let's end our senior year on a good note."

CHAPTER FIFTEEN

The summer was what I hoped it would be. I lived, breathed, and dreamed of the world champs—and then when I had the smallest amount of free time, I spent it as a normal eighteen-year-old, enjoying the summer with my friends before we all moved away to college. The breakup with Kennedy and the arguing with Liam set my mentality back by so much, I feared that I wouldn't be able to pull out of it by the time late July rolled around with the world champs. But I wasn't going to let that stop me. I knew that the pain I felt over the past few months wasn't going to be the only time in my life I would feel that way, and if I truly wanted that medal, and if I truly wanted to have a chance at going to the Olympics, I really just needed to tell myself I could do it and push through the pain.

And I did it. I qualified for the Rio Olympic trials the next summer, and my two world championship bronze medals lit up my suitcase in Kazan airport security. I was way more embarrassed than I thought I would be.

My family surprised me with a welcome home/going away/joint graduation party with Liam. We only had a week and a half left of summer before everyone moved: Liam to Ithaca College, me to Berkeley. All of our friends and family showed up. So that was, like, at least seventy-five people out in our backyard, sucking up the last rays of summer as it colored all of our skin a light shade a pink. All of our guests swarmed around me to hear about Russia and begged to wear the medals. Let's be honest: everyone showed up just for the medals, not for Liam and me, the two of us decided.

My stomach was so full from all the food Mom insisted on ordering for the party. My feet hurt from all the standing and walking to make sure I spoke to every family member, neighbor, and friend who came. And then I couldn't forget about the sprints I had to break out in to chase Erick and Meghan around the yard because they tried stealing the medals. My brain was almost on empty from having so many small-talk conversations with family members who didn't know how to talk to me—what was my major going to be (nonexistent for the time being, but I was thinking psychology), where was I going to put my medals (probably leave them in my room in Aspen Grove so no one could steal them), how after four years I was probably going to stay in California (oh yes, I already had it planned—my parents didn't know that yet), and how the Berkeley boys needed to watch out for me (okay, Aunt Karen. Don't hold your breath for that).

As people started to leave, Mom and Dad cleaned up abandoned plates left on the tables while I tried hunting down Liam to round up my two medals. My uncle Ben was in charge of collecting them back from Erick and Meghan, but turned out, Liam still found a way to get his grimy hands on one of them. I heard his voice coming from the front of the house. So, I peered around the side and saw that dark red Jetta parked in the street. Kennedy stood on the driveway talking to Liam, both of them with smiles on their faces. In a total friendly way. Not a "let's bang on the driveway" way. Her tan skin had soaked up all the summer sun, and her hair was a few shades lighter.

The pain she'd left had slowly fizzled over time, but those feelings in my stomach churned all over again when I saw her. Last time I'd seen her was at graduation in late May. During the last two weeks of the school year after prom, our only form of communication was cordial smiles to each other in calc or if we caught each other's glances from across the cafeteria. Last time I spoke to her was the day I left for Russia when she wished me luck, but we hadn't actually spoken to each other face-to-face since prom.

She still had the ability to make my whole body feel warm when she smiled at me. Not like my body needed to feel warmer on a hot August evening after a whole day of standing. But she was the warmth I needed, a warmth I would always need.

"Hey there," she said, her smile still wide. "Miss World Champion."

Did I just suddenly get sunburn, or did Kennedy add to the redness on my face?

"Oh hey." As much as I wanted to remain calm, a pathetic grin popped up on my face, and I sounded and felt as if I was talking to my longtime crush for the first time ever.

I noticed one of the bronze medals dangling around Liam's neck.

"Hey, I've been looking for that one," I said. "Fork it over."

Liam gave Kennedy a good-bye pat on the shoulder and then handed me back my most prized possession. He leaned in to whisper, "Just so you know, she texted me to make sure you were still here." He winked and walked to the backyard.

The butterflies in my stomach felt as if they'd just ingested speed.

"What are you doing here?"

"Oh, I just happened to be in the neighborhood," she said, not too seriously. "Plus, I wanted to stare at that masterpiece." She pointed to the medal.

"I feel so used by everyone today. But I guess if you came all this way…" I said and took a step forward to wrap the medal around her neck.

She still smelled like apples and flowers.

"Holy crap, Quinn. This is unbelievable."

She studied the medal in her hands. The late evening sun

reflected off the shiny bronze that said "Kazan Russia 2015" on it, next to a bronze shape of Russia over a blue background. I'd been secretly wincing all afternoon, knowing how many germs and fingerprints were being caked onto the medal, but now that Kennedy would be the last one to hold it, I didn't want to wash it.

"I'm so proud of you," she said. The smile directed at me took up her whole face. "So incredibly proud. I watched you. My whole family did, actually."

"Guess you're my good luck charm. That can be the only explanation for how I got two of them, right?"

"No, that was all you."

I wasn't afraid to let my blush darken the sunburn on my cheeks. "Wanna take a walk?"

"I'm always up for a walk with you."

And so, we started our walk, just like in that familiar scene five years ago. Except for this time, my bronze medal hung on Kennedy's neck, and she held it in her fingers to gawk at it like I'd been doing ever since I got it.

"All four of us were pretty much screaming during your races. I was worried our neighbors would call in a noise complaint. And when I told my parents I was going to see you, they made sure that I would tell you that they said congratulations."

"I love your parents. Tell them thank you."

"They love you too. I think they're more upset that we're not together more than the fact that I'm bi or pan or whatever label society wants to give me. All summer, they were trying to get me to call you up. I don't think they understood me when I told them 'No, Mom and Dad. Quinn needs to focus on swimming. Not me. Get over it already.' It was kind of annoying. They really ship us, I guess."

I laughed. "Well, I'm glad I got approval from Brian and Michelle. You got approval from Debbie and Mark too."

We continued walking for a couple moments in silence.

Now that we got our small talk out of the way, I hoped the couple moments of silence would bring out the real reason she stopped by. Because there had to have been a reason for her to suddenly appear when we hadn't spoken to each other in months.

"So, why did you really stop by?" I said.

Okay, I was too nervous, excited, and scared to wait for her to come around to the essence of the visit.

"To see you one last time before you left. I wanted to tell you I saw your races, and I'm so happy for you. Also, to say good-bye. Maybe get some closure."

"Closure?"

She let out a slow, deep breath. Here came the essence. Here came my stomachache and another round of neck sweat. "I just need to make sure you don't hate me. I can't leave this place without ending on the best note possible. You're really important to me, so even if we're not together anymore, I don't want to not have you in my life again."

"Kennedy, I don't hate you. I can never hate you. I want you in my life too, but just so you know, I'm still going to find you extremely attractive, though. Hope that's not awkward."

"No, it's not awkward because I'll think the same thing about you."

We approached her old house. The family that moved into the house five years ago was playing outside. The dad tossed a wiffle ball to his son, who barely hit it. The daughter swooped up, snatched the ball off the ground, and proceeded to chase her little brother around the yard, both of them laughing uncontrollably. The kids couldn't have been older than ten, and I immediately saw the four musketeers in my memory playing flashlight tag with the other neighborhood kids alongside them.

"There were some good memories in that house," Kennedy said. "I miss it and the little Harry Potter closet underneath the basement stairs. Our secret spot, as we called it."

"God, I haven't thought about our secret spot in forever.

I wonder if they painted over all the things we wrote on the drywall."

"I hope so. I think we wrote all of our boy crushes on those walls, so clearly that's not relevant anymore."

"I can't remember ever having a crush on a boy. That must have been just you."

"Um, pretty sure you were in love with Michael O'Brien for, like, three years. You kept drawing hearts around his picture in our yearbooks."

The repressed memory resurfaced. She was right, and I was mortified. Michael O'Brien definitely peaked at age nine and went downhill after that. Guess that's what happened when you skipped school constantly to smoke weed and cigarettes. "Okay, that was, like, first through third grade. And then I started liking Jessie Moreno, but I didn't tell anyone because I thought it was against the rules of life."

"You liked Jessie Moreno? Why am I just finding out about this now?"

"I didn't know I had a crush on her until I knew I was gay and remembered that I always wanted to get her out in tag just so I could touch her. I was also a little bummed when she started dating Cole Shea in eighth grade."

"I think she and Cole Shea broke up this summer. Did you hear about that?"

"No! They've been together forever. I seriously thought they were going to get married right after graduation. Maybe I have a chance now."

"Maybe you do."

The memories lasted until we passed the next house, and the mood grew solemn again. A part of me wished that we weren't going off to college. Maybe there would be a time in the future where our stars would perfectly align after we had those four years to experience life for ourselves and knew what we wanted for the rest of our lives. After all that exploring, maybe our paths would cross again. I would wish on every shooting star in the sky that we would find each other again. With ourselves as whole as possible. With nothing in the way so we could let our relationship grow to its full potential.

"Can we make a pact?" I said.

"A pact? What kind of pact?"

"We do our thing in college. You know, find ourselves. Date all sorts of people. Do all of the stuff one needs to do in college, and if after we graduate and hopefully have already discovered who we are and we're one hundred percent confident and happy about that, if we somehow run into each other, we try it again. You and me, living openly, freely, and not giving any fucks about the world."

She smiled, and I suddenly wasn't the only one with rosy cheeks. "Yeah, I like that. Ambitious, but I like that."

We walked around the neighborhood at least four times. I asked her about her summer, and she told me how she made bank at the country club from schmoozing with the rich old men of Aspen Grove, and she hoped to spend it traveling abroad next summer, hopefully to Spain and France first.

"I got an A in French, so I volunteer to teach you some phrases," I said. "Gotta know some French."

"I know how to say 'hello,' 'good-bye,' and 'Hello. I don't speak French. Do you speak English?'"

"Great, the basics not to look like an American asshole."

"Okay, then teach me something in French. I don't wanna be an asshole, and I need to learn my French from the best."

"Well, that could be taken as dirty."

She smacked me on the arm. "I don't think it's appropriate if the teacher makes those comments to the student."

"Depends what you're into, but okay." I put my hands up to surrender. "*Je suis désolée,*" I said, and I hoped her smile was because she liked the sound of French coming from my lips. "For when you need to say 'I'm sorry'—for being an asshole."

"*Je suis désolée*," she said almost perfectly. My smile was definitely because I liked how French words came from her lips. God, her lips fascinated me, I could never get tired of staring at them. "How was that?"

"Perfect, actually. And kinda really sexy."

She pressed her lips together to hide a growing smile. "Great. I'm a natural." *Yes, you are.* "Give me another."

So, I taught Kennedy how to say "your girlfriend is hot," just in case she needed something to gain some experience. Homework for our pact. I only knew that phrase because that's how Meghan and I studied for our French class. We needed useful sentences just in case we ever needed to impress a really hot French woman.

And then I told her another phrase that Meghan and I purposely went out of our way to memorize. It was a long one, but it made Kennedy's smile grow wider.

"And what does that mean?" she asked.

"You have the most beautiful eyes."

It was a good thing Meghan and I did extracurricular French studying. Sure, I originally taught myself the sentence because I knew that down the road, complimenting a girl in the world's most romantic language would really benefit me in the end. But when I said it to Kennedy, I actually meant it. The way the last glimmer of daylight reflected deep shades of yellow and oranges in those eyes made them even more beautiful.

She shyly tucked a strand of hair behind her ear and let her gaze fall to the sidewalk. "Is that for me to use to seduce people, or is that just for me?"

"It's just for you."

She grinned while her cheeks turned pink.

By the time we approached my house again, only a little bit of dark blue daylight streamed across the night sky. The crickets chirped in the grass, and the fireflies flickered all around us. Kennedy walked me up to the porch, buying just a few more minutes of me and the summer we should have had together. I wished my driveway was five miles long so our walk wouldn't end so soon.

"Well," she said.

I rested my back against the front door. Out of all the room she had on my porch, she chose to stand about a foot away from me. My heart thudded in my chest, and her eyes darkened on my face. I looked at those lips again and wanted them to move so I could see how they danced when she spoke. She slipped the medal off her neck and then put it back around mine, grabbing the ends of my hair so they wouldn't be tucked underneath the royal blue ribbon. When she did so, her eyes and lips were one step away from landing on mine.

"I feel like this scene is awfully familiar," I said, feeling more scared and anxious than I had five years ago. More history hung between us. More desire skated on our lips.

"It does." Her eyes fidgeted all over me as if she wanted every single detail of my face perfectly sketched into her memory. I did the same, though I wasn't sure how I would forget someone that beautiful.

"Would it be weird if we maybe take the extreme leap and Facebook friend each other so we can keep in touch?" I said.

"Oh God, that's so embarrassing that it hasn't happened yet. That I can do."

"So we can stalk each other when we miss each other."

"Which will probably be all the time."

I reached out for her hand. "I already miss you now, so it will definitely be all the time."

I slipped my fingers into hers, and feeling her hands gripping mine sent a spark running up my arms. I needed more of her. I'd needed more of her when we danced at prom and her breath kissed me instead of her lips. If I had to go through four years without her, I needed to be reminded of what it was like to be happy with her. I needed her lips to kiss away the awful four months we had without each other.

"God, how are you so beautiful?" I said. The question wasn't rhetorical. I needed a scientific answer.

My free hand slipped through her hair, my thumb grazing her soft, sun-kissed cheek. Her face nestled into my hand, and finally, after all this time, my hand cradled her face. I was holding her. I pulled her face into me until her forehead touched mine. Her fingers gripped harder on my hand, and her cheek begged for more of my palm.

I couldn't wait anymore. I couldn't let the moment pass, and I couldn't let our future be stained by the uncertainty of another front porch kiss. So, I pulled her face into mine, and finally, the wonderful taste of her replenished my lips. Her hand let go of mine and grabbed my face. Our tongues reunited, and the touch of her tongue caused me to send a moan into her mouth. Her stomach caved into mine, and her pelvis held me in the same spot, and the top of her thigh pressed between my legs, and God, the feeling of her against all my sensitive areas forced another murmur out of me.

I tried to slow down the overwhelming feeling of love I had for her and kissed her as thoroughly as I could, so each inch of her skin was marked by me. Her lips. Her neck. The other side of her neck. Her right cheek. Her lips. Her left cheek. Her forehead. Her nose. Her wonderful lips. Her tongue. The feelings I had for her swallowed me whole. The few inhales of air we took only lasted a few seconds before we went back to each other. The more we kissed, the more we felt alive, the more we surrendered our feelings to each other. The way she kissed me was so confident and strong, it was like kissing a whole different Kennedy. I'd kissed her so many times, each in a different phase of her life. Five years ago, when she wasn't even sure who she was. Four months ago, when she was ashamed of who she was. And now, when she finally seemed to love and accept who she was.

Watching her go through that journey over all those years of self-discovery and ending with the kiss on my porch was one of the most beautiful things I'd ever had the chance to witness.

Because she finally learned to accept herself for who she was, and hopefully, that meant she saw all the beauty and wonderful qualities that I saw.

Finally able to breathe, my lips let go of her so my eyes could have their turn of enjoying the last bit of her too.

I started missing her all over again.

"Quinn," she said so softly. Her forehead stuck to mine, and her eyes were still tightly closed. "Promise me you won't forget. About our pact. About me."

I couldn't forget her even if I tried. We managed to be apart for four years, and still, I couldn't shake her from my life. She always found a way back in my mind, and I knew if our paths crossed again in four more years, that meant we were meant to be together. How many stars did I have to wish on for that to happen? Because I would spend all the time I had searching for them. She was a constellation I always wanted to look for.

I couldn't let her go.

My fingers ran through her soft hair, trying to collect one last smell of apples and flowers permeating the breeze under my nose. I held her face tighter, and my thumbs grazed her soft cheek one last time before the night ended.

"I won't forget. I promise."

About the Author

Morgan Lee Miller started writing at the age of five in the suburbs of Cleveland, Ohio, where she entertained herself by composing her first few novels all by hand. She majored in journalism and creative writing at Grand Valley State University.

When she's not introverting and writing, Morgan works for an animal welfare nonprofit and tries to make the world a slightly better place. She previously worked for an LGBT rights organization.

She currently resides in Washington, DC, with her two feline children, whom she's unapologetically obsessed with.

Books Available From Bold Strokes Books

A Bird of Sorrow by Shea Godfrey. As Darrius and her lover, Princess Jessa, gather their strength for the coming war, a mysterious spell will reveal the truth of an ancient love. (978-1-63555-009-2)

All the Worlds Between Us by Morgan Lee Miller. High school senior Quinn Hughes discovers that a broken friendship is actually a door propped open for an unexpected romance. (978-1-63555-457-1)

An Intimate Deception by CJ Birch. Flynn County Sheriff Elle Ashley has spent her adult life atoning for her wild youth, but when she finds her ex, Jessie, murdered two weeks before the small town's biggest social event, she comes face-to-face with her past and all her well-kept secrets. (978-1-63555-417-5)

Cash and the Sorority Girl by Ashley Bartlett. Cash Braddock doesn't want to deal with morality, drugs, or people. Unfortunately, she's going to have to. (978-1-63555-310-9)

Falling by Kris Bryant. Falling in love isn't part of the plan, but will Shaylie Beck put her heart first and stick around, or tell the damaging truth? (978-1-63555-373-4)

Secrets in a Small Town by Nicole Stiling. Deputy Chief Mackenzie Blake has one mission: find the person harassing Savannah Castillo and her daughter before they cause real harm. (978-1-63555-436-6)

Stormy Seas by Ali Vali. The high-octane follow-up to the best-selling action-romance *Blue Skies*. (978-1-63555-299-7)

The Road to Madison by Elle Spencer. Can two women who fell in love as girls overcome the hurt caused by the father who tore them apart? (978-1-63555-421-2)

Dangerous Curves by Larkin Rose. When love waits at the finish line, dangerous curves are a risk worth taking. (978-1-63555-353-6)

Love to the Rescue by Radclyffe. Can two people who share a past really be strangers? (978-1-62639-973-0)

Love's Portrait by Anna Larner. When museum curator Molly Goode and benefactor Georgina Wright uncover a portrait's secret, public and private truths are exposed, and their deepening love hangs in the balance. (978-1-63555-057-3)

Model Behavior by MJ Williamz. Can one woman's instability shatter a new couple's dreams of happiness? (978-1-63555-379-6)

Pretending in Paradise by M. Ullrich. When travelwisdom.com assigns PR specialist Caroline Beckett and travel blogger Emma Morgan to cover a hot new couples retreat, they're forced to fake a relationship to secure a reservation. (978-1-63555-399-4)

Recipe for Love by Aurora Rey. Hannah Little doesn't have much use for fancy chefs or fancy restaurants, but when New York City chef Drew Davis comes to town, their attraction just might be a recipe for love. (978-1-63555-367-3)

The House by Eden Darry. After a vicious assault, Sadie, Fin, and their family retreat to a house they think is the perfect place to start over, until they realize not all is as it seems. (978-1-63555-395-6)

Uninvited by Jane C. Esther. When Aerin McLeary's body becomes host for an alien intent on invading Earth, she must work with researcher Olivia Ando to uncover the truth and save humankind. (978-1-63555-282-9)

Comrade Cowgirl by Yolanda Wallace. When cattle rancher Laramie Bowman accepts a lucrative job offer far from home, will her heart end up getting lost in translation? (978-1-63555-375-8)

Double Vision by Ellie Hart. When her cell phone rings, Giselle Cutler answers it—and finds herself speaking to a dead woman. (978-1-63555-385-7)

Inheritors of Chaos by Barbara Ann Wright. As factions splinter and reunite, will anyone survive the final showdown between gods and mortals on an alien world? (978-1-63555-294-2)

Spinning Tales by Brey Willows. When the fairy tale begins to unravel and villains are on the loose, will Maggie and Kody be able to spin a new tale? (978-1-63555-314-7)

Love on Lavender Lane by Karis Walsh. Accompanied by the buzz of honeybees and the scent of lavender, Paige and Kassidy must find a way to compromise on their approach to business if they want to save Lavender Lane Farm—and find a way to make room for love along the way. (978-1-63555-286-7)

The Do-Over by Georgia Beers. Bella Hunt has made a good life for herself and put the past behind her. But when the bane of her high school existence shows up for Bella's class on conflict resolution, the last thing they expect is to fall in love. (978-1-63555-393-2)

What Happens When by Samantha Boyette. For Molly Kennan, senior year is already an epic disaster, and falling for mysterious waitress Zia is about to make life a whole lot worse. (978-1-63555-408-3)

Wooing the Farmer by Jenny Frame. When fiercely independent modern socialite Penelope Huntingdon-Stewart and traditional country farmer Sam McQuade meet, trusting their hearts is harder than it looks. (978-1-63555-381-9)

Shut Up and Kiss Me by Julie Cannon. What better way to spend two weeks of hell in paradise than in the company of a hot, sexy woman? (978-1-163555-343-7)

Emily's Art and Soul by Joy Argento. When Emily meets Andi Marino she thinks she's found a new best friend, but Emily doesn't know that Andi is fast falling in love with her. Caught up in exploring her sexuality, will Emily see the only woman she needs is right in front of her? (978-1-163555-355-0)

Spencer's Cove by Missouri Vaun. When Foster Owen and Abigail Spencer meet, they uncover a story of lives adrift, loves lost, and true love found. (978-1-163555-171-6)

Unexpected Lightning by Cass Sellars. Lightning strikes once more when Sydney and Parker fight a dangerous stranger who threatens the peace they both desperately want. (978-1-163555-276-8)

Without Pretense by TJ Thomas. After living for decades hiding from the truth, can Ava learn to trust Bianca with her secrets and her heart? (978-1-163555-173-0)

Escape to Pleasure: Lesbian Travel Erotica, edited by Sandy Lowe and Victoria Villaseñor. Join these award-winning authors as they explore the sensual side of erotic lesbian travel. (978-1-163555-339-0)

Ordinary is Perfect by D. Jackson Leigh. Atlanta marketing superstar Autumn Swan's life derails when she inherits a country home, a child, and a very interesting neighbor. (978-1-163555-280-5)

Royal Court by Jenny Frame. When royal dresser Holly Weaver's passionate personality begins to melt Royal Marine Captain Quincy's icy heart, will Holly be ready for what she exposes beneath? (978-1-163555-290-4)

Strings Attached by Holly Stratimore. Rock star Nikki Razer always gets what she wants, but when she falls for Drew McNally, a music teacher who won't date celebrities, can she convince Drew she's worth the risk? (978-1-163555-347-5)

The Ashford Place by Jean Copeland. When Isabelle Ashford inherits an old house in small-town Connecticut, family secrets, a shocking discovery, and an unexpected romance complicate her plan for a fast profit and a temporary stay. (978-1-163555-316-1)

Treason by Gun Brooke. Zoem Malderyn's existence is a deadly threat to everyone on Gemocon, and Commander Neenja KahSandra must find a way to save the woman she loves from having to make the ultimate sacrifice. (978-1-163555-244-7)

A Wish Upon a Star by Jeannie Levig. Erica Cooper has learned to depend on only herself, but when her new neighbor, Leslie Raymond, befriends Erica's special needs daughter, the walls protecting Erica's heart threaten to crumble. (978-1-163555-274-4)

Answering the Call by Ali Vali. Detective Sept Savoie returns to the streets of New Orleans, as do the dead bodies from ritualistic killings, and she does everything in her power to bring their killers to justice while trying to keep her partner, Keegan Blanchard, safe. (978-1-163555-050-4)